Praise for *Still Life in Shadows*

"Alice J. Wisler is a master artist with words. **Her characters come alive** from the first page, and draw you into their world, holding you a willing captive until you turn the last page. *Still Life in Shadows* is a unique and compelling story, which Novel Rocket and I h˙ˑ˙ˑˑ commend."

—ANE MULLIGAN, senior edit○ˑ

"Novelist Alice Wisler crea˙ˑ ˑ ˑ lot that keeps turning up surprises ˑˑ ˑˑ ˑˑ ˑˑ ˑˑ ˑˑ ˑ ˑ ˑˑ ˑ ˑ ˑˑ ˑe even pray."

—EUGENE H. PETE˙ ˑ ˑ ˑeritus of Spiritual Theology and tran˙ ˑ ˑ ˑe *Message*

"As an Alice J. Wisler fan, I was expecting yet another great read; needless to say, I wasn't disappointed. *Still Life in the Shadows* is a wonderfully crafted and **compelling story**. It held my heart captivate from the first page until the very last line. I highly recommend this book. You don't want to miss this one!"

—DEBRA LYNN COLLINS, Christian fiction writer

"**A touching novel** about how an embittered man is forced to face the Amish community he ran away from years ago. Told by a thirty-year-old auto mechanic and an autistic teenage girl, Alice Wisler's *Still Life in Shadows* speaks of the complexities of family, of belonging, and the tricky task of forgiving. Especially when it comes to yourself."

—JULIE L. CANNON, author of *Twang*

"Alice Wisler's characters come to life on the pages of *Still Life in Shadows* as they face real problems and find out that sometimes the hardest thing to do is go home again. While this book might not be your typical Amish story as it explores what happens when a man leaves the Amish fold, **it is one you'll be glad you read.**"

—ANN H. GABHART, author of *The Outsider* and other Shaker and historical novels

"Complex and raw, *Still Life In Shadows* is a poignant story in which Alice Wisler has created characters who evolve from the stark, monochromatic lines of a newly begun painting into the richly brushed colors of a masterpiece. This was a beautiful novel filled with heart and truth."

—JESSICA NELSON, author of *Love On the Range*

"Alice J. Wisler took me by surprise with this intriguing spin on the Amish genre. *Still Life in Shadows* is a beautiful story about the complexities of faith, friendship, family, and the daring lengths one man will go to save those he cares about. An excellent demonstration of God's love, this story has the power to change hearts."

—TINA ANN FORKNER, author of *Rose House*

"Alice Wisler's *Still Life in Shadows,* captures a clearer glimpse into the Amish life. You will fall in love with the real-life characters and will be cheering them on the whole way. Their caring support of each other gives the real depiction of what a family looks like, even if it's not what their society says. And with their eyes focused on God, they can't help but to prosper in whatever community they choose to live in."

—KATY LEE, author of *Real Virtue*

Still Life in Shadows

Alice J. Wisler

MOODY PUBLISHERS
CHICAGO

© 2012 by
ALICE J. WISLER

The author is represented by MacGregor Literary, Inc.

Edited by Rachel F. Overton
Interior design: Ragont Design
Cover design: Dugan Design Group
Cover image: iStock RF from Alamy.com
Author photo: CK Photography

Library of Congress Cataloging-in-Publication Data

Wisler, Alice J.
  Still life in shadows / Alice J. Wisler.
    p. cm.
  ISBN 978-0-8024-0626-2
  I. Title.
  PS3623.I846S75 2012
  813'.6—dc23

                                    2012016644

We hope you enjoy this book from River North Fiction by Moody Publishers. Our goal is to provide high-quality, thought-provoking books and products that connect truth to your real needs and challenges. For more information on other books and products written and produced from a biblical perspective, go to www.moodypublishers.com or write to:

River North Fiction
Imprint of Moody Publishers
820 N. LaSalle Boulevard
Chicago, IL 60610

1 3 5 7 9 10 8 6 4 2

Printed in the United States of America

For all yearning to belong

Still, my soul, be still; do not be moved by

lesser lights and fleeting shadows.

Keith and Kristyn Getty and Stuart Townend

1

Kiki had to get out, get going, or she'd punch a hole in something. This two-bedroom house was as cramped as a coffin and nearly smelled like one, as the aroma of fried food saturated the walls. Mari had told her to stay close, dinner was almost ready. But who wanted to wait around inside as her sister stir-fried green peppers, onions, and potatoes—again?

In her room, Kiki laced her neon green tennis shoes as quickly as her fingers could maneuver the frayed strings. She grabbed Yoneko, her cotton tabby-cat puppet, and scrambled to her feet. Too quickly. The blood all rushed from her head. She steadied herself against her closet door and waited for the sensation to pass. *Slow down, slow down, for Pete's sake.* Then with tiny steps, she ventured into the hallway.

Her sister Mari—a lanky figure still wearing the tea shop's frilly apron—stood in front of the stove. With her back to Kiki, she turned vegetables over with a spatula and hummed some song—probably from the last century. Mari liked those old romantic songs by the Beatles and Bob Dylan because, as she put it, they had *meaning* for her heart.

Kiki held her breath; she was good at that. *One, two, three.* She'd held it for ninety-nine seconds once. No way could anyone, especially not that braggart, Angie Smithfield, compete with the record she'd set. Still holding and counting to herself, she made no sound as she slipped toward the screened back door. She opened it cautiously, making sure not to bang it against the frame.

Quiet as a mouse. If Mari knew what she was up to, the game was over. Mari would yell, then Kiki'd yell and do what Dr. Conner said she must not do—throw a clenched fist at her bedroom wall.

There, dimmed by the fading sun on the crooked driveway, stood her best friend—her maroon bicycle. She tossed Yoneko into the wire basket that wobbled by the handlebars, hopped on, and released the kickstand with a swift push. Just a little cruise before it was time to eat. Just down the street and around the corner. Exercise was good for her. Hadn't Dr. Conner told her that?

She pedaled fast and then slow, pretending she was a cyclist on some reality TV show, going for the prize. With the evening breeze in her short-cropped black hair, she smiled. Riding was almost as beautiful as hearing the choir at church sing the benediction about God being close to us, like our very breath. When she rode, it didn't matter that she was often a girl in the shadows watching others her age gather to talk about boys, leaving her out.

The dry mountain road curved around, and the climb was steep. But once she passed the Ridge Valley Apartments, the road sloped and she could coast down it with ease. To the left, right, suddenly she was in town pedaling past the hardware store, the tearoom, the Smithfield Funeral Home, and then a right curve by Russell Brothers Auto Repair Shop.

She'd watched these men, greasy with car fluids, jack up a Chevrolet or Ford in the two bays and use their tools to fix what they needed to. They had so many shiny tools. Her fingers itched to touch them, to use them on her bike. One of these days, she'd ask them—ask the man who always wore a beige shirt and John Deere ball cap—if she could borrow a tool or two. Her bike's front wheel was squeaky, especially after she cruised in the rain. But now a sign on the shop's glass door read "Closed." That meant everyone had gone home. She edged her bike toward the parking lot, a wide section to the left of the shop. Today it was barricaded by four bright orange cones, cones standing tall in a line where the lot met the leaf-blown sidewalk.

Past those cones was a spacious place to ride, without a parked car or truck in sight. She bet she could go fast. The space called to her; she could hear it. She would just ride around it, the autumn air in her face. She wouldn't hurt anything—those cones probably just meant they didn't want people parking there when they were closed. She heard music in her head—not one of Mari's ancient songs, but one of her own that sang, *Kiki is the champion, Kiki rides faster than the wind.*

She pedaled quickly into the lot. Immediately her bike slowed, grew sluggish. She pedaled harder. What was wrong? She looked at the pavement. For Pete's sake, it was soft and gooey, like the oatmeal Mari made for breakfast on chilly mornings before school. She pumped her legs hard; that always made her bike sail. But today it was only getting the front tire stuck. She tried again, but the bike teetered to the left. To regain balance, she dropped her feet from the pedals onto the ground. Like the tires, her shoes made fresh imprints into the pavement.

She saw all the faces that could get mad, grow red with frustration. "Yoneko," she said to her puppet, "we gotta get out of here." Her tires were coated with a gray film, and as she rushed home, flecks flew from them and dripped off her tennis shoes.

A few neighbors called, but she just kept racing toward her one-story house with the peeling front porch. In the driveway, she slid off her bike and guided it against the side of the house, behind an overgrown azalea bush. She pulled Yoneko from the basket and looked at her sneakers. They were caked. She tried scraping their soles against the gravel driveway and then in the grass. Knowing that there wasn't much time till dinner, she sat down in the yard and quickly tugged them off. Dropping them inside the basket, she hoped that no one would see the dirty bike or her shoes. *No one will ever know,* she thought as she mounted the steps to her back door.

Inside, she took a few breaths.

"Kiki!" Mari's voice was loud from the kitchen.

"Yes?" Kiki made her way down the hall, her socks slipping along the hardwood.

"Where were you?" Mari searched her eyes, then filled the room with a vast sigh. "Come on, time to eat."

Kiki stared at the plate of fried food her sister had placed at her table setting. She dreamed of chicken baked in crushed onion rings, like she saw on a TV commercial, mashed taters, a side of macaroni and cheese, and a slice of creamy chocolate pie. But there would be none of that. Her sister only knew how to make one recipe, and this—this measly dish—was it.

2

At sunrise, Gideon Miller, dressed in a beige shirt and black pants, ambled into his kitchen. As he spread apple butter on wheat toast, he thought of the harvest in Carlisle. Something about autumn mornings made him nostalgic for the open fields and watery-blue skies of his hometown, the distant mountains framing the landscape like a postcard. He thought of his mother, in a gray apron and bonnet, hanging clothes on the line. He saw his father, heaving bales of hay into his barn nestled in the ninety acres of farmland, his face stern because he did not know how to smile. Even after all these years away, Gideon's childhood crackled like dry leaves into the crevices of his memory. Why did he allow these thoughts? Seeing it was already seven, he placed his plate into the dishwasher and grabbed his John Deere ball cap from the hook on the living room wall.

Pushing aside anger from his youth, he set out to walk the mile to work. Walking was his fitness program. At thirty, he was not getting any younger. Or thinner. The brisk trek to the shop each morning, then back to his apartment after work, helped him feel no guilt when he went to the tearoom for a coveted piece of blackberry pie. Their pie was just like his aunt Grace made back in Harrisburg, the crust flaky and the filling not too sweet. Good blackberry pies weren't easy to come by.

He saw the damage to the pavement as soon as he rounded the corner. The cones were still there, spaced like he'd left them yesterday at closing. The cones were supposed to keep everyone out, but hooligans were oblivious to those rules.

Ormond Russell sat at the desk he kept in the middle of the shop's musty office, seven feet in front of the storage room. Ormond, too old to be much good now, had taught Gideon everything he knew—from diagnosing engines to changing spark plugs. The shop was his, named after his father, the late Edgar Russell.

"What happened to the driveway?" Gideon bellowed. His voice made the hair rise on the back of his own neck. Why was it that whenever he yelled, he sounded just like his father?

"Beats me." Ormond looked up from the *Twin Star* and sipped from a chipped mug of coffee. He wiped a hand over his gray mustache. "I parked across the street by the hardware store. I listened when you told me yesterday the parking lot was out of commission from being newly poured."

"There are tracks all over it."

"Tracks? The train don't run through here, now do it?" Ormond chuckled as he often did when he was amused by his own jokes.

Gideon usually laughed with Ormond, but not this morning. Not after he had spent half a day smoothing new concrete. "Someone will pay." His father's phrase—*someone will pay*. He'd used it that day, his neck pulsating with purple veins, when the gate to the orchard had been left open.

Gideon thought of calling Henry Kingston, Twin Branches' sheriff, and filing a complaint, but the phone on his cluttered desk rang and delayed that concern.

"Hello, Russell Brothers Auto Repair."

"Uh, hi."

"Yes?" Gideon drew the receiver closer.

"Is this Gideon Miller?" The voice was strained.

"It is."

"Gideon?"

"Yes." Was this another prank call? Silence was heavy on the other end. "State your business, please."

"I'm Amos." There was a pause. "Amos Stoltzfus, son of Ruth and Amos in Lancaster."

Gideon knew Lancaster County. They produced some of the best apple butter of any Amish community. "Well, Amos. What can I do for you?"

"I'm told you can help me."

Gideon heard the accent then, there was no denying it. His gut told him this was not going to be a conversation about a car that needed new tires or to be towed from a desolate mountain road. As he watched Luke Sauder enter the shop and head to his bay to finish work on a Ford truck brought in yesterday, he recalled six years ago. It had been autumn then, too, when Luke called him from a gas station in Huntington, West Virginia, asking if Gideon would help him and his thirteen-year-old sister Rebecca to escape. They'd managed to get rides—on public transportation and from an uncle who owned a furniture store in Cincinnati. Their uncle took them as far as Charleston, West Virginia, but they needed a way to get to him in Twin Branches, North Carolina. They were out of money.

Today's caller didn't use the word *escape*; he asked if he could learn how to become *English*. Only he asked it in Pennsylvania Deutsch, the German dialect, making Gideon's skin grow clammy with memories.

"Where are you now?"

"Outside of Harrisburg at a truck stop."

"That's a long ways away."

"I know. But if I get to you, can you help me?"

How could he say no? It was what he did, part of who he was: someone to believe in. "I can. Call me again when you get to the Smoky Mountains. Try to get a ride to Gatlinburg, in Tennessee."

13

"Thank you." The lightness to his voice made Gideon relax.

"How did you hear about me?" he asked before hanging up.

"Everyone knows about you, Gideon. You're the Getaway Savior."

Gideon worked off his frustration by ordering three cases of motor oil from his supplier and completing the inspection for a 2003 Jeep owned by the local librarian. Then he repaired the parking lot. When he finished, he duct-taped a cardboard sign with "do not trespass" in bold letters to one of the cones, looked at his work, and figured that should do the trick. Inside the shop, he interrupted Luke and Ormond's discussion on the recent University of Tennessee football game to emphasize that under no circumstances were they to let anyone walk or park on the lot. Then, as his stomach rumbled, he washed his hands and set out to Another Cup, the local tea shop, for a sandwich and some green tea.

He sat at the counter where he always did, in the corner near a jukebox he'd never heard play. He didn't bother with the menu—he wanted hot green tea and a roast beef on rye. He'd heard green tea was filled with antioxidants, good for the body, and now that he'd tried it, he liked it. As he ate, he read the newspaper, his shop's copy that he had persuaded Ormond to hand him. While Ormond focused on the sports page, real news always fascinated Gideon. Growing up, he'd had no idea there were shootings in the Middle East, plane crashes, and oil spills. Life had been about his remote community alone.

When the new manager approached him, he grinned at her and put his paper aside. Mari was her name. She was young, probably twenty-five, thin, dark hair and eyes. When she smiled, it was like being at the beach on a summer day. Last time they'd talked, she said she'd just moved here from Atlanta to take on the manager job at this tearoom. Today she eyed his green tea and said she was surprised.

"Surprised? Why?"

"Never met a man who drinks green tea." Her voice was gentle, her dark eyes flashed warmth.

14

"In Asia, doesn't everyone?"

"Sure. But we're in little Twin Branches, and most of the men I know here don't touch hot tea."

"I'm not from around here. Maybe that's why."

"Where are you from?"

"Pennsylvania." He didn't want to add he was once Amish.

"I've been there a few times. Isn't that where they have all those funny people who ride in horses and carriages?"

He swallowed hard, then said, "Uh, well . . . Where did you grow up?"

"Far from here." Picking up a cloth, she wiped down the counter to the left of him. "Everyone thinks I grew up in China. Can you believe that?"

Gideon felt a little silly; he'd assumed she was Chinese.

"They ask me about crazy things that have nothing to do with my ancestors." Seeing his clueless expression, she said, "Japan."

"Oh, of course," he said much too loudly. "Japanese, right."

"My great-grandparents came to the States from Kobe. I've never been there, never been to Japan at all." Her gaze shifted to the wide window behind him. "They felt life would be better here. But I don't know." She sighed and slipped her hands into her apron pockets. "There are no perfect places, are there?" Her face clouded and her jaw grew tense and he was afraid she might cry.

"These mountains here are nice," he said with feeling. She didn't respond, so he continued. "Especially now that it's fall, the colors are really pretty. Have you been up to Cove's Peak?"

"I dread the winter."

He wanted to see her smile again, so he thought of one of Ormond's jokes, one about the difference between a cougar and a lawyer. But as he set out to tell it, he realized he'd forgotten the punch line. He stood to pay his bill.

Della—an older woman with a pile of dyed, blond hair and heavy makeup who called everyone Sugar—entered from the kitchen. She took his twenty, handed him change, and said she hoped he had a good day. He wished her the same; it was the American Way.

When he turned to tell Mari goodbye, she was nowhere in sight. The cloth she had been using lay abandoned on the counter. His eyes rested on the clear canister that held fresh pies. He considered getting a slice of blackberry to go, but it was best he got back to work.

3

Principal Peppers' office was like a busy intersection, the kind Mari warned her not to ride her bike across. Teachers, the vice principal, and even a bus driver all wanted to discuss something with the middle-school's headmaster.

And here Kiki sat again, in the same chair across from his desk as she had been in last week. She studied his desk, eyes glued to a silver name plaque with his first and last names engraved on it. *Dusty Peppers*. No wonder people made fun of him. Between his name and his love of Hawaiian shirts, he was recognized and talked about wherever he went in Twin Branches. Kiki had heard that he once ate three bowls of peach ice cream at the state fair, then topped it off with a fried Twinkie.

"I called him," the VP said. She met Principal Peppers' gray eyes, then looked Kiki up and down. Her frown never left her wrinkled face. "He's on his way over."

Kiki's feet itched. She wished she could remove her shoes and scratch them. She heard Angie Smithfield's voice in her head, ringing like a phone that wouldn't quit. *"Miss Stevenson! Miss Stevenson, Kiki's in big trouble."*

How did Angie know these things? How could the girl accuse Kiki of riding her bike over the parking lot at the auto shop yesterday? Kiki was sure she'd not been seen.

Principal Peppers reassured the driver it was school policy to not tolerate disrespect on the bus. Should the behavior continue, the eighth graders who were tossing cantaloupe slices out the bus windows would be banned from riding. The bus driver thanked him and left.

Kiki's pulse raced. She was alone with Principal Peppers. Swallowing hard, she wished she had her puppet Yoneko. Mari told her not to bring Yoneko to classes because middle-school girls did not carry toys around at school. *Toys.* Didn't her sister realize Yoneko was more than a toy? Mama had sewed the cat's front paw back on with orange thread last year, making the stuffed puppet whole again.

"So," the principal said from behind his massive desk. He took off his wiry glasses and rubbed his eyes. "Kiki, what is this I hear about you?"

The urge to get out—get moving and away from this scene—raced across her mind. But her feet were like boulders. And they still itched. She saw her cement-caked sneakers, the ones she'd hidden until Mari closed her bedroom door last night and went to sleep. Then Kiki had rushed outside to start her cleanup. She'd used the garden hose on both shoes, scrubbing the soles with a kitchen scouring pad she later threw in the garbage. Had Angie seen her then? Kiki'd slipped back into the house with wet feet, dried them on a towel, and hoped she'd wiped the hallway well enough so that Mari would never guess what she'd done. Perhaps she'd been so concerned about not waking her sister that she hadn't noticed Angie spying on her next door.

The principal was peering at her, his glasses back on his face.

His eyes matched the blue-gray of his shirt. She liked that color. It was neither bright nor dark, one of those in-between tones that made her think of the arrowheads she had in her collection.

18

"Are you happy here?"

Happy? *Happy*. She rolled the word around in her mind. Did anyone care about happiness? Had that stern woman from social services with the bad hair and teeth asked if she was happy to be leaving Mama's house in Asheville? No, she had just said Mama was unfit to raise a child.

"The school year just started, and already you've been in here three times."

Kiki recalled the last time. They'd called Mari. Then Mari, stressed from having to leave the tearoom, had to listen to Principal Peppers explain that Kiki had thrown her math textbook onto the floor and threatened to burn all the stupid math books.

She could not face Mari being mad at her today. "Please don't call my sister. For the sake of Pete, please, please, please."

The principal sighed. He shuffled the pages in a manila file the VP had handed him.

Kiki was not only good at holding her breath, but she could also read upside down pretty well. The name on the file was hers. She bet that if she looked inside, it would have in large, mean letters: *Retard*.

But she was not a retard, she was autistic. That's what Dr. Conner said. And it wasn't bad to be autistic. That's what he told her whenever she shouted how she hated being this way. Being autistic just meant she was unique. The key was learning how to make her uniqueness work in a complex world. *Complex*.

Suddenly Kiki wanted to ask the principal if he knew what that word meant. She looked across the desk at him as he burrowed through her file.

Before she had a chance to speak, he asked, "Did you get into trouble at your school in Asheville?"

She wanted to say, "No way!" but that was a lie. In all her thirteen years, she couldn't recall ever *not* being in trouble. But she wouldn't tell him that. She opened her mouth to say something—she wasn't sure what would come out. Then the door scraped open and in walked the man from the auto shop, wearing his work clothes and smelling of the identical aftershave her social studies teacher wore.

"This is Mr. Miller." The VP motioned the newcomer toward the chair by Kiki and then closed the door.

Without looking at Kiki, Mr. Miller sat down.

"Thank you for coming by," the principal said. "I'm sorry to bring you down here, but I thank you for your time."

Kiki lowered her eyes. With a sidelong glance, she focused on the man's hands, soiled with grease and dirt under his nails. Her fingers got that way sometimes, especially in Asheville when she helped Ricky repair bicycles. Ricky had taught her how to use a wrench and a screwdriver.

"As we told you on the phone, Mr. Miller, Kiki, here . . ." He coughed, cleared his throat, and apologized.

Had it been a different day, a day she didn't feel so shaky, Kiki would have offered to get him a glass of water. She liked to get Mari water whenever her sister got a tickle in her throat.

"Apparently," the principal said, "Kiki rode her bicycle over your parking lot when the concrete was wet."

Perhaps, Kiki thought, this man would be kind. Perhaps he wouldn't yell or scold or—

"I want her to stay away from my shop."

Kiki's stomach morphed into a ball of jelly.

"Well." The principal cleared his throat. "Well." He coughed into his hand. "Kiki, what do you have to say to Mr. Miller?"

"I'm sorry. Sorry, really sorry."

The principal nodded her way. Perhaps that meant she was supposed to say more. "I didn't know it was wet."

With heat in his voice, Mr. Miller said, "I spent all afternoon pouring the concrete, and then I had to do it all over again."

Kiki felt the man's anger seeping from his skin and coating her like a bad dream. Perhaps this was a dream, and she'd wake up. She held her breath and starting counting.

"Maybe Kiki could show you how sorry she is by coming to your shop to help out."

The principal's voice was soft. Kiki raised her head, stopped counting, and smiled into his face. He might have a funny name, but today she didn't mind.

"I think that Kiki could work off her indebtedness to you," the headmaster said.

Her heart bloomed like it did when Mama made mashed taters for dinner, even if they were the kind from a box. The warmth from the bloom was almost as sweet as when the soloist at church sang "Silent Night" during the Christmas pageant. "Yes! I can help you! I am a good worker."

"Kiki, you may sit down."

She hadn't realized she'd jumped to her feet. Reluctantly, she sat.

Principal Peppers directed his next statement to Mr. Miller. "She could help you after school for a few days."

"Oh, please! I can work at your shop!"

"No," the man said. "That will not be necessary." He turned to Kiki. "Just stay off my property."

She winced.

He stood, one hand gripping the chair. With his jaw as firm as his voice, he added, "Please." Then he shook the principal's hand and left.

Kiki slumped into her chair. This was not good, not good.

"You may go," Principal Peppers said, his eyes now focused on papers spread over his desk. His black pen moved across a page. He licked his index finger and rubbed it against another page.

"For Pete's sake." Something inside made her spring out of her chair. "I could help him at his shop."

"He doesn't want help."

"I'm good with tools."

He looked at her. "Kiki, he wants you to stay away. You need to abide by his wishes."

Kiki felt like hitting the wall, felt like making the brown-and-gold-framed awards with *Dusty Peppers* written in bold letters, sway. If she did that, the school would call Mari. She stuffed her hands inside her jeans' pockets and, with loud steps, left his office. If only Yoneko was here, she'd cuddle the animal's soft fur and shut out this unfair world.

4

Back at the shop, Gideon busied himself with a 2002 Mustang the youngest Stuart son had brought in for a brake job. The Stuarts, like most of the mountain folks around Twin Branches, loved to hunt and fish and could use rifles and fishing lines almost before they could feed themselves with spoons. The Mustang's body was in good shape, but Gideon didn't think all the *Born to Hunt* and *I'd Rather be Fishing* stickers added anything to its value.

Yesterday Gideon had replaced the master cylinder, and today he was replacing the rear rotors and pads. As he worked on the car, he fumed. Did that girl who'd ruined his parking lot really believe he'd want her getting under his feet at the shop? He didn't need her help. He sighed and wondered why it bothered him that he was so peeved. *She's a kid. And she's not right in the head. You can tell by looking at her.*

Ormond interrupted his thoughts by handing him the cordless phone. The call was for him. Gideon wiped his hands on a shop rag. How would he ever get anything done today?

"Can you pick me up?" the caller asked.

"Who is this?" The accent was familiar, but there was nothing wrong in making sure.

"It's Amos. I called you the other day."

"Hello, Amos." The kid sounded more desperate. Had being in the *real world* already thrown him for a loop?

"Can you pick me up?"

"Where are you?" He stuffed the rag into his back pocket.

"Gatlinburg. I got a ride here this morning from Charleston."

The kid had made good time. Gideon paused to determine if today was the day his contact in Gatlinburg made the trek to Twin Branches. He opened the bottom drawer in his tool cabinet and took out a crinkled paper with Bruce's delivery schedule. If Amos could get to Bruce's depot by one o'clock tomorrow, he would be willing to drive the kid to Twin Branches. He'd driven many teens here from communities in Pennsylvania, Ohio, and Indiana—kids wanting to escape bonnets, buggies, and the Old Order.

Gideon gave Amos directions. "You want to go to Lyle's Produce at 676 Fairmont Place." As many times as he'd given this address, he knew it by memory.

"6176?"

"Do you have a pencil? Paper? Write it down. I'll wait."

Gideon heard some muffled voices, then Amos said, "I got the paper and pen. What was that again?"

Slowly, Gideon repeated the address of the trucking company that carried fresh produce over the mountains each Wednesday. "When you get there, ask for Bruce. He'll drive you here."

"What if he wants money? I'm out."

Of course, these kids were always out. "I'll cover it when Bruce gets here."

The driver would take him to 102 Azalea Avenue, the apartments where Luke lived. Hiber Summers, the landlord, offered inexpensive furnished places for Gideon's "brethren," as he called them, because he was a kind man. He also enjoyed having his 1988 Volvo serviced for free

24

and detailed at least three times a year—a little arrangement he and Gideon had.

"I'll be at the apartment tomorrow afternoon when Amos arrives," Gideon told Ormond. Bruce usually got into town around three. He'd greet Amos and get the lad situated in an apartment. *Lad.* Even after all these years, he called young boys lads, just as his parents had.

"Where is this one coming from?"

"Lancaster. He sounds really young."

As he continued with the Mustang, Gideon recalled that day when a lad had come to his father's farm. Gideon had seen the gate to the orchard wide open, the goat wandering around outside of it. But the scene his mind played over and over was the one after his father had noticed someone had been in his orchard.

The evening air was cool, the shed door cold and hard. Gideon placed his ear against it and thought he heard a whimper, like a calf when it was hungry. "Are you all right?" he asked. There was no reply so he tried again, this time his voice a little louder. "Are you all right?" The autumn wind circled his head, ruffling his brown curls. He was about to ask if the lad would like a bowl of soup when footsteps rounded the corner. His hands shook and his legs froze, though he knew he must run before his father caught him.

No more! Gideon nearly said it aloud as he lowered the car to the ground. He gave the lug nuts a few more tweaks with the ratchet. Then he opened the door and climbed in. He revved the engine and backed the Mustang out of the bay. He usually had Luke take the cars for runs to make sure they were operating smoothly. But he felt the need to drive. Just a few spins around the town, stopping every so often to test the brakes. Though he rarely drove his own 2006 F-150, there were times he needed to get behind the wheel and go.

Therapy, Ormond called it. "Driving clears your mind," he insisted. The old man, who had taught him years ago about repairing cars, knew a thing or two about the human condition, too. "Some days you just gotta let her rip, feel the wind in your face, and know that God gave us motorized vehicles for a reason. Driving sure beats going home and kicking the cat."

When Gideon got back to the garage from a late lunch—complete with a slice of blackberry pie, two cups of green tea, and a fairly nice conversation sprinkled with a few smiles from Mari—he saw her.

What is she doing here?

She was dressed in billowy blue sweatpants that engulfed her small frame and an equally baggy T-shirt. Gone were her jeans from earlier today. With her arms folded across her chest, she stood talking to Ormond.

"You!" He felt his veins grow hot.

The girl glanced at him timidly. "I rode my bike here."

"I told you no at school today. The answer is still no."

"But I'm a hard worker."

"That doesn't matter. I can't use you." Had someone advised her to use that hard-worker line on him? He'd heard those words from so many he'd helped to leave their Amish communities. What did they value about their upbringing? They'd ask each other this. Most said they appreciated that they'd been taught how to work hard.

But Gideon, when he felt like playing devil's advocate, would tell these young escapees, "Even a workhorse cannot survive on labor and whippings." Wide-eyed, they'd stare at him. "I still have a scar," he'd tell them. "Trust me. No child should be punished like that." Then he'd shut his mouth as the room grew silent, faces uncomfortable, some wanting to ask about this scar but uneasy to do so.

To the young girl today, Gideon repeated, "I can't use you."

Ormond looked up from his newspaper. "Kiki tells me that a friend taught her to use tools. She says she can fix bikes."

Gideon shook his head and stalked out to the bays. Luke was checking the oil under the hood of a white Mercedes.

"Luva Smithfield wants us to take a look at her new car," Luke said. "Just bought it this summer. She told me to treat it as I would my own.

26

My own! The only thing I know about owning my own Mercedes is in my dreams."

Well, this was no surprise. Most people thought Luva owned Twin Branches, so it was no wonder she could afford a car like this. The first day she'd driven it back from the dealership in Asheville, she'd slowed down Main Street, a proud smile on her face. She'd waved at passersby as if she was riding in the annual Twin Branches Christmas Parade.

As Gideon noted the shiny rims, the girl slipped up behind him. "I'm a hard worker. I can fix bikes. You can ask Ricky. He'll tell you how good I am."

She has no glassenheit, Gideon thought. Glassenheit—that blessed word for humility his father always shouted. It lodged in his mind along with his father's harrowing voice. As though pushing the word and memory away, he swatted the air with a broad hand. "Just go. Now."

"For Pete's sake, give me a chance."

"We repair cars here, not bicycles." He saw her maroon bicycle leaning against the edge of the building and thought of the damage it had caused. Inside the basket was some sort of stuffed animal. "Go," he said, hoping his tone was strong enough to make her leave. He gestured toward her bike in case she needed any more convincing. Turning abruptly, he walked back inside the office for a bottle of water. He took a cold Deer Park from the tiny fridge and unscrewed the cap.

"Please." The voice came from behind him.

She was relentless, but so was he. "I said no."

As Gideon started back to the bay, Ormond rattled the paper and peered over it at the girl. "Come back tomorrow," he whispered. "Gideon will be gone from three on." He gave her one of his wry smiles. Then he chuckled, warm and low, as he did when he told a joke.

Gideon pretended he had not heard any of it.

5

The Ridge Valley Apartments were built on the corner of Azalea and Woods Avenues. Although they once might have been appealing, now they stood like squat mounds of dry clay against the mountain range. A mossy stone fence surrounded the cluster of buildings, and ivy tumbled over the entryway onto the ground beneath. A lone spruce stood by the leaning signpost that read "Come Make Ridge Valley Your Home."

Gideon checked his watch. Bruce should be arriving in his semi any minute, with Amos in the passenger seat. He made himself comfortable on a bench near one of the buildings. He thought of Mari—the way she rested her hand against her neck, the tapered fingers adorned with silver rings. Today she'd seemed less moody, relentlessly teasing him about his green tea and asking how work was going. He told her about how some kid had ruined his parking lot. As he told her a few of the details, although not the kid's name, he realized it was really a small thing compared to the headlines in the daily paper. Mari agreed, making him think he should just let it go. But back at the garage, once he saw Kiki, he couldn't.

The sound of an engine hammering along the road grew louder as a long truck pulled to a stop in front of the Valley Ridge Apartments. Gideon recognized the truck, saw Bruce sitting behind the wheel. The passenger door opened, and Amos slithered out. Gideon greeted Bruce over the roar of the engine, handed him an envelope containing his delivery fee, and waited for Amos to gather his belongings.

Dressed in new Levi's and a navy T-shirt advertising Pabst Blue Ribbon beer, Amos stood before Gideon. A lit cigarette hung from his mouth. Gideon observed it all, even the watch on his wrist. Amos was already looking like a real Englishman.

"How long have you been on the road?"

"You mean when did I leave Lancaster?"

"That's right."

"Five days ago. At first I was just going to stay in Harrisburg, but then I decided to leave Amish country altogether."

"How old are you?" Gideon asked as Amos pulled a black duffel bag off the floor of the cab and thanked Bruce for the ride.

"Seventeen. I know, I look younger." Then he smiled and gave Gideon a spontaneous hug.

Gideon recalled when he left his parents fifteen years ago. The pleasures were here, the forbidden fruits his parents did not tolerate. He had embraced them all—Jim Beam, Marlboro Menthols, and the Rusty Saddle Bar and Grille. He gave up smoking and drinking within a year. He didn't like the taste of smoke in his mouth and nose—or the burn of whiskey in his throat. As for the local bar and grill, there had been a cute blonde pool player who frequented the establishment, but when she got engaged, he stopped heading there after work. Instead he walked home to his shows on cable. And he drank Gatorade and discovered bologna sandwiches.

"Seems to me," Gideon said as they climbed the stairs to the apartment reserved for Amos, "you made good time."

He showed Amos around the sparsely furnished one-bedroom apartment. He had no idea if the kid knew about refrigerators, dishwashers, or garbage disposals, so he explained how each appliance worked. At last he said, "I'm sure you'd like to rest." He pointed to the double bed in the bedroom. "Linens are in the closet." He flicked on the overhead light. "You know about electricity?" He was glad when Amos smiled.

"Once you get on your feet you can furnish this place the way you'd like. Right now it's not much, but it's safe and dry." He handed Amos a copy of his terms and conditions to sign. This was standard procedure for all those he helped.

Amos dropped his duffel bag onto the wooden floor beside the bed, causing the room to echo. From the pocket in the front, a Snickers bar popped out.

Gideon recalled how his candy bar of choice had been Twix. He never could get enough of that sweet flavor when he first left the home place. His father insisted that his children never have a taste of carbonated drinks or candy bars. They were not to fill their appetites with *English junk food*. Now the gold and red Twix packaging reminded him of long ago, another time, when he was just discovering the rest of America.

Amos studied the document. He rubbed his chin as he turned over the two pages, then looked at Gideon. "I'm kinda tired. What does it say?"

"It says I pay your first month's rent of $340—and during that time, you work at the auto shop. After that you are free."

"Free?"

"Free to keep staying here, paying your own rent, or free to live elsewhere. If you don't work for me during the thirty-day period, I can terminate your contract with the apartment's landlord, and you'll be evicted."

Amos's mouth opened. "Evicted?"

"Thrown out."

Gideon patted the boy's back. "Welcome to the real world, Amos. I hope you like it." He handed Amos a pen and showed him where to sign. Then he folded the pages and fit them into his back pocket. When he reached the front door, Amos called after him, "Do most?"

"Do you mean, do most escapees stay or go back to their communities?"

"Yes, that's what I meant." Amos stood at his elbow now.

Gideon thought for a moment. "I know of only one kid I helped who ended up returning to his family in Goshen."

"What happened?"

"Let's just say he sowed his wild oats and then ran out of money."

"Couldn't he get a job to support himself? That's what I plan to do." Amos's chest seemed to expand, pride filtering through his squared shoulders.

Gideon shrugged. "I think he missed his family." He felt a large sigh here would add weight to his statement, but no sigh formed in his lungs. "The real world is not an easy place for everyone, Amos. Even for the English born into it." Amos wouldn't fully understand his words. It would take time to grasp them in the fibers of his being and feel their value.

"Come on over for dinner," Gideon said. "D'you like chitlin stew?"

Amos's face showed he had yet to experience the food culture of the South.

Gideon retrieved a dog-eared business card from his pocket and scribbled his address on the back. "I live in another set of apartments about a mile from here."

Amos took the card and glanced at himself in the mirror on the stark wall. "Do I look like I could fit in?"

"Depends on what you want to fit into."

The boy studied his features. "I'll never grow a beard. I won't look Amish."

"It's not just about looks. The heart has a way of coming into play." Gideon could have said more, could have explained how it took some time away from a religion so entrenched in a culture and a lifestyle before you could recognize what you wanted to keep and what you wanted to toss. The tossing held its own set of demons. But as the boy yawned twice, Gideon decided to let him get some rest. He'd save his sermons for their dinner conversation.

The truth was, Gideon thought as he made his way back to the shop, the one kid who went back to life in Goshen—Ezra Wagner, a wide-eyed boy with a frothy laugh—was not around to tell the story. Although his family had welcomed him back, and he'd joined the church, married a Yoder girl, grown a long brown beard, and worn the customary black attire each Sunday, he wasn't happy. One night he'd packed a small bag and left again. Months passed; he didn't come back to Twin Branches or to Goshen. To this day, Gideon had no idea where he was.

But there were rumors. There would always be rumors, and rumor had it that Ezra had moved to California and married a local girl he met at a bookstore. Ezra never told her he was already married to Annie Yoder because to the day he died, she was to be his wife. Mr. Yoder had made that clear. Divorce was not an option in the Old Order Amish community of Goshen, Indiana.

Ezra was still on Gideon's mind when he entered the shop, but what he saw in his bay jolted him quickly from his thoughts. There she was—that girl—seated on the floor, with her bike leaning beside her on its kickstand. He stifled the urge to tell her to get out.

Ormond and Luke hovered around her as she removed the front wheel.

She smiled at them and then, without any sign of strain, put the wheel back on.

Gideon had watched his own mother swiftly and effortlessly use a treadle-powered sewing machine to create clothes for his family. He was still in awe of her expertise, and since that time he'd not experienced that sense of wonder. Yet here was this girl, this troublemaker. What was her name? With the help of a pair of open-end wrenches, she'd taken off the wheel and replaced it. Just like that.

Seeing Gideon, Kiki announced she was going to adjust the brake pads. She spun the front wheel and the back, working the brakes as they made a shrill noise. Then, using an Allen wrench, she turned the spring adjusters for the front brake. With the handle of a screwdriver, she tapped the wheel and then tried the brake. "No more squeaking!" Delight filled her face.

As though on cue, Ormond and Luke clapped.

She approached Gideon. "Did you see me? Did you see me? Can I have a job here?"

Gideon sucked in air. Amos would need work to pay off his rent, and the shop already had Luke, Ormond, and him on payroll. The shop did not get enough business for another employee.

Her dark eyes were pleading.

He looked away. Walking to the tools scattered around her, he picked them up. "There is a place for everything, and everything has a place."

"I know that!"

"You have to pick up the tools after every job."

She took the wrenches and the Phillips head from him, raced them back to his rolling tool chest, opened the top drawer, and placed them inside. With a flourish, she pushed the drawer, watching it shut tightly. "All done!"

Luke applauded.

"She does good work," Ormond said.

A silence followed. Gideon realized all eyes were on him, waiting. "Come back tomorrow," he heard a voice say, then realized he'd just spoken.

"Really, Mr. Miller?" Kiki's face glowed like a harvest moon over the farmlands of Carlisle. "Are you being serious?"

"Yes."

"Seriously?" Her voice had a funny singsong quality. "Cross your heart and all that stuff?"

"Yes."

She threw herself against him, wrapping her thin arms around his waist, burying her face into his chest. "Thank you, thank you, thank you!" Then she came up for air and hopped on her bike, steering it carefully out of the garage.

Gideon shook his head. "Strange kid."

"Ain't she something? I do like her persistence." Ormond stretched his arms high above his head and grinned. "Do you recall when you first stepped foot in here fifteen years ago?"

"No." Gideon did not care to hear Ormond repeat that anecdote.

"You were so green, still breathing Amish air," Ormond said. "But you begged me to teach you how to fix automobiles." He let out a long laugh. "Automobiles, you said, as though you hardly knew how to pronounce the word. I never told you this in all these years, but I believe a part of you might have died that day if I had sent you away."

Gideon sat at his desk, pretending to be occupied with a memo pad and pen.

"What if I had said no to you?"

"Do we need to order any more brake fluid?" Gideon called to Luke, who was washing his hands in the small sink by the fridge.

"Last time I checked, we had three quarts of the full synthetic left."

"Well?" Ormond persisted, standing in front of his desk. "What if I had told you no?"

Gideon looked at his watch. "Seems like it's nearly time to go home." He turned to Luke. "Will you close up the shop today? The new kid is in 2F, upstairs from you. I've invited him over to dinner tonight, and you're welcome to join us." Gideon knew that Luke lived on ramen, Campbell's soup, and TV dinners. He never turned down a home-cooked meal.

"I'll be there." His eyes flashed with appreciation. "I'll stop by and pick up the new guy."

"Well?" Ormond awaited his answer.

Gideon slipped past Ormond, avoiding his eyes. "See you tomorrow," he called over his shoulder.

He walked back to his apartment, admiring the persimmon-and-marigold-colored leaves as they floated to the pavement from a cluster of trees. He heard Ormond's question every step of the way. He knew the value of giving people a chance—his people. This girl, this Kiki, was not one of his.

But he had not been one of Ormond's people. Ormond had never met an Amish brother before. He had only seen a buggy in a photograph, and he had never tasted apple butter or shoofly pie. Ormond had chuckled often as he patiently taught Gideon how to repair automobiles. He believed in what he saw in Gideon. Russell, Ormond's father, had not been so sure. But Ormond never gave up.

6

She was racing, racing, riding like the wind. *Here comes Kiki—Kiki the wonder girl!* With each push of her bike's pedals, her elation rose. Mr. Miller, the man at the shop, said she could come back tomorrow! She'd showed him how good she was. He was probably heading home now to tell his wife and children what a fast worker she was. Kiki felt like celebrating. She knew Mari would be home soon and expecting her to be there, but there would be nothing wrong with going by the Piggly Wiggly first for a Coke. She felt the quarters in her pocket, grateful that she hadn't lost these like she'd lost the ones last week. That had been embarrassing, standing at the drink machine with no coins. In despair, she'd let out a moan, then she'd given the base of the machine a few swift kicks. In the movies, it worked—drinks popped out like a jack-in-the-box. But that day nothing happened. Kiki wanted to cry, until a hand touched her shoulder, and there stood her neighbor, Mrs. Luva Smithfield. Mrs. Luva told her not to worry, she had money. A Coke had never tasted so good to Kiki as it had that day, and Mrs. Luva had even given her more quarters for another day.

Today was that day. Kiki put three quarters into the beverage machine, selected a regular Coke, and waited. Mari always told her not to be impatient. With a sputter, out came a can. "Cheers!" she said as she lifted the drink to her lips. "Cheers to me!"

Two boys coming out of the store laughed at her antics, but she didn't care. Let them laugh. She doubted that they knew how to fix a bike like she did.

When she was sure that the can was empty, she tossed it into the recycle bin, jumped onto her bike and with a few spins around the park, took the long way home. She wished it was already the next day so she could be at the auto shop working on bicycles and getting the attention of the others. They liked her! They were going to let her work there!

But as she coasted her bike into the driveway, her elation over her moment of glory faded. She heard voices she recognized coming from next door in the backyard of Angie's grandmother. Kiki eased off her bicycle, listening to the laughter coming from beyond the wooden fence that separated her house from Mrs. Luva Smithfield's large bungalow. Kiki secured her bicycle inside the garage, grabbed Yoneko, and scampered through the back door. Sailing into her bedroom, she pushed back the curtains and stared out her window.

The early October day was giving way to night, but in the shadows she saw them by the swing set beside the apple tree. She squinted to see Angie and two other girls from school. From her lone window, she watched them tumble with headstands and cartwheels into the soft grass. Their jackets and hair were dotted with leaves. She knew they were practicing for gym class. Everyone was supposed to be able to do a cartwheel and headstand tomorrow.

With one hand on the blue-green curtains and the other holding her cat puppet, she watched their moves. Her heart wanted, wanted so much, to be with them, to be able to sail out of the house as quickly as she'd entered and cry, "Hey, guys! What are you doing?"

But she knew too well what they were doing. They were having fun—without her.

Their laughter and squeals filled the evening air. Why didn't they want her? She could laugh. She even knew how to flutter her eyelashes the way the women did on her favorite TV show, *Gilligan's Island*. She had a tube of lipstick, one she'd taken from Mama. But no, none of that mattered. Angie called her a baby, right to her face.

Even when she heard Mari call out that she was home, Kiki stayed by the window. In a moment, another figure came to the grassy backyard from inside the bungalow. Angie's Uncle Reginald. He was over six feet tall and wore heavy boots and a leather jacket. Kiki heard he drove trucks for a living and hated anyone who was not fully white. She pulled the curtains tight, turned on her desk lamp, and put her hand into the puppet. She made the cat move—up and down like it was gliding. Mama would do that. Mama had named this cat that she bought for twenty-five cents at the Thrifty Mart. Mama had wanted to call it *no-raneko*, which meant *stray* in Japanese. Kiki begged for another name, so Mama christened it Yoneko, which she said meant *rice child*. "Rice child?" That sounded strange, but Mama said all cats in Japan ate rice, just like all children did.

As Kiki looked at her arrowhead collection, she wished she was a Japanese child in Japan so she'd get rice for dinner. But she could already smell the aromas from the kitchen, the usual scents—onions, green peppers, and potatoes.

Her first arrowhead was a gift from her grandpa before he died. When he closed his eyes for the last time, a frail figure on the heirloom feather bed, she was given twenty-nine arrowheads he'd accumulated in the mountains of North Carolina. That winter afternoon, as her throat clogged with tears, she blew her nose on a tissue Mama handed her, thinking how it smelled of honeysuckle. "There now, my *musume* (daughter)," Mama had said. "You love arrowheads. And these are all yours." She felt glad about getting the collection, but crushed that her grandfather would no longer polish them with the silky cloth as he sat by the stereo and listened to a gospel radio station.

She loved rubbing her index finger over each arrowhead and feeling the pointed edges. Grandpa called these his prizes. He'd kept his collection in a cedar box, the kind that smelled like a forest with the sun shining over the treetops. But when Kiki was handed them, they were in a red bandana, tied at the ends. She once asked Mama where the cedar box went, but Mama shook her head and said sometimes it was best not to know too much.

After dinner, Mari cleared the table and told Kiki to do her homework. Kiki frowned.

"You have math homework, don't you?"

How could her sister tell? "I don't wanna do it."

"Kiki, remember what Dr. Conner told you?" Mari looked deep into her eyes.

Of course she remembered. But what was the point in learning math? "I'm never gonna use it, never gonna use that stupid math."

"Just go do it."

"I hate math."

"If you want to stay in mainstream school, you need to follow the rules." Mari's eyes were like bullets, and Kiki wanted to avoid looking at them.

"Math is not a good rule. It's a stupid subject." She flicked a fried onion off the kitchen table and onto the floor.

"Kiki, pick that up!"

With a loud sigh, she did. Along with trying to do well in all her subjects, Dr. Conner reminded Kiki not to make Mari mad.

Again Mari told her to get into her room. There was no way she could escape doing her homework. As she slid her chair back, the phone rang.

Mari answered, then said, "Sure, she'd like to speak with you, too."

Kiki drew her arms across her chest. "I don't want to talk to her tonight."

With her hand over the mouthpiece, Mari pleaded.

"I don't want to. I have nothing to say to her."

Mari gave her a stern look, and Kiki knew there were times you just had to do what you were told to do. Even if your brain didn't see the need. Like math homework. She took the phone and said as cheerily as she could, "Hi, how are you?"

Mama's voice was low and soft, just as she remembered it. "I am missing you."

"Really? Well, I'm doing just great!"

"Good, good for you." Mama paused, most likely trying to come up with something to ask. Mama often asked questions. "How's school?"

"Fantastic!" She didn't usually use that word, but it sounded perfect for what she wanted to convey.

Mari's eyes widened.

"That's nice," Mama said. "I hope to see you soon. I bet you've grown. How tall are you now?"

"I'm not a giant yet."

"I hope Mari can drive you to see me one day."

Her voice was so clear, like Mama was seated right beside her. If she just moved her free hand out, surely Mama would take and grab it, blowing kisses against her fingers.

"I want to see you soon. I love you, Kiki."

"Yeah, I hope so. Here's Mari." Kiki stood, thrust the phone into her sister's hand and left the room. She pounded her feet all the way down the hallway to her bedroom.

She thought she'd slam the door. Instead she collapsed onto her bed, turned toward the wall, and muffled a sob. She stroked Yoneko's fur, the smooth patches that were not worn, running her finger along the foot Mama had sewed. She saw the cramped house in Asheville, every inch teeming with furry critters, puppets, Mama's loves. If Mama really loved her, why did she choose them over her? Why couldn't Mama clean those puppets out of her house and live like a normal person?

She felt tears on her cheeks, then a hand on her back.

"Thank you for talking to her. You made her happy."

"Those stupid puppets make her happy, not me!"

Mari sat on the bed, and Kiki turned to face her. "Remember I told you that Mama isn't well? She has a problem."

Kiki chewed on her clenched fist. She hoped Mari wouldn't go into another lecture about how some people suffer from addictions.

Mari just massaged her shoulder. "She does love you."

"Why can't she throw away all those puppets and clean her house?"

"I don't know . . ." Mari's voice trailed off. "Hey," she said a minute later, "why don't we have some cookies?"

Kiki sat up. "What kind?"

"What do you think?" Mari smiled into her eyes.

Kiki brushed a tear from her cheek. "Oatmeal?"

"You bet!"

Kiki laughed. Maybe this evening wasn't going to be so bad. Maybe over cookies, she'd even tell Mari that she was going to fix bikes at Russell Brothers Auto Repair. As her mood rose, she grabbed her pirate hat off the closet floor and fit it over her head. Its broad brim curved like hands bent to cup a drink of mountain water from a stream. Two red and gold feathers sailed out of the back. Kiki had wanted a flamboyant Jack Sparrow pirate hat—or at least one with a shiny brass buckle that if polished enough, you could see your reflection in. Yet this hat was all Mama found when she went out to look for a Halloween costume for Kiki two years ago. Although it wasn't exactly what she wanted, there were times you should just be happy with what you got.

Over a glass of milk and two cookies, Kiki came close to telling Mari her good news. But she didn't want to make Mari angry, so perhaps it was best to keep her news to herself. She'd just head over to the shop tomorrow after school and get home before Mari returned from work. Or she'd call Mari at the tearoom to say she was going to a friend's house to do homework. That would be a lie, but it would make Mari happy. Sometimes little lies weren't bad, were they? She'd have to ask Pastor Clayton.

The next day at school, Angie said her friends were going to have a bike-riding contest next week—and Kiki was not invited. Kiki tried to ignore Angie. Today she wouldn't let her ruin her good mood. In two hours and seventeen minutes she was going to run home, get on her bicycle, and ride to the auto shop. Tonight after dinner, for sure, she'd call Ricky to tell him how she amazed them at fixing her bike and so now she had a job. She saw Ricky's tender eyes, his smile, and knew her friend would be happy for her. He'd say things like, "That's awesome" and "Way to go, Kiki!" She'd smile into the phone and feel warm all over.

7

Amos arrived at the shop at eight o'clock, sleep still in his eyes. Gideon tossed him an old shirt and a wrinkled pair of work pants he'd found on one of the shelves in the storage room. A kid who had left Goshen, Indiana, had worn them—for all of two days. That boy hadn't seen any beauty in changing oil or looking at engines. After a short stay in Twin Branches, he'd gone to High Point, where a relative got him a job as a salesclerk in a furniture store.

As Amos changed in the restroom, Gideon dismissed the memory of the young Goshenite. He sat at his desk, staring at paperwork that needed to get done yesterday, then he took a walk to the bays, opening the garage doors since Luke hadn't done that yet. He breathed in the clean, crisp, autumn air and, by habit, looked to the right. The lilac-colored morning glories that had flourished in August were now only memories, except for one single bloom that had yet to fade. In his last spring in Carlisle, his mother had planted morning glories. His brother, Moriah, had picked one for her when it flowered in July, then wondered why the bloom wilted and didn't open again the next morning, even though Mother obliged and placed the flower in a vase of water.

The delicate heart-shaped flower made him think of Mari. Like the vine that threaded through the chain-link fence between the auto shop and Benson's Laundromat, she seemed to have found a way to creep into his heart. Back inside his office, he sat at his desk, picturing her face, the way she smiled, the tilt of her face when he ordered his lunch.

"How do I look?" Amos was in the doorway, changed and hopefully ready to learn. The stained beige shirt swam around his narrow shoulders, and the black pants dragged on the ground. Gideon nodded his approval. If the boy stayed on and proved to be a good worker, he'd order work clothes to fit him. "Go find Luke," Gideon said. "I'll be with you in just a minute."

As Amos trailed off, Gideon knew that if he was going to focus on training the new kid today, he needed to concentrate on engines and oil changes. That should keep him from spending so much time thinking of Mari.

Using the 2007 Jeep Limited that had been dropped off the night before, Gideon explained to Amos the parts of the car under the hood. Then, since the Jeep was in for its annual inspection, Gideon explained how to test the headlights, parking lights, and taillights. He hooked up the car to the diagnostic machine to show Amos how to test emissions.

As Amos stared at him blankly, Luke nudged Gideon. "I think he doesn't know what fuel injectors are. You need to start slow, like you did with me."

Slow? He *was* instructing things in his slow voice. *How much more elementary can I get?* Then an idea came to him. "Luke, why don't you take over?"

Luke and Amos had gotten along well last night when Gideon invited them over for dinner. The two talked like old friends as they ate curried pork chops, scalloped potatoes with a cheddar cheese sauce, and baked apples. Luke asked about several relatives he had in Lancaster to see if Amos knew them. And when Luke took out his banjo, Amos hollered as though a pig had bitten him. "A banjo! I've read about those. Teach me how to play."

While Gideon cleared the dishes and made a pot of green tea, Luke strummed. Then he handed the instrument to Amos, who held it lovingly, as though it might break, and ran his fingers across the strings. Luke leaned over and showed him how to play three chords. Neither was interested in a cup of hot tea, so Gideon poured one for himself and drank it as he loaded the dishwasher.

He could see the two young men were having fun. They connected. He wondered why he had trouble connecting to people. He scraped a dish with a fork and ran some water over it; the remains of parsley from the potatoes swirled down the drain. He thought about friendships. Ormond had taken him fishing a few times in the Great Smoky Mountains National Park and at Fontana Lake. He never caught anything, but Ormond's fetch of trout was always numerous.

Henry and his wife had invited Gideon over for meals, and when the trucker Bruce was in town for any length of time, Gideon enjoyed conversing with him. He wasn't a recluse. Even so, he wondered why he felt so lonely.

Gideon stood at the open garage door as a flock of geese soared into the shimmering autumn sky. He inhaled the fresh air and let it expand into his lungs. He loved living in North Carolina. What could be finer than the serenity and beauty of the Smokies?

A blue Toyota with a maroon bicycle strapped on the trunk turned into the lot. The bike looked familiar and so did the two inside. The passenger door swung open, and Kiki jumped out. Mari parked the car and emerged from the driver's seat.

Then it dawned on Gideon. Kiki must be Mari's daughter.

"I came home from school and had to go to the doctor, Dr. Conner." Kiki took her bike from the trunk rack and wheeled it inside the garage. "Dr. Conner made me late getting here."

Mari smiled at Gideon. "She says you are going to let her work here?"

"She says she wants to."

"I'm sure she does. She likes tools."

Gideon nodded. "She impressed us all."

"I have to get back to the tearoom. Tell Kiki to ride her bike straight home when she is done with her work here."

"I will." Gideon waved to Mari, then turned to where Kiki had put her bike in his bay. He told her to bring it into the shop, out of the way of cars he and Luke—and perhaps Amos—would be repairing.

"But where will I get tools?" she said. "For the sakes of Pete, Mr. Miller, I need tools so I can work."

"Gideon," he said. "If you are going to work here, you need to call me Gideon."

"Gideon." She said the name as though it was a foreign word.

"None of this *Mr. Miller* stuff, okay?" When she nodded, he pulled out an Allen wrench, a Phillips screwdriver, and a flat screwdriver from his work chest. He motioned to the inside of the shop—away from the bays—and she pushed her bike along.

Gideon found a spot for her to work near the storage room, out of the way of the others. He had no idea what she was going to do, but assumed she wanted to tinker with her bike. If that occupied her and kept her out of his hair, it suited him fine.

"I got home and had to go to Conner's." Kiki sat on the floor in front of her bike. "I wanted to come here right away, but I had to go to Conner's."

"That's okay." Gideon reassured her it was all right that she had not been able to come immediately after school.

"I need a towel," she said as he placed the tools beside her.

He entered the storage room and brought out a few shop towels. "Use only one or two of these each day. They cost a lot."

Kiki cleaned her bike's spokes with one of the towels. She seemed different, now that he knew she was connected to Mari. It didn't take a rocket scientist to realize the two could be related, since they both looked Asian. Mari must be Kiki's mother. *Mother.* The word wasn't one he wanted to associate with this woman he found so intriguing. He let his thoughts focus on the child, and why she was so intent on being here.

After a while, he shook his head. *If she wants a place to hang out and it makes her happy, okay,* he thought. *But I'm not paying her to tinker with her own bike. Plus, in a month, Amos goes on our payroll. Speaking of Amos, where is that kid?* "Where's Amos?" Gideon asked Ormond and Luke.

"Went home." Luke checked the pressure in the front tire of the car at his bay. Ormond stood beside him, telling some joke about a banjo and a piano.

"Home?" Gideon looked at the round white clock on the wall behind Luke's head. "It's 4:37."

"My watch says 4:36." Ormond lifted his hand to glance at his Rolex.

Gideon wasn't in the mood. "What is he doing heading home this early?" The shop didn't officially close until 5:00.

No one spoke.

Gideon looked at Luke. "Do you know why he went home before closing time?"

"He said he was tired."

"Tired? Tired? Who said he could leave?"

Luke looked at Ormond, who looked back at Luke.

Gideon closed his eyes and saw a film of red. When his eyes opened, Kiki had joined them.

"He's not a hard worker," she said.

Ormond grinned, and Luke nodded.

"Does anyone want to go over to his apartment and tell him to get back here?" When no one offered, Gideon grabbed his jacket from the wall. He would give Amos a piece of his mind. *No.* He steadied his breathing. He'd wait. He'd set a good example for the others as

47

co-owner. He'd wait till the shop closed. Then he'd meet with Amos and talk the laziness out of that boy. He'd tell this farm boy that one didn't walk out early from a job unless given permission. How did he expect to learn anything if he couldn't even work a full day?

8

Gideon's walk to work the next morning was heavily seasoned with questions. His first was, why? Why was he interested in someone that he couldn't have a relationship with? Why did he feel such a longing to get to know Mari when she'd never be the woman he could marry and grow old with? She was divorced. Growing up, his parents spoke of those who got divorced as evil, removed from God, denied of His blessings. A marriage union was supposed to last forever. Amen. If Mari was Kiki's mother, then she must be either unwed—another unacceptable situation—or divorced. Either way, how could he ever continue being hopeful about a possible future with her? By the time he got to the auto shop, he felt weary, like he needed a nap.

Seeing Ormond at his usual perch with the newspaper, Gideon approached him, standing in front of his desk, his hands in his pockets.

"Uh . . . Um . . ." His voice sounded like a faulty muffler, in bad need of replacement. "What do you think about people who get divorced?"

Ormond read a few more lines from the sports section and then laid the paper down by his coffee mug. "What do I think?"

"Yeah."

"About divorce?"

Gideon clarified. "About what the Bible says and all that."

"Are you asking me some biblical interpretation about divorce?"

"I think so."

"At this early hour? I'm only on my first cup."

"Yes." Why couldn't Ormond just answer the question? He attended Valley Baptist each Sunday; he should know these things.

Ormond smoothed his mustache with his thumb. Pensively, he studied his fingernails as though seeing the dirt in them for the first time. "My sister's husband beat her with a frying pan."

Gideon gulped. He'd forgotten that horrific incident that happened just a year after he'd arrived in Twin Branches.

"And yes, filing for divorce and running as far as you can away from a monster like that is the only thing to do." Through clenched jaw, he added, "And pray he gets time locked up."

Gideon let out a low sigh. Ormond was an easygoing man, calm and humorous, except for when, as he called it, *fire rumbled under his skin.* Then his soft demeanor turned cold, eerie. Gideon was sorry he'd made Ormond remember the terrifying event of years ago. He knew Ormond's sister had been in the hospital with broken bones and ribs for a week after that night. Gideon had only been sixteen, but he'd visited her in the hospital with a bouquet of daisies. Daisies and a handmade card were all he could afford.

Ormond took a swallow of coffee. "Some men are monsters. They've lost any human resemblance; let themselves be stripped of the light and love bestowed on them by their Creator."

Gideon's thoughts rushed to his father. Did that man ever hold any love and light? He was the epitome of beast and monster. The shed, the tree limb, the whack across that lad's bottom, and then the hard blow against his own backside—these images were not easily dismissed in Gideon's mind. Every time he saw his scar in the bathroom mirror, he wanted to retaliate with some act of violence. Gideon made his way to his office and, clutching the edge of his desk, lowered himself to his chair. He breathed in and out, unaware what a toll simple breathing took on him.

A rap on his door caused him to raise his head. There stood Luke. Feebly, Gideon motioned for the young man to enter.

"Customer wants to see you. Something about spark plugs you ordered for him."

Gideon drew in a breath. "Give me a minute."

Luke eyed him cautiously and then said, "Do you want me to help him?"

When Gideon didn't respond, Luke said confidently, "I can do that," and walked away.

Gideon tried to compose himself. He felt his frustration mount, his veins hot with the thick tar of anger. He would never return to his hometown. He couldn't, because that would mean he'd have to take the strongest stick he could find, square up to his father, and let his emotions flail. Of course, they'd toss him into jail. They locked up those who beat the tar out of men.

At first Gideon thought the damp, foggy weather contributed to the wariness he felt brooding in the chilly air. But as he rounded the corner, the two sheriff's cars parked diagonally at Another Cup's parking lot confirmed it was more than just a feeling. Officers didn't usually come here, not even for tea. Inside the tiny eatery stood Sheriff Kingston and his deputy, Tomlin, their hands on their hips close to their holsters.

"What's going on?" Gideon sidled up to his usual spot at the counter.

Henry hiked up his pants. "Got a little trouble going on." He spoke like he had marbles in his mouth. Gideon once thought it was chewing tobacco, but the sheriff did not chew or spit. "We don't like this kind of trouble."

Gideon's breath caught, and he scanned the room. Mari was taking an order at one of the tables. As long as she was all right, things couldn't be that bad.

51

"Things just ain't like they once was around here," Deputy Tomlin said.

"What do you mean?"

"Well." He drew a breath and looked at Henry. "Bad riffraff from across the mountains." He jerked his thumb toward the door.

Gideon knew he was pointing west toward Gatlinburg. Twin Branches prided itself on being "a quaint mountain town, pretty as a postcard and warm with Southern hospitality." That phrase was printed in curvy gray lettering on the Welcome to Twin Branches sign.

Henry accepted a Styrofoam cup of coffee from Della, thanked her, and turned to Gideon. "But they're gone now. And we best be heading back to the station." He neared Gideon and lowered his voice. "Going to come over to our house for Thanksgiving this year? Mebane wants you to know you're invited."

Although it was only October, Gideon figured he could commit to saying yes. He doubted he'd get an invite anywhere else. "Sure, tell her thank you."

Henry and Tomlin scanned the eatery one last time before wishing everyone a good day.

When they left, Della came out from the kitchen with two plates of bacon, eggs, and grits. She smiled at Gideon on her way to deliver the food to a table behind him. "Be with you in a moment, Sugar."

"What happened here?"

She stopped and whispered, "Two rednecks trying to get something for nothing. Complaining about the food, refusing to pay their tab. You know how those kids from Gatlinburg can be."

Gideon spread out the day's *Twin Star* on the counter, but he could not concentrate. He watched Mari as she answered the phone and then went into the kitchen, her dark hair swinging over her shoulders. She looked exceptionally pretty this afternoon. He liked the way her makeup accentuated her brown eyes.

You can't ask her out, a voice inside his head said. *She's been married and divorced from Kiki's father. Or maybe she never got married, just had a baby and Kiki's father didn't hang around.*

Before asking what he'd like for lunch, Della spit her chewing gum into the trash can behind her. Every time she did this, she followed the same pattern—she'd give a light cough, then turn her head and shoot the gum into the trash.

Each time Gideon knew what she was doing. Just like when she pretended to be reading a menu with her reading glasses, but she was actually peering over them at any man who entered the restaurant.

"How's business today?" she asked.

"Pretty good."

"I need to bring our Ford in. It's making funny noises."

"You should. Funny noises are never good when it comes to cars."

"Look at you," she said. "You are going to make some woman happy one day."

"Who?"

"Oh, someone perfect for you." She winked.

He didn't really think she had anyone in mind. She was just a romantic at heart; the Lifetime Movie Network was probably a constant at her house.

"Well, I know you're hungry." She smiled. "Need a menu?"

"I'll have a roast beef sandwich with horseradish on the side."

"Fries?"

"No, thanks." If he was going to order pie, he had to cut back somewhere. "And green tea, please."

As Della took the ticket to the kitchen, Mari made her way behind the counter. "You should try something else today. Don't you think variety is the spice of life?"

He looked at the display of pies and couldn't see how the apple or pecan would satisfy him like the blackberry did. "I don't know . . ."

"We have so many kinds of tea. You should try something besides green." Behind her a large chalkboard listed the specials of the day in fancy, colorful letters.

He'd ordered a turkey sandwich from it once. It'd come with a cup

53

of broccoli-cheese soup. But she was gesturing at the selection of teas. "Herbal mint?" he read from the board.

"If you like mint."

He didn't know about mint in anything except for his toothpaste. When a glob accidentally went down his throat, it was never pleasant. He leaned on the counter and read aloud. "Lemon sassafras. Raspberry apple. Orange and hibiscus?" Were his eyes playing tricks on him? "These all sound like shampoo."

She laughed. "The blackberry." She pointed to where it was printed in yellow chalk on the right side of the menu. "That's what you should try."

"Blackberry tea?"

"You like the pie, the tea might be your new love."

He smiled at her. *Careful,* he thought as she made her way to a table of women asking for more sweet tea. *Mari is not the kind of woman you should be pursuing.* He burrowed his eyes into the newspaper. Growing up, he'd learned that God did not smile on the divorced—or the pregnant women without husbands. It was best not to get too close to her. And as for the tea, he was a creature of habit. When she returned, he told her he'd decided to stick with the usual. "I know, I'm not adventurous."

As he finished his sandwich, Mari cut him a large slice of pie and poured a fresh cup of green tea. He noted her long lashes and smooth skin. She not only made delicious pies, she was also beautiful to look at every day.

"Kiki likes coming to your shop," she said. "I know she can't do much, but thank you for letting her have a place to do something. In Asheville, there was this after-school program she went to. She loved it there."

"I'm glad to help." Gideon almost felt true to his words. "What was going on here earlier?"

"You mean why Henry was here?"

"Yeah."

54

"Two thugs from Tennessee thought they could treat this place like a street corner bar."

He wasn't sure what she meant.

"You know, coming on to Della and me. Teasing us, then complaining about the food and service. It got loud, so I asked Henry to come by."

"Looks like he took care of it." Gideon couldn't see why men would be interested in poufed-out bleached-blond hair that looked much too fake. But Mari, yes, he could understand the attraction.

"He did a good job." Mari filled the napkin dispenser with white napkins from a cardboard box . "I called him, and he was here in minutes."

"You can always call me. I mean . . ." He felt his face grow hot. Why did talking to someone like Mari seem so unnatural? In his part of Carlisle, men didn't know how to flirt with women. Now that he had learned a few tips on how to do it, he felt silly for his attempts. "I mean, if you ever need help, I'm just down the road."

She smiled. "Yes, but do you have a gun or a badge?"

"I could get one from Walmart if that would help scare hoodlums away."

"Kiki says that if I just sang one of my Bob Dylan or Beatles songs, no one would ever bother me again."

"I like the Beatles. I have their *Abbey Road* album on CD."

She began to hum "Here Comes the Sun." Although he hadn't listened to it in two years, he was glad he recognized the tune.

"I'll have to work on my Dylan. I don't know any of his songs."

"I bet you've heard this one." Softly, she sang, "Knock, knock, knocking on Heaven's door, just like so many times before." Mari's alto voice was pleasant. She hummed and said, "This is the part where Dylan plays the harmonica."

He admitted he'd never heard that song. "I guess I have some homework to do before I come back."

Her smile was wide and warm as he paid and left the tearoom. "See you soon," she called out.

He wanted to stop, turn around, and ask her to a movie or a walk in the mountains or dinner at a restaurant he'd seen recently. He wasn't sure of its name, but he'd passed it on his way to Bryson City the other week, and the diners seated under the canopy outside looked to be having a great time. He was pretty sure it served Italian food.

As he ambled back to the shop, he thought of how nothing ever worked out for him. Was he too strict? Not fun enough? He once sang in the rain. It was "Amazing Grace." Even so, he had a decent voice. Mother always said so. Too angry? He clenched a fist before he realized what he was doing. He tried to make his fingers relax. Had he not yet met the right woman? Perhaps. Once Luke said to him, "You really want an Amish girl. Maybe an English girl isn't going to be good enough for you."

Luke was engaged. Only three years after coming to Twin Branches, he had found romance in the arms of Ashlyn Kingston, the sheriff's daughter. They would be married next spring. Rebecca, Luke's younger sister, had moved to Charlotte to attend UNC–Charlotte and was now a pharmacist, living her dream. She'd succeeded in her education, proving that girls were capable of studying and obtaining degrees. Back in Lancaster, girls were forced to quit school after eighth grade and spend time quilting and learning the secret to delectable pies.

He wondered if Mari had been to college. He knew so little about her. Did she ever feel angry? He'd seen her sad eyes that one day at the tearoom. She said she feared winter. What else did she fear? Who was Kiki's father? Had he been kind once but turned and grown uncaring? Or had he never stuck around once he learned she was carrying his child?

Inside the garage, Gideon busied himself under the hood of an old Plymouth Voyager. He hoped the sound of his tools would be loud enough to drown out his thoughts.

9

To save time, Gideon decided to skip lunch at Another Cup. Instead, he consumed two chocolate Twinkies from the vending machine at the Laundromat. He knew it wasn't healthy, but those little cakes sure did taste good. He loved the inside filling; it reminded him of the chocolate pie his mother used to make for Sunday evening desserts.

Kiki was tightening the brakes on her bike as Gideon explained engines and carburetors to Amos who stood nearby, munching on an apple. Gideon hated to admit it, but he'd gotten more enthusiasm out of a lion sunning himself at the zoo. What was wrong with this guy? How could he be Amish and be so lazy?

Thinking that perhaps the lad might be interested in something other than under the hood, Gideon said, "I can show you how to remove a tire. Why don't you come over here?"

Amos tossed the apple core into the trash can and wiped his mouth with the back of his hand. With deliberate weariness, he ambled over to Gideon.

Gideon tried to ignore the kid's lack of eagerness to learn. He asked

Amos to bring him two jack stands. The boy had no concept of speed.

"What did you do on your farm in Lancaster?" Gideon asked.

"Milked cows, picked corn." His brown eyes glazed over; Gideon assumed it was from lack of sleep.

"Did you like doing that?" Gideon asked.

"Did I like it?" He frowned. "Had no choice. You remember how it is." After a moment, Amos said, "We had an apple orchard, too."

An apple orchard. Those three words together never missed their opportunity to evoke a pain in Gideon's heart. Like a whirlwind, the words took him back—always back to that night outside the shed after his father had locked it. He wanted to know that the boy inside was alive, wanted to believe that his father hadn't killed the lad when he beat him with a branch from the apple tree. Of course, the boy did make it home after the beating, he often reminded himself. But in his dreams, there were times the boy died, and he was always screaming for Gideon to help him.

Amos interjected, "May I get some water to drink?"

Gideon shook off his tangled thoughts. "Sure, help yourself." Amos had already taken a break since arriving this morning—he'd smoked three cigarettes while standing in front of the shop, just watching the world go by. What harm could another break do to his flawed work ethic?

Mari pulled up in her car and when she bolted through the open bays and saw Kiki, her temper flared. "Why didn't you stay at home? I told you I'd pick you up there." She shot a frustrated look at Gideon, who wiped his hands on a cloth and wondered what was going on. He did know that kids could be exasperating; his own mother had told him that.

Kiki frowned at Mari and continued tampering with her bike. She let the wrench clack against the spokes, the noise echoing throughout the shop.

Mari stood over the girl. "It's time to go."

"Why?" She hit the side of her bicycle with a screwdriver, and Gideon suspected this was a deliberate attempt to make Mari annoyed or to make her go away.

"Kiki," Mari's voice was firm. "Your appointment is in ten minutes. Let's go!"

"I don't wanna go to the doctor! Sheesh! I had to go yesterday."

"Come on, Kiki."

"No!" She crossed her arms against her chest, her hands slapping against her shoulders. "I have to work here."

"Kiki, don't be difficult. Put on your listening ears and come on."

"Quit trying to sound like Mama!"

Mari looked at Gideon, her face begging for help.

Gideon felt he was operating in slow motion. *Mama?* Had Kiki said that word in reference to someone else? Someone other than Mari?

As Kiki continued making noise with the tools and Mari's face showed despair, Gideon stepped out of his own fog and moved toward the child.

When he approached her, Kiki got up, the wrench still in her hand, and leaned against the wall of the garage. With her chin jutted out, she clamped her lips together and squeezed her eyes closed.

"Kiki." He swallowed the urge to shout. Certainly, the girl wouldn't throw a tantrum and hit him with the tool, would she? He was grateful when Mari stood by his side. Trying to speak softly, he said, "When you come back, we'll have . . ." He paused as Mari looked at him. Have what? What did the kid like? "Chocolate," he said. There, that was a safe bet; who didn't like chocolate?

"Chocolate gives me gas." She spoke quickly and then let her lips seal into a tight bow.

Noting his shocked expression, Mari smiled.

Gideon's tension eased. He thought again and came up with, "Popsicles. How about those orange ones?"

"You mean Creamsicles?"

He nodded. "Exactly."

Kiki's arms released from their stance of protest. Her breathing resumed, and as her mouth relaxed she said, "Okay, let's go." She handed the wrench to Gideon, a sign of surrender.

He saw gratitude in Mari's eyes as Kiki made her way to Mari's parked car. The girl pulled open the door and plopped into the passenger seat, folding her arms across her chest again. Gideon watched the two drive off, the brakes of the Toyota squealing before Mari merged onto Main Street.

Like an early morning mist, the realization of his naïveté settled onto him. He'd made a mistake thinking that Mari was Kiki's mother. He was just like his father—always jumping to conclusions. Always assuming the worst about a situation and acting before really thinking about it.

Back inside his office, he let the stupid feeling subside and began to think about possibilities. A date? Dinner somewhere nice was what he'd like to do on a first date. Would Mari go for that?

Ormond rattled his paper and called out that the Clemson Tigers beat Duke yesterday. "I love it when any team beats Duke," he said. "Any team." He went on to say he'd watched the game on TV and wondered if Gideon had happened to catch it.

Gideon, still contemplating about Mari, walked over to the older man's desk. "You know I don't watch sports."

"You're missing out." Ormond grinned at a photo of Clemson fans with orange paws painted on their cheeks, cheering over the victory.

Gideon gave a weak smile, his thoughts far from any excited sports fans. He respected Ormond and decided that seeking his advice about a woman couldn't hurt. Ormond had been happily married for forty-nine years. "Uh . . . well . . ."

"Something on your mind?" Ormond turned the page, folded the paper, and ran a palm over the comics.

"Yeah . . . I was . . . Do you think . . . ?"

"All the time." Ormond chuckled.

Gideon studied his fingertips, picking at dirt underneath both thumbnails. "Do you think I should ask her out?"

"You should take her to the music festival in Gatlinburg."

He'd been there once with a girl back when he was still in his twenties. The evening they'd gone had been cool, and under a canopy they'd listened to a jazz band. He couldn't recall any of the names of the tunes, but he did remember how Sandy, the girl, told him she wasn't ready to seriously date him or anyone. As the band took a break, she gave the infamous line about just being friends. Gideon was sad to hear that she wasn't interested in him, but agreed that if she needed time to "find herself," that was best. Two weeks later, he'd heard Sandy was dating a doctor from Hendersonville.

Ormond lifted his gaze from the paper to look at Gideon. "Or the Oktoberfest," he said.

"When is that?"

"It runs through the month of October. Does she like bratwurst?"

"I don't know." Gideon didn't think he'd ever seen Mari eat anything. He knew she made pies early in the morning before Another Cup opened for business. Did she ever sample the ones she made? He felt a bit foolish for not knowing more about her culinary tastes.

"Well, she has to like strudel," Ormond said as he lowered the paper onto his desk. "Everyone loves that."

"What about dinner at that Italian place?"

"Does she like Italian food?"

Ormond was certainly full of questions this afternoon. Gideon felt like he was playing a game of Twenty Questions. "I don't know much about her." He realized this was probably one of the truest statements he'd made. What did he really know about Mari? Up until a few moments ago, he'd had her pegged as either an unwed mother or a divorcee with a child.

Ormond took a sip from his coffee cup then resumed his paper reading. "You know," he said, "she's new to the area. She could probably use a friend."

Gideon liked the sound of Ormond's words. He busied himself

61

with an inventory check of the storage room, making notes on his clipboard, and thinking of how he could ask Mari for a date.

When he walked past Ormond's desk, the old man stood to stretch his legs. "So all that advice I gave you about divorce isn't necessary anymore?"

"What?"

"You thought she was divorced, didn't you? Thought an Amish man couldn't date a divorced woman?"

There was no pretending with Ormond. He must have known when Gideon asked about the Bible and divorce, that he'd had Mari in mind. "Did you know she was single when I asked you all those questions?"

Ormond adjusted his glasses and sat back down. "I guess I just felt I should wait until you figured it all out. I knew Mari and Kiki were sisters all along." Then he laughed as if he'd just given the punch line of one of his favorite jokes.

10

Gideon woke before the sun sprinted up into the sky. He felt the relief from days ago wash over him anew as he thought of the connection between Mari and Kiki. Sisters. He could deal with that. He knew he was old-fashioned, but the chains of his childhood belief system were not weak. He'd left his home, his church, and culture. He wore English clothes and owned a truck. But there was something about women he'd been taught from his mother's knee. "A good girl is not quick to give of herself, and a good girl stays married. No matter what." That standard had stayed with him.

Looking back over his years under his parents' roof, he wondered if his mother had to remind herself of the last part of her mantra for the sake of her own sanity. *A good girl stays married.* Had she wanted to stray from her husband, the man who was beast-like as he demanded respect and yet could not give it, shouted orders, and listened to no reason?

Gideon dismissed those thoughts as he spread apple butter on multigrain toast. He poured a glass of apple cider from a jug he'd bought from Henry's wife. Mebane made her own apple cider and asked Henry to sell it when he went on his daily patrols around town.

Gideon tried a smile as he thought of Henry's wife, a short woman with a round face and porcelain complexion who held a fierce love of the mountains where she was raised and learned the skill of making the best apple cider. She'd taught their daughter, Ashlyn, to cook as well. That young woman's specialty was bread she steamed in cans in a pot of hot water. She often dropped off samples at the garage for her fiancé Luke and anyone else willing to give it a try. Gideon had been a guest at Mebane and Henry's many times, and their home was always cozy with love and respect abounding. Henry valued his wife's opinion on most topics—except for recycling. He couldn't see the need to take the time to wash out empty jars and bottles before placing them inside the bin. But even with his inability to match her views on the need to cleanse the cans and jars first, he admired her for going the extra mile. Gideon felt that his father could take some lessons from this English family. With Father, it was his way. Period. There was never any room for discussion.

Gideon pushed thoughts of his father aside as though they were empty oil bottles ready to be recycled. He wanted to dwell only on happy thoughts this morning. He sought to be smiling and lighthearted when he went to Another Cup for his tea and pie. Today was going to be the day. He spent extra care as he shaved and tossed on one more splash of cologne before heading out for his walk to work. As he walked out under a murky sky, a lone catbird meowed from a desolate maple tree, reminding him that winter was just around the corner. To the east, a few crows cackled and then got lost in the distance as a hawk spread her wings, circling for some tidbit on the nearby ground.

He had to admit that he continued to feel a little imprudent for assuming that Mari was Kiki's mother. Since Mari looked to be about twenty-five or twenty-six, and Kiki was thirteen, that would have meant Mari had been awfully young when she'd conceived Kiki. She would have been barely a teen. He shuddered to think of how his great-great-grandmother on his mother's side had had her first child at thirteen.

She went on to have eight more after that. Story had it that one of her sons had found her body in a cornfield. She'd died of a massive stroke at the age of thirty-seven.

At the shop, he greeted Ormond and later Luke. By nine, he tried to hold in his frustration that Amos was nowhere in sight. He asked Luke if he'd heard anything about the young man's whereabouts. Luke looked up from under the hood of a 1998 Camaro and said he had not seen Amos since yesterday.

When the boy ambled in to work twenty minutes later, Gideon glared. "You are to be here at eight when we open," he said.

Amos rolled the long pants legs up so that they no longer dragged. Scratching his chin, he said, "I overslept."

"Do you need an alarm clock?"

"A what?"

Slowly, with emphasis. "A clock with an alarm that goes off to wake you up in the morning."

"I have a cell phone that beeps when I set it."

Gideon was impressed that the kid had found the alarm on his phone. "Be here at eight tomorrow," he stressed and then told him to help Luke with the pastor of Second Presbyterian's car that had just arrived for a tune-up. He was tired of reprimanding Amos. Days ago he'd headed over to his apartment to remind him of the contract. "You signed it, you need to keep to it. You are getting free rent by working for me for a month."

The boy had stared up at him and then sat on the wicker chair in his living room, looking weary from just breathing.

"Are you getting enough sleep?"

"I don't know. I guess."

Gideon had left the apartment after that, uncertain as to what to do. He'd helped others who were only passing through on their way to someplace else, realizing that Twin Branches and the Russell Brothers Auto Shop was not to their liking. But those boys and girls were clear about what they wanted. Like Luke's sister, Rebecca, and others who had connections in Raleigh or Atlanta, they each desired to experience what a larger town had to offer. He was fine with that; they didn't have to feel obligated to stay in these mountains. But none of them had been as lazy and ungrateful as Amos was proving to be.

Again, Gideon needed to rid himself of ill thoughts today. He was about to head over to the tearoom to see Mari. He wanted to feel courageous and brave. Suave and warm would help, too. He was going to ask her out. He studied his hair in the restroom mirror. His curly locks had a tendency to look forlorn if he didn't keep them in check. He took off his cap and swiped a hand over them so he didn't have hat hair. He smiled into the mirror. Even though he'd spent a majority of the morning working under the hood of a Honda, he could still smell his aftershave.

Briskly, he walked to Another Cup, hope expanding in his chest. He couldn't recall when he'd ever felt this ready and eager to ask a woman out on a date. As he entered the shop, he smiled.

Since it was past one o'clock, the heavy lunch crowd was gone. Only the three tables by the large window were occupied. Still smiling, he sat at the counter. When Della took his order, he asked where Mari was.

"She's in her office in the back, I think."

He ordered his usual green tea and roast beef sandwich, asking for extra horseradish on the side. He ate, relishing each bite. Before finishing the sandwich, he pointed to a slice of blackberry pie that sat under a glass dome to the left of the counter.

Della's bosom heaved as she laughed. "You are the most pie-eating man I know."

"Guess I've always had a severe sweet tooth."

"Sugar," she said, "so do I. My downfall is those chocolate-covered pretzels and a good chick flick on the Lifetime Movie Network."

As he ate the moist piece of pie, he pretended to read the newspaper but spent more time peering over it in the hopes of seeing Mari. How long did she need to stay in the office in the back? Trying to make his lunch last longer, he'd purposely eaten the pie slowly, chewing each bite more times than necessary. He accepted a refill of tea, taking small sips. Lifting the last forkful of pie to his mouth, he felt his heart sink. Perhaps today would not be the day after all. He'd have to pick up his newspaper and head back to the shop, seeking out another time to ask her for a date.

Suddenly, she emerged from the kitchen's double doors. His heart pounded as she walked over to him, greeted him with a smile, and asked how he was.

He wiped his mouth with the napkin he'd laid across his lap. How embarrassing it would be if later he realized he'd been talking with pie smudged across his mouth. But the napkin picked up no blackberry stains from his lips. He wiped again, just to make sure. "I'm doing well. Um . . . Yeah. How are you?"

"Better than I was. We had a bit of a problem this morning with our water heater, but it's fixed now."

"That's good." He clenched the napkin in his hand, wondered where to put it. "I mean . . . that's too bad the heater caused a problem."

"But good that it's okay now?" She asked it like a question, like she was helping with what he meant to say.

He smiled. "Yes, exactly." He found a spot for the napkin by his empty plate.

"The repair cost me over two hundred dollars. With this tourist season nearly over, I hope I can recoup that." She seemed sad, and he so wanted to see her smile.

So he smiled again, watching for her reaction.

"I suppose it could be worse. You know, it could always be worse. That's what I tell myself."

"Yes," he agreed. "That's a good thing to remember." Then he decided he must do what he came to do. After a sip of tea to clear his throat, he looked at her. "Would you like to go out with me to the Bavarian festival in Gatlinburg this weekend?"

At first there was a smile. Then the smile faded as she said, "No, I don't think so."

He forced the lump down his throat. "No?" The word sounded hollow.

"I can't leave Kiki alone on a Saturday for very long."

He wondered why she couldn't leave her. She was thirteen, quite capable of being on her own, wasn't she? Yes, the child was a bit slow, but couldn't Mari just give her a DVD to watch and pop her some popcorn? He watched Mari move from him, and when her back was to him, taking orders for a couple at the opposite end of the counter, Gideon decided that the conversation between her and him had ended.

After that, he opened his paper and read until he realized that each headline was running into the next. He couldn't concentrate on what the governor was proposing for the state of North Carolina or about how a man was arrested at Chimney Rock for desecrating the tourist spot with a can of lavender paint.

As he left the tearoom, defeat clouded his mind. With each step back to his workplace, he heard her reply, "No, I don't think so." How could she say no to him? How could she steal his hope from yesterday? He'd planned out what to say and how to ask her out so carefully. And now—dashed. No more. The pie soured as it mixed with the sandwich inside his stomach. The day seemed darker, gone was the autumn luster it had held earlier.

What was the matter with him? Why did he take life so hard? Ormond often reminded him that he needed to laugh more, fret less, and certainly not let his past continue to eat away at him.

About a year after Gideon had obtained his GED, Ormond commented that Gideon could benefit from a creative writing class. Judith Lane Russell, Ormond's sister-in-law, taught at the community college and just like Ormond, she encouraged Gideon to attend. Gideon figured he'd write about lush fields and horse-drawn carriages, the natural and typical aspects of an Amish life. How surprised he was when his notebook filled with descriptions and anecdotes about his remote and unrelenting father instead.

My father is an angry and bitter man, dressing in those emotions each day. They are part of his attire, like the suspenders he's worn since he was a boy.

"You write well," Judith observed after reading a few paragraphs. "Writing like this serves as therapy, too, you know."

Therapy? What did she mean? All he knew of therapy was from TV shows where the psychiatrist sat in a chair with a pen and notebook while his patient lay on a couch, confessing he was not going to let his life be ruined any longer. Yet the more Gideon wrote during that continuing education creative writing course, the more he'd vowed not to let his father destroy any more of his life.

"He's not going to control me from here," Gideon muttered aloud as he took his last heavy strides toward the shop.

The first person he saw when he stepped into the garage was Amos—Amos seated on an overturned paint bucket as though he had nothing to do, no place to go. Gideon bit back the urge to give him a piece of his mind. He waited until Luke received payment from a customer and she drove off in her minivan, pleased that Luke had done such a fine job.

Then he called Amos into his office. The boy slithered in as though he were some sort of reptile.

Gideon wasn't sure where to start, so he just took a stab at it and hoped his words came out gentle but firm. "You aren't happy here. You need to look for another job."

Amos nodded and then seemed to be deep in thought.

Gideon was about to repeat himself when Amos interjected, "I have."

"You have what?"

"Looked for another place to work. Cars just aren't my thing. I realize that."

"You do?" Perhaps the kid had more going on upstairs than he let on. But who would hire him? "So you have looked elsewhere?"

"Yes." Amos's face shone.

69

"Where?"

"The tearoom up the street. The woman there said I could have an interview."

"Which woman?"

"Kiki's sister. What's her name?"

"Mari?"

Amos nodded. "I call her Miss Yanagi."

"When's your interview?"

"Friday." Amos looked at his feet. When he made eye contact, he muttered, "I guess I should have told you before now."

Gideon wanted to say that he doubted he'd get the job if he didn't look more awake or comb his hair or act enthusiastic. But he recalled how excited the boy had been when he first jumped off Bruce's truck. Perhaps that spark was like an ember inside him that would come to full flame during his interview. Gideon started to say something, but the phone rang and he went to answer it instead, motioning for Amos to get back to work. Or whatever it was that he was doing before Gideon had called him into his office.

"Russell Brothers Auto Repair." Gideon hoped the caller wouldn't be long-winded—he wanted to get back to licking his wounds and wondering why Mari had refused him.

"Hey bro, how are you? Long time no see."

Gideon felt his skin grow clammy. The voice held a distinctive lisp. Moriah? But why would Moriah be calling him? "Who is this?"

"It's me." Laughter followed. "Moriah."

Gideon imagined him at a truck stop somewhere outside of Harrisburg, a duffel bag at his feet, eager to leave the farm. "Where are you?"

"Sunny Orlando."

Orlando? Why did he choose Orlando? "As in Florida? You've traveled far."

"Yeah, got here about three years ago."

"You've been gone from home for three years?" Gideon felt his throat catch; he swallowed hard.

"I had to get out of there. He's a beast."

Gideon shivered as though cold water had been splashed against his face. He didn't need any clarification when Moriah spoke of a beast.

"So I heard through the grapevine that you welcome anyone. Does that include me?" Moriah gave a light laugh.

As he spoke, Gideon made some mental calculations. The last time he'd heard his brother's voice, Moriah had been five. That would make him twenty-one now. He had a lisp back then; it was a shame he still had it now. "Hey, I'd like to come for a visit."

Gideon tried to clear his head. He still wasn't sure this was his baby brother from their hometown outside of Carlisle. Except for the occasional mispronunciation of *th*, this boy sounded self-assured, bold, and friendly. He didn't have a trace of an Amish accent. "Up to Twin Branches?"

"I found it on the map." He laughed and said finding it wasn't an easy thing to do. Twin Branches was smaller than Carlisle.

"How did you know I'm here?"

"Everyone knows, bro. They call you the Getaway Savior." He laughed, bringing Gideon back to long days in the sun plowing the fields and milking the Jersey cows, watching the clothes drying on the expansive clothesline behind the old homestead.

"So if it's okay with you, I'll be stopping by to see you. One day you'll hear the doorbell ring, and it'll be me."

"I look forward to that," said Gideon and then felt his words sounded as though he was speaking to a stranger and not to someone he had carried on his back from the orchard. When he placed the phone back in the cradle, he sat at his desk, his mind racing. He hoped his brother would come to see him. Although Gideon had been in contact with a few relatives who were in Ohio, he hadn't seen any family members since he'd been in these mountains. He wondered what Moriah looked like. He'd been a blond-haired kid with chubby cheeks, causing the older women to playfully tug at his face and kiss his forehead.

That's two of us, thought Gideon. *Two of us who have now left the*

71

Beast. He'd heard from his aunt Grace that his three older sisters were all married now, promising God to be good Amish women, create lavish quilts, and raise large families. Gideon knew that they'd never leave Pennsylvania; they'd never trade the familiar for the unknown. They would forever let *uffgevva*—submission—be their lifelong mantra.

His thoughts rushed to recollections of straw-brimmed hats, walks to the schoolhouse carrying lunch pails, and chatter among friends during a softball game at recess. He remembered the excitement in Moriah's eyes that day when their cousin Sadie married Jacob Swartzendruber, the last event he had attended before running away from his home. He'd left the festivities early to pack his bag and then stowed it under his bed until his planned hour of escape. He'd not only packed his clothes, but apples and oranges, and even a few slices of ham for the road. He remembered the determination he'd felt then, fueled by the consuming desire to leave his home once and for all. *He'd show him.*

Gideon got to his feet. If he busied himself, he could forget his father. On the way to the garage, he reminded Ormond to do the payroll for the two-week pay period. While Ormond had given Gideon co-ownership of the shop, he still had to cut and sign the checks. There were times he forgot, and Gideon had to gently remind him that it was time to get out his checkbook.

11

Kiki walked home from school slowly, her fleece jacket tied around her waist. She stopped and knotted the sleeves twice before nearing her driveway. School had seemed long and tedious today, and she had wanted to scream out many times, especially during math class, but held her breath instead. Her book bag, heavy against her shoulder, reminded her that she had lots of homework. She saw Angie in the front lawn of her grandma's house, peering over a bicycle that lay by one of the bare dogwood trees.

Her first reaction was to suggest that she and Angie go on a bike ride together. Then she remembered. She had to go to the repair shop to work. "Hey," she said. She saw that the bike's back tire was as flat as one of the arrowheads she inherited from Grandpa. "How did that happen?"

Angie straightened. "We were racing on Saturday over behind the funeral home and I hit something."

Kiki bent over to study the tire. "Glass, I bet. Yeah, glass."

Angie scowled at her.

Come on, Kiki thought, *why do you have to be so mean like that?* She pushed the expression aside and brought the bike to its upright position. "Take it to the shop," she said.

"To the Russell Brothers' place?" Angie shielded her eyes from the sun.

"Yeah, we fix bikes there."

"We?"

"I work there now." Kiki felt pride fill her heart with warmth at just hearing her own words. Angie might laugh at her and not want her company, but at least Kiki had a job.

A truck pulled up and parked by Angie's grandma's front lawn. Out stepped a large burly man in a pair of Levi's with a tattoo of a coiled snake on his arm. "Angie, get in the truck."

"Why?"

"Your mama wants you home now." Kiki figured Angie's uncle Reginald had to be one of the most despised men in all of Twin Branches. She recalled how when she and Mari had first moved into the house to rent, Reginald had glared at them from across the yard, muttering about how the neighborhood was going downhill fast due to the recent Chinese invasion. Kiki had wanted to glare back at him, but Mari gave her a stern look and told her to start unpacking.

Angie looked at Kiki, still holding the bike by the handlebars. "I guess I have to go," she said. "He's such a moron sometimes."

"What about the bike?" Kiki asked.

"Just leave it." Angie walked toward the truck.

Gruffly Reginald said, "Go on home, China Girl." Kiki wanted to say that her relatives were from Japan, not China, but she only kept her eyes on Angie's bike, right at where the name brand had been scratched off. Kiki could only make out an R and a T. She kept her eyes on those letters as Reginald continued harpooning slurs at her. *Ignore him,* her inner voice told her, the one Dr. Conner advised her to listen to. *Ignore him.*

She knew what she was going to do as soon as Reginald left. If only he would go. *Leave,* she repeated in her mind, until at last, his truck was out of sight. Then Kiki lowered Angie's bike onto the grass. She rushed into her house, tossed her book bag on her bed and then raced out. Slowly, avoiding the potholes, she guided Angie's bike to the shop. Not only was the tire flat, but the brakes made a clicking noise. She would show them all. She'd fix the flat tire and the brakes. It would be good as new, good as new. Kiki, the bike repair hero!

Twenty minutes after sitting by the storage room with an assortment of tools, Kiki had Angie's bicycle sounding and looking in good condition. She figured a sliver of glass had punctured the tire, and she doubted the shop had a new one. But after she removed the tire and the tubing, she saw that the tubing just needed a patch. Luckily, Gideon had a can of glue and a patch he let her use.

"You do good work," Gideon said as he watched her. "Whose bike?"

"Some tattletale girl named Angie Smithfield."

"The funeral home family?"

"That's it." With a sour expression, she muttered, "She also told on me."

"Told on you?"

Kiki didn't meet his questioning look. "About the parking lot."

"Oh, I see. That's how she got the tattletale name."

Kiki let out an exasperated huff. "She's too nosy. Nosy Angie Smithfield. Just because her family owns this town doesn't mean she has to act like she's the boss over me."

Ormond sipped from a cup of iced tea. "I always say that those Smithfields wear their money like a nicely pressed suit."

"Well, none of them will press me like a suit! Angie's not the boss over Kiki Yanagi." Kiki stood erect like a statute and saluted.

Gideon stifled a laugh and then suggested that they steer the bike into the empty bay so that he could fill the tire with air from his compressor.

Kiki had never seen a compressor in action before. Ricky always added air with a bike pump he had to maneuver with his own strength.

She recalled how his powerful muscles flexed whenever he lifted a bike to the work area inside the gym at the after-school center. Then he'd pump air into each tire, his ability to swiftly fill them leaving Kiki in awe.

Kiki noted the tools scattered at her feet. "Mr. Miller?"

"Gideon," he corrected.

"Okay. Gideon, then. I need something to put my tools in. Do you have anything?"

Gideon said he'd look around and minutes later handed her a wooden box about the size of a shoebox.

"This is a nice box," she said, her attention suddenly far from Angie's bike. Running her fingers over the wood, she felt the grooves where the nails were. She opened and closed the lid, opened it, and placed the three tools inside.

"Gideon made that box," Ormond said with a look of nostalgia. His eyes met Gideon's, then he smiled and turned to Kiki. "He used a piece of cedar. When he first came here, making things from wood was about all he knew how to do."

Kiki rubbed the brass latch. "Really? He made this?" She couldn't help but think of how beautiful it was, a real work of art. She looked up at Gideon. "You are talented!"

"Thank you."

"In Amish-land, that was what he was good at," explained Ormond. "Apparently, he made these and sold them at a local craft store, didn't you, Gideon? He made a few here and gave them out as Christmas gifts his first Christmas here."

Gideon reminded Kiki of a little boy who was too shy to admit that he had a skill. She wanted to hear him talk about the box so she said, "What's it called?"

"It's called a keepsake box."

"Keepsake." Kiki let the unfamiliar word fill her mouth and slip off her tongue. "Keepsake. A keepsake box." She looked at Ormond and Gideon and suddenly let out a snicker. "For Pete's sake, give me the keepsake."

When Ormond laughed, she was encouraged to repeat her ditty. "For Pete's sake, give me the keepsake."

Now that she had repaired bicycles and had been given a keepsake box for tool storage, she'd better show others that she had a business. As she pedaled home, she saw a gray piece of paper on a telephone pole, asking about a missing dog. A flier! That's what she needed to spread the word about her bicycle repair business.

As Mari made dinner, Kiki set out to design a flier on their computer. She wrote *Bikes Fixed for You* at the top of the page and then remembered that bikes could also mean motorcycles and she didn't know how to fix them. She changed the words, typing in, *Get Your Bisycle Repaired!* But when she asked Mari to take a look, her sister told her she'd misspelled bicycle. *How embarrassing is that!*

As the aroma of fried potatoes, onions, and green peppers saturated the house, Kiki rubbed her temple and wondered what else she could say about her business. "Ahh," she cried out in frustration. "This isn't working!"

Mari told her to calm down. Then she soothed Kiki's brow with a cool hand.

"Let's eat dinner, Kiki."

"Then I can finish it after that?"

"Don't you have homework?"

She had loads of homework, way too much, as usual. When she was the queen of the world, she would never let homework be allowed. *Seven hours doing work at school was enough, why did teachers expect more from you at home?*

"Kiki, do you have any?"

"Some."

"You better do it then. You can work on the flier this weekend."

"Will you help me?" Kiki knew she needed help, and Mari was good at English with all its crazy nouns and verbs.

"Yes." Mari turned off the stove and said dinner was ready.

After dinner, Kiki went to her room, tried to concentrate on her math homework, and then put it aside to put on her pirate hat. Observing herself in the full-length mirror on her closet door, she shook her head in different directions because she liked to watch the two feathers on the top of the hat bounce with her movements. Pretending she had a sword, she flicked her wrist and called, "Aye, you can't win over me. I'm the best there is. Aye, aye."

Ricky had helped her perfect her pirate talk. One day they'd watched the first *Pirates of the Caribbean* movie in the rec room. Although a few of the other kids joined them, none were as taken with the pirate's life as Kiki had been. After seeing that movie, she'd asked for a poster from it, and Ricky bought her one for her birthday. She'd found a space big enough on her bedroom wall to hang it. She knew the actor Johnny Depp was Jack Sparrow in the movie, and she found him extremely handsome.

With the hat fitted snugly on her head, Kiki quietly tiptoed down the hallway, entered the kitchen, and picked up the cordless phone that sat on the counter by the refrigerator.

Mari was in the living room; the sound of *Frasier* reruns softly came from the TV. From memory, Kiki punched in the familiar numbers, numbers she had often dialed when she lived with Mama in Asheville.

With sweaty palms, she waited as the phone rang.

A woman answered.

Using her most grown-up voice, Kiki said, "May I speak to Ricky, please?"

"Ricky?"

"Yes."

"Ricky no longer works here."

Kiki thought she hadn't heard correctly. "Ricky," she repeated. "Ricky Lopez?" For the sake of Pete, how could the woman not know who he was?

"I'm sorry. He no longer works here."

"Why not?" She squeezed the phone closer to her ear.

"I don't know."

Like a flash across her mind, Kiki saw the gym where Ricky had taught her to shoot hoops, coaching her with patience, although she was not any good. Then there was that afternoon she found him tinkering with a bicycle on the outdoor court and when she asked him how he repaired a flat tire, he showed her. She'd observed with interest.

Now this person on the phone said she had no idea where Ricky was. "Well, when will he be back?" Kiki asked.

"I said he doesn't work here anymore."

"But, but why not?" Suddenly, her adult voice caved into that of a desperate child's.

"I have no clue, honey. I just know he isn't here."

Kiki clung to the receiver, even after there was a beeping noise and she knew the woman she'd been talking to had hung up.

12

By Wednesday of the next week, Gideon wondered if he had imagined the phone conversation with Moriah. He played parts of it over in his head, but even so, today he was beginning to think he'd dreamed the whole thing. What if he was so homesick to hear another immediate family member's voice that his mind was playing tricks on him? His brother had said he was on his way here from Florida. Gideon hadn't even asked what kind of car Moriah drove.

On the same Wednesday, Gideon decided that perhaps it was time to end a habit. Before Mari had become the new manager at Another Cup, he'd eaten a lot of takeout for lunch. Maybe it was time to go back to doing that. Luke had made a comment that he was spending *hours* over at the tearoom, and if Luke noticed then that meant that either Ormond already did, too, or he would. Ormond was a big teaser.

Each afternoon Ormond picked up food from Ole Loner's Barbeque, and although the pulled pork looked too greasy for Gideon's taste, it would have to do today because that's what he'd ordered.

Spreading a napkin across his desk, Gideon arranged his glass of sweet tea and Dixie plate of pork, coleslaw, and baked beans on top of it. As he sipped his tea, he tried not to ponder on a cute manager with thick black hair and eyes that lit his heart.

The next day he asked Ormond to get him a half-rack of ribs instead of the pulled pork. When he asked if there were other sides, Ormond handed him a coffee-stained menu he kept inside his desk. Gideon requested corn on the cob and green beans. He figured something a little less caloric might be what he needed. He wasn't getting any thinner. *Of course*, a voice inside his head whispered, *you could give up all that blackberry pie*. But why would he want to do that? As far as vices went, blackberry pie was a harmless one.

That afternoon, he stood by his open bay looking out at the parking lot. A cloud of despondency loomed over him, like something was brewing in the air. Even the ribs from lunch seemed sour in his stomach.

The lone morning glory over by the fence behind the metal Dumpster had not bloomed in weeks. He'd have to wait until next summer to feel connected to its faint purple petals again. They were the same color as the teacups his mother had on a shelf in the living room back on the farm. His father had scolded that they were too fancy for a proper Amish wife to own, much less display. His mother merely said that purple was mentioned in the Bible as a color of royalty and displayed them anyway.

Still heavy in thought, Gideon did not recognize the man who walked briskly his way then stopped a few feet in front of him. Gideon noted the man's long, sandy-colored hair, pulled back in a ponytail. He was dressed in a pair of jeans worn out at the knees and a gray T-shirt. A charcoal leather jacket swung over his shoulder.

The minute he pulled his sunglasses off his eyes, Gideon knew. Frozen, unable to move or find his voice, Gideon stood with his mouth open. This must be what it felt like to be paralyzed. The man laughed and threw his arms around Gideon's shoulders, knocking Gideon's cap off his head.

As Gideon welcomed his embrace, he felt all the years he'd missed of this kid's youth. He smelled Irish Spring soap, cigarettes, and nostalgia—all gripping his heart in every tender crevice. When he found his voice, he said, "Moriah! It is you. You look good."

His brother laughed again, stepped back, and smiled into Gideon's face. "You haven't changed a bit."

Gideon teased, "Still wearing suspenders and a straw hat, right?"

Moriah retrieved his older brother's cap from the floor of the bay and placed it on his own head. Draping his jacket on a plastic chair by the tool chest, he said, "I'm glad I made it. This is a tiny town. The man I got a ride from said that if you sneeze, you'll miss it."

Gideon laughed and playfully snatched his John Deere cap from Moriah's head and fitted it on his own. He watched Moriah take a pack of Marlboros from his T-shirt pocket. He offered his brother one, but Gideon declined. He wondered when Moriah had picked up the habit. Or maybe it wasn't a habit yet—maybe it was just another way to denounce all that their father believed was right.

As Moriah lit up, Gideon said, "What took you to Orlando?"

"A girl." He wiggled his eyebrows.

"A girl? Where did you meet her?"

"On the beach. She was wearing a pink bikini." He grinned, blew out a puff of smoke. "She taught me to surf."

"You went straight to Florida from Carlisle?"

"No, I went to visit Uncle William in Missouri. Did you ever meet William Bender?"

Gideon thought the name sounded familiar. "One of Mom's relatives?" With all the family tales she used to tell around the dinner table, it seemed she was related to everyone.

"That's right." Moriah inhaled one last time before extinguishing his cigarette. "I went to help him out on his dairy farm and then never went back home after that."

Gideon thought of his own story of departure. That night of his cousin's wedding, he'd snuck out of the house to meet an English friend down the road. The friend was headed to Virginia Beach for the summer but had been willing to first drive Gideon to the Shenandoah Valley of Virginia. In Staunton, Gideon had helped out on an uncle's farm until he made his trek into North Carolina.

Moriah swung an arm around his brother. "The farm life there was okay. I did go out with this pretty girl who lived across the street. But . . ." He paused as though he was debating whether or not to tell more about his relationship with her. "I wanted to get away from farming. You know, like you did. And here I am now!"

Dismissing his brother's enthusiasm, Gideon blurted, "How's Mom?" Although he'd only written to her once since he'd left home—Ormond had insisted that she needed to hear he was safe—he thought of her often.

Moriah lit another cigarette. Between blowing smoke rings, he said, "She's the same. She'll always be the same." Gideon wasn't sure just what he meant by that, but decided not to ask.

"I don't miss them at all. Good riddance is what I say, you know?"

Gideon felt the strain in his own jaw. Moriah made leaving a family seem easy, as though there was no room for remorse or regret. Clenching his teeth, he fought the urge to say something sarcastic.

The rest of the afternoon, Gideon tried to keep his questions to a minimum, especially after Moriah complained that he could be a drill sergeant. He introduced Moriah to Luke and Ormond. When Kiki came by after her doctor's appointment, Gideon said, "This is my long-lost baby brother."

"Your brother?" said Kiki. "I thought after you, your parents decided you were enough and not to have any more kids." She grinned. Then with a careful look at Moriah, she smoothed out her hair with her hand and moistened her lips.

Moriah laughed. "Had they been normal, they would have. But they are Amish and believe that the more kids, the better your chances are at getting into Heaven."

"Really?" Kiki looked at Gideon for his reaction.

"No," interjected Gideon with force. "That's not true."

"I believe it is," said Moriah, the smile gone from his young face. "Why else do they reproduce like rabbits?"

Gideon wished Moriah would be quiet. It bothered him that his brother could lash out criticisms without considering the effect his words had on others.

"Rabbits?" Kiki repeated. "Rabbits?"

"It's an expression." Gideon's tone was strong, hoping it would make his brother realize that he needed to curb this conversation. Turning to Moriah he said, "Do you have dinner plans?"

Moriah said he had no plans, but he was hungry. "Haven't eaten since this morning, and that was so long ago."

Quickly, Gideon did a mental assessment of what was in his fridge and freezer at home. "You like grilled chicken?"

"Sure."

"I like grilled chicken," said Kiki. "And macaroni and cheese. And pie and milkshakes." She smiled. "I like fowl roasted over a spit, too. That's what pirates eat when they're looking for treasure." In a serious tone, she explained, "Fowl means bird."

Moriah smiled wide, his teeth sparkling like an ad for toothpaste. "A girl after my own heart." Then in a singsong voice, he belted out, "It's a pirate's life for me! Aye, aye! A pirate's life for me!"

"I like pirates!" Kiki cried. "I was a pirate at Halloween."

Moriah nodded. "I like them, too. They get to ride on cool ships and look for treasure. They never have to be home at a certain time. They just wander."

Gideon wished it wasn't so, but Kiki was looking at Moriah with a contented, dreamy expression, like she thought he was the most handsome man around. The truth was, he was. Gideon sucked in his jealousy, slapped Moriah on the back, and offered a small smile. "Good, good," he said, although he wasn't sure why.

In his apartment kitchen, Gideon washed russet potatoes to roast, patting them dry and then covering them with dabs of butter and sprigs of fresh rosemary. He'd seen a chef on the Food Network make potatoes this way and ever since then had made his own. Finding a pack of frozen peas, he decided to add them to the menu. He'd spice them up a bit with some oregano and onions. "You still like peas?" he called out to Moriah, recalling a toddler in a high chair cramming peas into his miniature mouth.

There was no reply, so Gideon entered the living room where earlier Moriah had been stretched out on the sofa, his shoes off, his bare toes wiggling. The room was still— there was no sign of his brother. He checked the bathroom, both off his bedroom and the half bath in the hallway. "Moriah?"

Back in the kitchen, Gideon opened the oven to make sure the chicken was browning. He removed the pan, stirred the pieces and then added pepper to them.

Peering out his kitchen window, he hoped to see his brother, perhaps on the grassy common area beside his apartment building. Maybe he'd gone out for a cigarette. But although he craned his neck to scan as much of the view as he could, Moriah was not on the lawn.

Half an hour later, just as Gideon was about to take the chicken and potatoes from the oven, Moriah sprung open the front door to the apartment. A six-pack of Coors dangled from his hand. "Hey," he grinned. "I thought we could use something good to drink."

Moriah placed the cans on the kitchen table and opened one. Handing it to Gideon, he said, "Here you go."

"No, thanks."

Moriah took the beer and lifted it to his lips. "You're missing out."

Gideon merely stated, "Beer makes you fat." He was not about to tell Moriah his own obsession with drinking when he was first loose from the reins of his parents. Upon his arrival in Twin Branches at the age of fifteen, he had drunk so much he fell asleep in an alleyway. The next morning he was discovered by a child on her way to school. The child called her mother to come look at the homeless bum. Never, he vowed, would he humiliate himself that way again.

Moriah ate like a famished mutt Gideon had once seen by the Dumpster outside the repair shop. "You're a great cook," he said as he chewed his last bite of chicken. "Where'd you learn?" Retrieving his paper napkin off the floor, he used the edge of it to wipe his mouth.

"TV shows. Emeril Lagasse and Gordon Ramsay." He doubted his brother had a clue as to who these culinary masters were, but Moriah surprised him.

"That Gordon Ramsay sure knows how to help restaurants that are in trouble. I saw a few shows on how he helped failing restaurant owners get back on their feet."

"I've seen some of those episodes, too."

"TV is awesome, isn't it?" Moriah leaned back in his chair. He lifted his can of beer above his head. "Here's to TV and music, movies, fast cars, and fast women. All the things a good Amish town will never have." Lowering the can, he drank. When the beer was gone, he crushed the can and placed it on the table with a ceremonial flair. Lifting his shirt, he said, "Let me show you this beauty. This is my pride and joy." And there, on his exposed belly, was a tattoo of an ornate ship with sails, a skull and crossbones on one of them. "This is what I got done in Orlando. What do you think?"

Gideon studied the colorful tattoo on his brother's torso, just inches above his belt. He had no words to say how he felt about this body art. As a child, Moriah had loved anything to do with pirates. He would draw pictures of their ships, their treasure chests, and even their faces, complete with dreadlocks, eye patches, and beards. Once, Father saw one of the pictures, and as the veins popped in his neck, he ripped it up with two large hands. He demanded that Moriah never draw anything that vulgar again and then, certain that his boy was getting these horrible pirate infatuations from those *wretched English boys*, told Moriah he could never associate with anyone but the Amish. Now, free from his father's rule, Moriah had chosen to have a drawing of a forbidden ship on his very skin. This was permanent, unable to be torn apart by an outraged man. "He would kill you," Gideon said.

"He would. Too bad he can't. He'll never see me again."

Gideon felt the air cool; the mention of their father brought a chill over the room.

"I'm so glad to be out of there. Free at last!" Looking around the dining area, Moriah said, "Do you ever think of buying your own house instead of renting?"

In fact, Gideon had. A two-story home with a wraparound porch just half a mile from the auto shop had interested him nine years ago. He'd contacted the Realtor, taken the tour, and liked what he saw. But when he got to thinking about the high mortgage rates, property taxes, and whether or not he wanted to invest in a house, he'd backed out. The Realtor called a couple of times, insisting she could get him a lower interest rate, but he declined, telling her that his apartment was fine— just the right size and location. The niggling voice inside his head knew that those sentiments were only the partial truth. He planned to get married someday. Wouldn't it be better to wait till the right woman came along and then together they could purchase a home to their liking? But tonight he chose not to reveal any of that and simply said, "Owning a home is a lot of work."

"Yeah, you're right. Better to be free from the hassle."

Thirty minutes later, the last beer consumed, Moriah let out a burp and said, "I'm tired."

"You can sleep on the sofa. It makes into a bed."

As Gideon helped his brother put a fitted beige cotton sheet on the mattress, he asked, "What are your plans?"

"What do you mean?"

"When do you have to get back to Orlando?" Gideon fitted a pillowcase on a fluffy pillow he found in his linen closet. He sniffed the pillow as he worked, grateful that the stale smell of being forgotten in a closet over time did not permeate.

Moriah stretched out on the sofa bed, the pillow under his head. "Ahh," he moaned as he closed his eyes. "This is nice. I'll probably be asleep in a minute."

Gideon rephrased the question. "How long will you be here?"

"Here?"

"Yeah, how long?"

Moriah rolled over and tugged at the sheet until it covered his lean torso. "I have no plans to return to Florida."

"You aren't going back?"

"Uh-uh."

"But what about a job? What about your friends in Florida?" What about that girl in the bikini he met on the beach?

Moriah's lips curved into a smile. He opened his eyes just long enough to say, "I want to be here with you, bro."

Gideon wanted to feel good about his sentiments, but something made him leery. What was wrong with him? He should be elated that his brother had found him and wanted to spend time with him. This was an opportunity to grow closer, to give each other kudos for risking it all and leaving the Amish life. They could go see movies together, go out for pizza, have discussions about religion.

He was about to ask what kind of pizza Moriah liked when suddenly his brother groaned. "I need to get up. Forgot to brush my teeth."

As his brother rummaged through his duffel bag for his toothbrush and a tube of Aquafresh, Gideon's suspicions grew. Moriah had said on the phone that he was coming for a visit and that he liked living in sunny Orlando. Why did he want to stay in Twin Branches now?

As Moriah brushed his teeth in the bathroom off the hall, Gideon said, "You'll need a job."

Moriah spit into the sink and laughed. "That's right, the Miller boys aren't lazy. We work from sunup to sundown and then some."

Ten minutes later, lying in his own bed, Gideon thought of where he could get a job for Moriah. What was the kid good at? Would he be like Luke, good with cars, or more like Amos, unable to handle grease and tools?

His thoughts grew hazy as sleep took over. He dreamed of the farm. In his dream it was a clear day with billowy clouds, the kind that looked like marshmallows bouncing along like hot-air balloons. The sun shone on the orchard and fields, a lone wagon hitched to a horse sat by the road that led to the farmhouse. Suddenly, a flock of people, his parents among them, were running toward him, shouting that something was wrong. A storm was coming. Gideon told them they were crazy to be worried, the sky was bright. Even so, everyone rushed inside, securing the doors and locking all the windows.

A voice cried out, "Where's Moriah?" The scene shifted, and there was a large gathering in the barn.

"Where is Moriah?" asked his mother, pulling at the arm of one of the bishops.

The man closed his eyes, as though in deep prayer. "Confess your sins," he said. "Confess."

Rain seeped through the roof. The crowd huddled, trying to avoid getting wet. Black cloaks covered small children, protecting them from the downpour. The wind rattled the barn walls.

Gideon saw the faces of all his siblings. Except for one. "Where did he go?" he begged each person. Someone offered him a piece of rock candy, the kind he'd bought for Moriah from a shop just a mile from their home. It was gritty in the palm of his hand. He didn't care for candy now, couldn't they see that? He wanted to find his brother.

But no one could find Moriah.

The dream, so vivid, woke Gideon. Jumping out of bed, he made his way into the living room. Moriah was asleep, snoring softly. Gideon felt his heart slow with relief. He got a drink of water before returning to his bedroom. It was amazing how dreams could make you thirsty.

13

The story had intrigued her ever since she first read the illustrated book—a present from Mama. And now, she had someone who was interested in reading it with her. Kiki leaned her bike against the main door to the shop and removed her worn copy of *The Lost Pirate Ship* from her bicycle's basket. Then she grabbed Yoneko from the same basket and cradled both book and puppet in her arms. The cover of the book showed a majestic ship sailing on a dark sea. Two seagulls soared in the velvet blue sky and one sat perched on the boat's stern. It was an awesome cover, and Kiki recalled how she first felt when she saw it, her ears itching to hear Mama read the tale of the pirate ship to her.

She expected to see Ormond. You could ask Ormond anything. He knew the whereabouts of all his employees. He was a fixture in the shop, never in either of the bays with tools, but always at his desk. Kiki thought how nice it would be to own a shop and have everyone else do all the work. When she ran that thought by Mari the other night, Mari told her that Ormond probably used to do a lot of work, but now that he was in his seventies, he was able to spend more time doing what he wanted to do. Most likely, he only came to Russell Brothers to be a daily presence there, keeping tabs on the others. Mari said that was one advantage to being an owner of a place. But today, the old man wasn't at his usual spot reading the paper. Kiki hoped he wasn't sick.

Gideon does all the work, she thought as he greeted her with a quick hello before heading to the cash register to ring up a bill for a customer who'd had his Ford inspected. *Gideon keeps everyone on his toes.* She wanted to ask if any bicycles needing repair had come in while she was at school today, but she'd wait to ask. Mari was constantly telling her not to interrupt. *Be careful. Don't be pushy.*

Kiki slumped against the storage room door with both puppet and book. *Where was Moriah?* She wished he'd get to the shop. He was a new employee, yet Kiki had yet to see him do much work. Perhaps he wasn't going to be a mechanic very long. Amos quit after Mari hired him at Another Cup. Mari said not everyone was cut out to work on cars, that not everyone had the needed skills.

Kiki jumped up when Luke returned from a late lunch. "Where's Moriah?"

"What am I? Chopped liver?" Luke smiled as he popped open the hood of a Subaru that was parked in his bay.

Kiki had no clue why Luke was bringing up the subject of liver. Just the word made her queasy.

"There he is." Luke gestured out the bay door to the parking lot, and sure enough, Kiki saw Moriah, his ponytail resting along his back. He was talking to a man in sunglasses outside at the edge of the parking lot. The man was in a sleeveless T-shirt, his bare arms adorned with colorful tattoos.

As Moriah entered the shop through Luke's bay, he gave Kiki a wide smile. "Hello there, Bike Girl."

She showed him the book. "It's got cool pictures. Wanna see?"

"Sure," he said. Within minutes, the two were seated side by side at Ormond's desk, reading the story of a pirate ship that set out to find treasure. The ship, decked out with large billowing sails, got lost in a storm because the captain ventured far beyond his usual sailing perimeters into uncharted seas. The storm caused bow damage, but the other ships came to the rescue and repaired the broken parts with the warm waters from the Caribbean Sea.

Kiki had the story memorized, so reading it aloud to Moriah was easy. She turned the pages, making sure that he had plenty of time to view each illustration.

With the story completed, she sighed. "I love that book. And it's not a baby book, either."

"What?" He gave her a quizzical look.

"I took it to school one day, and Angie said it was for babies." The way Angie had teased her still stung.

"Well, Angie needs to know that pirates are sophisticated adults."

Kiki gave a wide smile. Moriah understood! "I have a poster on my wall of a pirate ship that belonged to Blackbeard."

"Blackbeard, huh? I saw a movie about him."

"Have you seen the *Pirates of the Caribbean* movies?"

"Every single one. And I bet you have, too."

"Yes," she said, the memory of watching the first one with Ricky on her mind. Since that movie, she'd pretended to be Keira Knightly, the lead actress in it, riding with Johnny Depp on the frothy seas. "I'd like to have my own real ship."

"Where would you store that?"

"My backyard."

Moriah laughed then said, "Gideon was going to make me a ship. I wonder what happened to the wood I gave him?"

"Gideon can make a ship?"

"He's a good furniture maker. He made me a keepsake box. It was beautiful."

"He gave me one he made but not as a real present, just to use for my tools here."

"Ask him to make you a ship."

"Must have been a huge chunk of wood you gave him." Kiki tried to imagine how large a piece of wood would be needed to craft a sea-faring vessel.

"No. It was tiny." He grabbed a memo pad off Ormond's desk. "About this size."

"How would he have carved out a ship from wood only the size of a memo pad?"

"It had to be small. I knew that my father didn't like pirates, so the ship was going to have to be small enough to hide it from him in my room."

"Who couldn't like pirates? They are part of North Carolina's history." Kiki had even managed to get her sister to see the power and awe in a ship like Blackbeard's famous *Queen Anne's Revenge*. "I like to pretend I'm looking for treasure. Do you ever do that?"

Moriah leaned back in the swivel chair where Ormond usually sat. "I used to. I called myself the famous Moriah of the High Seas."

"Then I'll be Kiki of the Even Higher Seas."

He let out a laugh. "You have to be better than me, I get it."

"I even have a cutlass. That's a curved sword. I carried it with me when I went trick-or-treating at Halloween. It's only plastic, but it looks real. It looks really real."

"Did you know that Edward Teach is Blackbeard's real name?"

"Of course, everybody knows his mama didn't name him Blackbeard. Sheesh!"

Moriah smiled and Kiki felt as happy as she did when she heard the choir sing "Amazing Grace" or when she rode her bicycle fast over the sloping mountain roads. She was glad that Moriah was here. He made Twin Branches a happier place.

When Gideon stepped out of his office with a stack of papers, Kiki said, "Gideon, you need to make a pirate ship for us."

Gideon was preoccupied. Kiki could tell because Mari got that way sometimes, too. It seemed that most of the adults in her life let their faces cloud with worry lines. Principal Peppers once was so unaware of the circumstances that he slipped in the hallway even though the janitor had placed a big orange Caution cone on the floor.

As Gideon walked away from her, she said to Moriah, "I don't know if he heard me." She was about to call out to him and state again that she wanted him to make a pirate ship, but Moriah patted her arm.

"He'll do it one of these days," he said. "Sometimes with Gideon you just have to keep pestering him, and then he'll listen to you."

14

As the wind shot pellets of rain against Another Cup's windows, Gideon folded his newspaper and took a look outside. There was something about a downpour that he enjoyed, something cleansing, rejuvenating. Of course, it was always nice to be dry inside when the thunder reared back and roared like a hungry mountain lion, before the heavens ripped open and let her torrents flow.

As he sipped his mug of tea, Gideon wanted to feel as clean as the rain. Here he was in this cozy tearoom drinking a beverage he found tasty and healthy, having a nice break from the auto shop's routine.

Amos had just finished his shift waiting on tables, and he seemed happy to be employed here. Before leaving the eatery, he told Gideon that Mari had encouraged him to further his education and that he was seriously considering going to tutoring sessions in the evenings so that he could eventually get his GED. With a clap on his back, Gideon affirmed the young man's decision.

"I owe so much to you," Amos said, and with that, took off into the rain, an umbrella over his head.

Yet, instead of feeling contented over Amos's happiness, Gideon's thoughts swirled around Moriah. His brother was more interested in drinking a six-pack each night and smoking cigarette after cigarette than talking about what he planned to do with his days. Gideon had been proud to have his baby brother nearby at first, but now he wasn't so sure. Moriah seemed aloof at times; there was an eerie presence about him, yet other days, he was affectionate and elated.

Removing himself from his thoughts, Gideon glanced around, noticing that he was now the only customer inside. The shop was still except for the music of the raindrops on the roof.

Mari appeared from the kitchen with a thermos and refilled his cup of green tea. "Feels cold in here," she said, and poured a cup for herself. "My dad always said tea warms the spirit more quickly than kerosene." As an afterthought, she added, "We had a kerosene heater growing up."

Gideon wanted to lighten the mood with a joke or two, but his mind was blank. Looking at the paper, he considered bringing up an article he'd read about paving the roads in Twin Branches, but that really wasn't much fodder for a conversation. Finally, he asked, "Do you see your parents often? Are they still around?" He'd learned that one should never assume anyone's parents were living.

"I haven't seen my dad in years. He left us." She started to say more, but bit her lower lip and stopped. With her hands folded around her teacup, she gazed into the beverage. "My mother's a hoarder."

"Hoarder?" The word sounded strange to him, and the minute he said it, thunder cracked.

"Big-time. I've tried to think back to how it started. I go crazy wanting to come up with a reason."

"What does she hoard?"

Mari looked away, as though thinking about it pained her to the point of not being able to respond.

He stirred his tea, although by this time it was lukewarm.

"Puppets."

"Puppets?" Immediately, as though a prop for their conversation, he saw that mangy orange cloth cat Kiki carried with her. Wasn't that a hand puppet?

"She has tons of puppets. Literally, tons. She buys them at Goodwill and secondhand shops." She searched his eyes, as though waiting for some reaction to guide her to continue.

"Is she like those people on the reality shows?"

"Yes." Sucking in air, she again said, "Unfortunately, yes."

As the rain rushed over the roof of the tearoom, she moved from behind the counter to sit beside him on a wobbly stool.

He watched her take delicate swallows from her cup, and then seized the opportunity to lean in a little closer to her. She smelled of something sweet and floral. "So," he said, trying to concentrate on the topic, "is she in bad shape?" Those on the shows certainly were.

"My dad left her years ago. He was tired of living with puppets all over the furniture in the living room and bedroom. At first, he planned to help her toss them out. But she wasn't going to have anything to do with getting rid of them. He begged her. I remember so many times when I'd be lying awake late into the night and overhear my parents talking. 'Please, Yukiko,' my dad would say. 'Let's clean this place up. There's no room to walk in the hallways because they're crammed, stuffed to the ceiling, with puppets. Please, dear.'" Suddenly Mari stopped. A shocked look spread across her face, an expression that asked, *Have I told you too much?*

"I'm sorry."

"Why are you sorry?"

"Well, because I'm sorry that you have to go through this. It must be awful."

She squeezed his hand, stood, and smoothed out her apron. "I need to go." Glancing at the clock on the wall she said, "Kiki will be home soon from school, and with this rain, she'll want a ride to your shop for her shift."

He stood as well, picked up his cup and plate, and made his way through the double doors into the deserted kitchen after her. "Has your staff already left for the day?"

"We close earlier now." She took the dishes from him and placed them in the sink. "You know how business is slow around here during Thanksgiving and Christmas. So I decided to cut back our hours."

He helped her turn off the lights in the room and plug in the fluorescent Closed sign to the right of the entryway. It flashed on once and then burned red through the windowpane.

In the dimness she asked, "Do you go to church?"

"Church?"

"Do you attend anywhere?"

His mind flashed back to services in Carlisle. Sunday mornings, where chairs arranged in a meagerly furnished home filled by neighbors in dark colors, gathered to worship a God he had felt was too strict, too High German, and too harsh for his tastes. "It's not easy growing up Amish."

"Really?"

"Yes, really." He wondered if she got it, if she knew the impact of his confession.

"Don't they have good family values, wholesome lives, and all that? Amos told me that they take really good care of each other within their communities."

He sighed. Amos was right, but Amos had also left because of the confinement he felt within his own community in Lancaster. "What else did Amos tell you?"

"He said he likes the freedom that comes with thinking for himself. He also likes being able to wear T-shirts and jeans. And, oh, he wants to get a tattoo." Studying his face, she said, "Something tells me you aren't interested in getting a tattoo."

"No." He laughed. "I guess I'm still old-fashioned about some things." Moriah had told Gideon that he was old-fashioned about everything, but Gideon didn't feel the need to disclose his brother's opinion now.

"So . . . church," she said, bringing the conversation back to her original question. "I haven't seen a First Amish Church around, so I'm figuring that you haven't been in years."

He wanted to tell her that he was doomed to hell since he'd left his community, so what good would it do to attend church, but she seemed ready to leave for home; this was not the time for a discussion of God. He merely said, "It's a little complicated."

She smiled and nodded as though she got it, but he doubted she did. How could any English woman understand his roots, his resentment, the disorder within his heart from a lifestyle that represented order and peace?

"Would you want a ride back to the shop?" she asked.

"No, thanks."

"Kiki tells me you have a truck, but you prefer to walk everywhere."

He patted his stomach. "Gotta keep in shape, you know."

Together they left the tearoom, and once outside, he waited, watching her get into her car. The rain had eased. Now it was only like soft lyrical notes dripping off tree limbs onto a saturated ground.

As she backed her Toyota out of the parking lot, he stood under the ruffled awning that was anchored over the tearoom's door. Nearing him, she slowed her vehicle and lowered her window. "Don't say anything about Mama," she pleaded. "Don't let Kiki know that you know."

He guessed she meant about her mother's hoarding. "I won't."

Then he watched her car drive off—a right onto Main at the edge of the parking lot, heading toward home. Her brakes squeaked, and he wasn't sure if it was due to the rain or if they really needed repair. Perhaps he could propose that she bring her car in for a checkup. She might go for that.

His walk back to the shop was damp and filled with thoughts of her—thoughts that caused him not to mind the moisture against his face and hands.

15

When Kiki arrived at the repair shop the next Monday afternoon, she pushed her bike in through the front door. Only one of the garage doors to the bay was opened, and a car stuck halfway inside and halfway out into the parking lot. She thought she recognized the vehicle; something about it gave her stomach one of those floppy feelings like she got just before being summoned to Principal Peppers' office.

Inside, Gideon greeted her and said that Ormond was at the eye doctor's, and Luke was having a late lunch with Ashlyn. Then, when his phone rang, he went back to his desk. Kiki hoped it was people calling about her and her wonderful capabilities to fix bikes. She tried to eavesdrop, but another conversation rallied for her attention.

As she perched her bicycle by the storage room, she heard Moriah's distinct voice. Today it sounded like a sugarcoated donut. Quiet as a mouse, she walked over to the glass door to the garage. There, in the garage, stood Moriah talking to a young woman in a pencil-slim skirt and pair of knee-high black boots.

The woman dangled the keys to her Dodge Intrepid, letting them jingle in front of his nose. She laughed, whispered something, and he laughed, too. Kiki stepped closer to the door of the bay so that she could get a better view and hear what was being said.

The woman removed the lit Marlboro from Gideon's hand and inhaled. As smoke puffs rose to the garage's ceiling, she smiled at Moriah. "Welcome to Twin Branches," she cooed, and Kiki knew that this was not right. The sensation in her stomach told her that this woman shouldn't be batting her eyes at Moriah because she belonged to someone else. Kiki closed her eyes and tried to remember just who the man was that she had seen this woman with.

"Well, the day was just okay, but now that you are here, it has improved considerably." Moriah leaned closer to her. "It's not often that I get to hang out with someone as pretty as you."

Kiki thought that some of his words came out funny. But the woman didn't seem to notice.

"So where are you from?" Her lips were scarlet and her nails matched. She held the cigarette out to him—red on white.

"Orlando." Moriah accepted the cigarette from her and let his lungs absorb the smoke as he took a drag.

"Orlando? How long are you here?"

"As long as the scenery is good." He winked.

It was then that Kiki realized who she was—she was Angie's uncle's girlfriend. She'd seen them together having a meal at the Cloudy Glass Diner on Fifth Street when Mari drove her to her appointment with Dr. Conner a month ago.

"I'm Tamara." The woman smiled at Moriah. "What's your name?"

"Moriah."

"That sounds like a big strong name."

He smiled as Kiki thought, *I can bat my eyelashes, too, and I'm pretty. What does Moriah see in this woman?* Kiki doubted she knew anything about pirates.

Tamara left as soon as Luke came back from lunch. He asked Moriah if he'd filled out an order sheet describing what the customer

101

wanted repaired with her car. Moriah simply said, "She asked for a tune-up." Running a hand over his chest, he added, "I think."

Luke shook his head. "You gotta stay focused, Moriah. Focus on what the customer wants done to her vehicle, not what she looks like."

Moriah winked and laughed. "In Carlisle, I used to sneak out of my parents' house and go to this girl's house. She was gorgeous." With that, he headed outside to smoke a cigarette.

Kiki knew that she could bat her eyes like the women did on TV, like Marianne and Ginger on *Gilligan's Island*. Did Moriah think she was pretty, at least a little? She ambled over to where he stood, his bare arms round with muscles. She noted a tattoo of a snake on his left bicep.

"Hey," she said tentatively.

"Hey there." His smile was warm. "What have you been up to?"

"School, the usual." She twisted a few strands of hair, like she'd seen Marianne do on TV.

"Do you like school?"

"Some classes are okay, but not math."

"I never liked math either. Just doesn't make sense to me." He snuffed out his cigarette butt with the heel of his boot. Smiling at her again, he asked, "So you been fixing bicycles?"

"Yeah. I made fliers last weekend."

"Fliers, huh? You're a regular businesswoman."

Businesswoman. She liked that, especially when he said it.

Looking at his watch, he said, "I have to be somewhere."

"Where?"

As he studied her for a moment, she hoped he noticed that she'd used Herbal Essence's Honeyed Pear conditioner on her hair this morning. She ran a hand over the ends.

"If a man delivers a package for me, will you keep it safe?"

"A package?"

"Yeah. Will you hold onto it, keep it in a safe place for me?"

Was Moriah asking her to help him? Kiki beamed. "Sure."

"Great!" Moriah lit another cigarette. He gave her earlobe a light pull. "Thanks, Kiki. Don't tell anyone, okay?"

"About what?"

"The package that comes for me. Just take it from the man and hide it, okay?"

She ran his instructions through her mind to make sure she understood. "I'll take good care of it. I won't tell." A secret, she could keep a secret. Pirates kept their treasure maps hidden so as not to let others know where they planned to search. She was Kiki the Pirate of the Higher Seas; she wouldn't tell.

"Kiki, you're the best."

She watched him stride across the parking lot. He turned to wave, the sun casting light on his hair and shoulders. She smiled back, feeling as warm as the afternoon sun.

Suddenly he stopped, bent over, and picked something up from the pavement. Sprinting back to her, he said, "I found a penny." Pressing it into her hand, he said, "Could be a lucky one." Grinning, he walked away again.

Holding the penny tightly, she kept her eyes on him until he was out of her sight. "Moriah." Softly breathing his name made her heart pound. "Moriah," she said again and, fingering the penny, slipped it in her pants pocket.

Inside the shop she heard a squeak, and there stood a small boy with a crop of frizzy hair. A slender woman was by his side. Kiki recognized them both from her neighborhood. She was pretty good with names, and this was John Dimetra and his mother.

"We heard that you repair bicycles," the woman said. Her smile was light, friendly.

"Yes!" Kiki burst into energy, taking the bike from the boy and pushing it to the area where she worked. Her fliers were paying off! With Mari's help, she'd printed twenty on her computer three nights ago and placed them by the flags of the mailboxes on her street and the next one over. Mari told her not to put them inside each mailbox because that was considering tampering and against the law.

"The tires need to be replaced," said the mother, making her way over to Kiki, her hand resting on the handlebar. "This is an old bicycle we got from a neighbor, and the tires have dry-rotted." She patted the seat as one would the head of a small child.

"Sure!" As soon as Kiki said it, she realized there were no tires or tubing in the auto shop. She'd have to go buy some somewhere, Walmart or something. "I'll get this done. I can do this. It will probably cost fifteen dollars. Now that's cheap and I do good work, too."

She waited for them to leave before entering Gideon's office. Why did they have to take so long, commenting on every poster for tire advertisements that Ormond had displayed on the walls? Hoping they'd take the hint, she told them goodbye a few times until at last, they nodded and went out the door. Gideon sat at his desk sucking on ice cubes from a plastic cup.

She was about to call him Mr. Miller, thought better of it, tried to say Gideon, but she just couldn't—so she declined from using any names. "I need supplies," she blurted.

Gideon shifted a cube to the left side of his mouth. "Supplies?"

"John Dimetra brought his bike here, and it looks like it will need new tires. All new. Dry rotten or dry something-or-other."

"That's fine." Gideon had opened a notebook on his desk and appeared to be reading.

"No, it's not! We need tires so I can repair it."

"Tires?" He looked up.

"Yes! Quick!"

"How are they paying for this?"

"Didn't you read the flier I made?" She saw the edge of it peeking out from his messy desk. She'd handed him one the other day, and he'd commented that she'd done a good job.

"What does it say in your flier?"

"Payment required upon completion."

"Does John Demiter know that?"

"Dimetra!"

"Okay, whatever."

She let out a huff of air. "Hurry, get the supplies so I can fix the bicycle."

Gideon moved over to his computer, perched at the center of his desk. He typed a bit and then, looking at the screen, offered, "Here's a supplier in Gatlinburg. I could see if he can deliver what we need for your work at the shop."

Your work at the shop. She liked the sound of that. She told him what she needed and he said he'd order extra so she'd have supplies around for future repairs.

She tried to think, which was hard to do because excitement welled within her. "Patches!' she cried. "Sometimes bicycles have okay tires, but they're flat and need patches with glue."

"Patches with glue." He jotted words onto a pad of paper. "Anything else?"

She smiled, excited that he was taking her work seriously. When the phone rang in the bay, Luke answered and called out for Gideon. Kiki wondered if it was another Amish person wanting to leave Pennsylvania. She'd heard how helpful Gideon was to people from where he used to live. Gideon was a real role model.

She busied herself by looking at her keepsake box and then said she'd be fine when Gideon told her that he needed to leave the shop for a while.

Minutes after he left, a rusty tan truck pulled into the lot, smoke trailing behind it. Kiki watched a young man get out and ask Luke a question. Something jolted inside her. This was the man from the other day, the one she'd seen Moriah talking to in the parking lot. What if he was making the delivery Moriah had mentioned?

Kiki rushed toward the man and Luke just in time to hear, "Well, I have something for him."

"Is it for Moriah?" she asked.

The man's toned biceps were covered in tattoos and three gold chains draped like tree ornaments around his neck. He looked at Kiki although she could not see his eyes because they were shielded by a pair of dark sunglasses. "Yeah, it's for him."

"I can take it. He told me to take it."

The man studied her for a minute. "You?"

"Yes," she said, standing as tall as she could because that action made her more confident. "Moriah told me I was to take a package from you."

"Well, okay then."

From the passenger seat of his car, he removed a tiny box wrapped in brown paper. "Make sure he gets it. Keep it safe for him."

"I will." She watched him leave, smoke clouding her vision.

"Who was that?" Luke asked as he closed the hood of the car he was repairing.

Kiki tucked the package behind her back, hoping Luke would not see it. "Moriah's friend, I guess."

"He looks shady." Luke opened the driver's door and climbed into the car. "I think I've seen him before somewhere. He's a heap of trouble." With that he revved the car's engine and backed it out of the bay for a test drive.

Kiki wondered what Luke meant, but she didn't ask. She was too busy thinking of where she could store this package to keep it hidden. Moriah had instructed her to make sure it was safe. She immediately thought of the storage room. Finding an empty Pennzoil box, she carefully laid the brown square inside it. She tried to fold the flaps to seal the box like Mari did after opening produce that came to the tearoom. The wider left flap and the small one at the end and then the wider right one, no was it the left one first and the smaller one under it? Finding she was much too clumsy to get all four flaps to lock tightly, she gave up. Peering around the corner from the storage room to make sure no one was watching, she carefully lifted the container onto one of the shelves. There, it was safe.

She tinkered with John's bike, removing the tires from the rims, and caught herself daydreaming more than working. Her thoughts never left Moriah or the item. Curiosity consumed her; what could be inside that box? She thought of the shape—square and small. Perhaps it was a box with a piece of jewelry in it. *My birthday is coming up—maybe it is a gift for me. That could be why he wanted me to keep it safe and not open it. He did say not to open it, didn't he? Or did he?*

Gideon entered the shop, interrupting her thoughts. "It's nearly five, Kiki. Shouldn't you be heading home? Gets dark quickly these days." He looked out the window with his hands in his pockets, that stance that so many adults liked to take.

"My bicycle has a light."

"Do you have a helmet?"

"Helmet?"

"Yes, do you have one of those?"

Kiki shook her head. She knew that it was the law in North Carolina for kids to wear helmets, but the one she got last Christmas, she'd purposely left at Mama's house. Helmets made her head itch.

"When you get paid, you should buy yourself one."

Paid! Kiki smiled. She couldn't believe that Gideon—Gideon, the very person who had not wanted her to come to his shop ever again— was now going to give her money for her work. "You mean money? Like real American money?"

He laughed. "I don't suppose French francs would do you any good here."

"Real money?"

"Yes, Kiki."

"Thank you," she said as she swung her arms around his waist, nearly causing him to trip on his own shoes.

16

After a snack of oatmeal cookies, Kiki laid her arrowhead collection out on her bed and wished she had a nice box to keep her possessions in. A keepsake box like she had at the shop for her tools would be ideal. But even though she'd asked Gideon to provide her with one, his head was in the clouds these days. *For Pete's sake, he could build me one if only he would take the time.*

Ormond said Gideon used to make furniture as a child. If he could put together a table and chairs, then why couldn't he make a box? A box was much easier. *Oh, well,* she tried to console herself, *at least he ordered the things I need to fix bikes. I should count my lucky stars, as Mama used to say.*

She wondered what Mama was doing today. Probably at Goodwill, buying a few more precious puppets. Kiki knew that the social worker had told Mama to stop buying. Sternly, while tapping her pen against the palm of her hand, she'd told Mama to get rid of the furry cats, dogs, and monkeys that took up so much room in the hallways and bedrooms. But, as Mari had stressed, Mama was addicted. Not addicted to alcohol or cocaine, but to collecting puppets. She couldn't stop wanting them, buying them, hoarding them, inside her dilapidated house. At least here in this house, Kiki had room to move and didn't have to worry about knocking down a stack of puppets that practically blocked her path to the kitchen.

A knock at the front door set Kiki sailing toward it. There stood Angie, the wind blustering around her, sweeping her hair into her eyes.

"Hi." Angie twisted her fingers together and Kiki thought that maybe she had something in them she wanted to show. That was Kiki's first thought. Her next was: *Why's Angie at my house?*

"Thanks for fixing my bike." Angie looked up and brushed hair from her face.

"Sure. It was easy." Kiki knew she wasn't supposed to be too prideful, but she couldn't help it if God had given her so many skills.

"It rides really good now."

"I'm a pro," she said with a smile and thought about adding how fast she could use tools but then stopped herself. *No one likes braggarts.*

"I told some other kids to come to the shop."

"Thanks." Since Angie didn't seem to have anything else to say, Kiki added, "I'm going to watch *True Stories of Rescue Animals.* It comes on really soon. You want to watch with me?"

"Uh." Angie shifted from one foot to the other. "No. Umm, I have to go."

Kiki wished she didn't have to go anywhere. How nice it would be to have someone watch the show with her. "You really have to go now?"

"Yeah. Luva, you know, my grandma, well, she's driving me back home."

"You spend a lot of time at your grandma's."

Angie looked at her feet. "My parents fight too much."

Kiki wished she had parents around to fight. Her mama was alone now in that cluttered house in Asheville with walls that were stained with nicotine, surrounded by lifeless puppets. Who knew where her daddy was? She hardly recalled what he looked like. Some days she pictured him with a dark beard, and other days she had an image of him in a plaid shirt with a stiff collar, smelling of turpentine.

Again Angie said that she had to go. Kiki wondered if she was lying, but minutes after Angie walked back to her grandma's next door, a white Mercedes backed out of the driveway, and Kiki presumed that her classmate was seated inside. Satisfied, Kiki plopped down on the couch and got ready to watch her rescue animals show.

When she arrived at the repair shop the next afternoon, Gideon presented her with a box. Inside were supplies that he'd ordered for her. She saw plastic wrappings and cardboard containers that said "Bicycle Repair Kit" and "Tubing for Bicycles."

"What about two new tires?"

Gideon looked surprised. "Why would you need those?"

"I told you! Johnny's bike needs new tires." How could he have forgotten to get those?

Stepping into the storage closet, Gideon said, "Let's see. Could we put Michelin tires on his bike?" Then he laughed, and Kiki realized that he was trying to make a joke. Of course, the shop didn't store car tires inside this tiny room.

For a second she smiled, liking the fact that Gideon could tease her, but then she felt anxiety rise in her pulse. The secret package she'd hidden for Moriah was in there! Perhaps if she didn't look up at the shelf where she'd put it, Gideon wouldn't suspect anything. *Be calm*, she told herself. *Be cool.* Tentatively, she joined him in the closet. "Car tires? He needs regular bicycle tires."

Pointing to two rubber items that were propped against the wall, Gideon asked, "Would those do?"

He hadn't failed her. They were bike tires. Excited, she rushed into his chest, knocking a shovel onto the floor. With arms around his waist, she cried, "Thank you, thank you, thank you!" Now she could repair Johnny's bicycle.

"Can you keep it down?"

Both Kiki and Gideon looked to see Moriah at the door of the closet, Moriah, with a frown covering his splotchy face.

"What's the matter with you?" asked Kiki.

"Matter with me? You're acting like some sort of crazed creature. Keep it down."

"I got stuff for the bikes!" She held up both tires, steadying them with one hand. *Wow, I'm strong!* She could feel the flexing muscles in her arm.

"Who cares?" Muttering, he walked away from them, toward the fridge.

Moriah's words grated like nails against a chalkboard in her ears. How could he be so cruel? "Hey," she said, pretending she was not bothered by his rudeness. She ambled over to him, leaving Gideon in the distance. Whispering, she asked, "Do you want it?"

"What?"

"You know." She looked around to make sure that no one else was listening. Gideon was now in his office. "You know. The secret."

Moriah opened a bottle of water he'd retrieved from the fridge. After a swallow he said, "Nah."

"No?"

As he looked out above her head, his eyes seemed like shiny marbles, solid, but without any movement.

For a moment she just looked at his jaw, his blond hair tied behind his back, and his hands. She thought of one word only—handsome. Mama called some of her puppets handsome, but Moriah was better looking than any cloth puppet Kiki had ever laid eyes on.

She watched him walk to the bay where Luke was wiping grease off his hands. There was no time to argue or complain to him about his sourpuss behavior, she decided. Taking John's Schwinn out of the storage room, she sat down to work on it. She replaced the tires then rode the bike around the shop for a minute before heading out into the parking lot. Once again, she knew she'd done good work, but today that didn't matter as much to her. Moriah was nowhere. She called John to say his bike was ready and that he owed twenty-nine dollars.

111

When Ormond asked if she'd like to help him by washing out the coffeemaker and wiping the counter that it sat on, Kiki was glad for something different to do. Angie had said she'd tell others about the shop and to bring their bikes over, but Kiki didn't see anyone with bicycles this afternoon. Besides, she wasn't sure she could trust Angie to help her since the girl tattled and often made it a point to ridicule her.

Cleaning the coffeemaker was easy. Kiki let the glass pot fill with warm water from the tap, squeezed two drops of Palmolive from the bottle, and then, using a scrubbing pad, wiped the soapy inside. She rinsed out the pot, her mind jumping to Moriah and the box she was to keep safe for him.

Once her hands were dry, she made her way to the storage closet. By standing on her tiptoes, she was able to reach the Pennzoil box. Making sure no one was watching, she placed the box on the closet floor and opened it. Instead of finding the brown package, she found an empty box. *Empty!* Kiki panicked. She'd put the package in here only yesterday, certain that she could keep it safe. Who took it?

She hurried out to find Moriah, who was making his way to the parking lot. She called out to him, "Where is it?"

Turning, he stopped walking. "What?"

Rushing to his side, she cried, "The thing I was supposed to keep for you. The package."

"What are you talking about?"

Perhaps someone else had found the package and had it. Kiki ran inside and asked Luke if he'd seen it.

Luke stood at the counter by the coffeemaker with a cup of coffee. As he stirred sugar into it, he asked, "What package? Has Santa come early?"

Moriah stormed in after her. "Shut up!"

Kiki felt her knees quake. "What?"

"Don't be acting all loud about it."

"You gave it to me to take care of. I hid it like you told me. Then it was gone."

Under his breath, Moriah said, "I got it, okay?" He gave a little smile to Luke and with that, Luke's confusion faded. Taking his coffee, Luke walked toward his bay.

Kiki knew that smile at Luke was fake and that Moriah was pretending that everything was all right. Well, it wasn't.

"Just mind your own business," Moriah said after Luke was gone.

"What business? You mind your own!" Kiki knew her voice was loud; she felt her head grow queasy, like it did when she stood up too quickly.

Gideon came out of his office and asked what the commotion was about. Kiki looked at her hands as Moriah placed an arm around his brother's shoulders. "It's all good, bro. Kiki and I are just having a little fun." Then he smiled his wide movie-star smile, the one that always reminded Kiki of the smile that belonged to the Professor on *Gilligan's Island*. He patted Kiki's head then walked over to where Luke was changing oil in a vehicle. Next thing, they were both laughing, like old friends.

When Ashlyn stopped by after what she called a grueling day at the *Twin Star*, Moriah suggested that what she needed was a donut.

"Donuts?" Ashlyn laughed and Kiki thought how pretty her dark wavy hair was against her olive skin. She must have got her good looks from her mama because Sheriff Henry sure didn't have any to pass down.

Moriah winked at Kiki and said, "Wouldn't you like a donut?"

Kiki was relieved. Moriah was acting more like the friendly man she'd first gotten to know. With enthusiasm she said, "I would."

Without further ado, Moriah took off, his long strides cutting across the parking lot toward the Piggy Wiggly. Fifteen minutes later he sprinted back with a box of Krispy Kreme donuts. He grinned and set the box on the hood of the car Luke was servicing. Opening the lid, he exposed an assortment of a dozen donuts. "Dig in!"

The others laughed, carefully deciding which treat they wanted, while Kiki went for the lemon one. She knew it was lemon because a little bit of the gooey yellow filling inside oozed from the edge.

The donut was delicious; it made her mouth and tummy feel sugary and warm. She looked at Moriah who smiled at her. Perhaps he wasn't a meanie after all. Maybe he hadn't meant to be so thoughtless and ungrateful an hour ago. When no one was looking, she grabbed a sugar-glazed, popping it into her mouth so quickly, she could hardly move her jaw to chew. Mari wouldn't be pleased that she was consuming so much sugar, but thankfully, Mari wasn't here.

"You work at the paper, don't you?" Moriah asked as he drenched his throat with a large swig of bottled water from the fridge.

Ashlyn said that she did.

"Can you put me in the paper?"

Lightly, Ashlyn said, "Why do you want to be in the paper? For bringing donuts to us?"

Moriah laughed. "Even better than that! Put me in there for a good reason."

Reaching for another donut, Luke said, "What good are you going to do so you can get in the *Twin Star*?"

Moriah thought as he took another drink of water. "Something noteworthy. Something grand." Smiling at Kiki, he said, "Just watch. I'll do something to get in there."

Gideon came out of his office after that. Kiki thought he might order everyone back to work, but he didn't. He accepted Moriah's bear hug, laughed, and also accepted the last donut in the box. He didn't seem to mind that it was only an Old Fashioned.

17

Kiki drove her bike home in a fury. What was his problem talking to her like that? She'd done him a favor and yesterday he was rude to her. Then he was all nice, buying donuts for everyone. *Well, that didn't last,* thought Kiki. This very afternoon he was back to being rude, telling her to not talk so loudly and ask him so many questions. She'd only wanted to know what became of the item she'd carefully stored for him. Why couldn't he answer that question? Instead, he told her he needed her to take care of another package that was to come by. Then he'd left the shop and when he returned an hour later, he demanded that she tell him where the item was.

"No one dropped anything off for you," she'd said as she washed her hands.

"What do you mean?" The veins in his neck pulsed like angry ripples in a gushing stream. "I told you that someone was coming by."

"No one came by. No one did," she'd said as he groaned.

"Forget it then!" And with that, he cursed her and once again, left the repair shop.

Don't be rude, Kiki, Mari often told her. *Be polite.* Well, Mari needed to tell that to Moriah, because he certainly was lacking manners. "He's a retard," Kiki muttered, knowing that was a hateful word and she loathed it when anyone called her that. "No, he's crazy. He's no good."

The air was cool now and daylight, fading. Kiki was grateful to see her driveway and eager to get inside her house and make a cup of cocoa. She put her bike in the garage, then climbed the front porch steps and realized she didn't want cocoa, she wanted to sit and stew some more. *Sit and stew,* that's what Mama said Kiki did when she was upset. "Are you going to sit and stew? I'll leave you alone to sit and stew."

Kiki plopped down on the top step and put her head between her hands. "You are a moron, Moriah!" she shouted. *Why, oh, why did this day have to be such a bad one? When am I going to have a good day?*

Just then Angie stepped from the shadows over by her grandmother Luva's house and made her way to Kiki's front lawn. "Hi," she said. "What's wrong?"

"Nothing . . . Everything."

"Are you mad at someone or something?"

"He thinks he can do whatever he pleases."

Angie continued to stand in front of her, so Kiki, enjoying an audience, continued, "He's a no-good loser!" Spouting the line made her feel powerful. "He's not so great!"

"Who are you talking about?" asked Angie. She made a face like she thought Kiki was crazy.

Kiki took a breath, realizing she had not shared Moriah's name. Dare she tell Angie who she was talking about? What if Angie laughed at her? "Moriah," she said and waited for Angie's response. When there was none, she added, "He flirts with all the girls. I mean every single one of them."

Angie nodded and let a smile slip between her lips. "I've seen him. He is really cute."

Why did Angie have to say that? Kiki wished Moriah wasn't good-looking. Hotly, she shouted, "He is a big fat loser and he thinks he's all

116

that and a bag of chips." She yelled to shut out the music from her heart that repeated like a soft refrain, *I wish he liked me. I wish he liked me.*

"What did he do to you?"

"He asked me to take care of a package for him. And I did. And he never even thanked me." She was on a roll. Without taking a breath, she continued. "And then, he bought us donuts and acted all happy and laughing with everyone, but today he was back to being mean again."

"Guys," said Angie, disgust lining her face. "They are such problems." She made her way up to the top step and sat next to Kiki. "Don't let it get to you."

Kiki nodded. Having Angie seated beside her was strangely nice. But it didn't last long, because as usual, Angie said she had to go.

Kiki watched the girl walk toward her grandmother Luva's house. When Angie was out of sight, Kiki ambled inside to her bedroom. Her arrowhead collection was scattered on her dresser. She wished again that she had a cool box like the one at work to store them in. In the living room, she flicked on the TV to the animal show. She saw a commercial for dog food, a flashy boxer eagerly eating from a stainless steel bowl. *Why couldn't I have a pet like that?* She knew dogs made great and loyal companions. *There was Lassie and Skip and that movie called* Beethoven. *If I had a dog, I'd take good care of it.*

Wishing, she was always wishing. One day, she'd told Dr. Conner she wanted something grand to happen to her so that she didn't have to keep wishing her life away. He'd said that she could have good things happen to her. She just had to be patient.

18

Gideon was relieved that Amos seemed to be fitting in well at Another Cup. The two had agreed that Amos would pay off the rent he owed Gideon for his first month, and then lease the apartment under his name so that Gideon was not responsible for the payment. Amos seemed lighthearted again, the same boy who had stepped off of Bruce's truck, only a little more familiar with the ways of the real world and much more confident. "I think of home," he told Luke, Moriah, and Gideon one night when Gideon had them over for a dinner of beef stroganoff and seasoned carrots. "But then I think of now, this experience, and I don't want to trade it for anything."

Moriah smiled. "Well," he said as he lifted a glass of sweet tea. "I'd like to work at Another Cup, too. You've got great scenery there. The owner is a doll."

Gideon gulped. His brother's freedom to flirt around women was starting to bother him. What had living in Florida taught him? Had he taken some course on picking up women? Quickly, he tried to think of where the conversation had begun and get back to it. "Uh, Amos." See-

118

ing that he had the boy's attention, he continued, "Do you think you'll go back to Lancaster for a visit?"

"No way. My dad would never let me come home now that I've left. I snuck away and left no trace of where I was headed."

"How many times?" Moriah asked.

Amos raised a puzzled look.

"How many times did you try to run away before you actually succeeded?"

Amos's face lightened. "Let's see. Three. How about you?"

"I planned it all out and left and then realized I'd forgotten my wallet, so I came back after walking two miles and tried again two nights later." Moriah beamed. He looked at his brother. "Gideon made a clear escape his first try."

Gideon didn't want to get into the memories of that night. "So," he said to Amos, "you're here to stay?"

"It's a nice place," said Amos as he helped himself to more stroganoff. "I like the church here."

"Church?" said Luke. "Which one are you going to?"

"Mari invited me to her church and I went. Different. But nice."

Gideon wanted to change the subject. He had no interest in hearing more about Mari's church. He supposed that she invited everyone to her church as he recalled how she'd asked him about attending that rainy afternoon at the tea shop.

Halfway through dessert, Moriah looked at his wristwatch and said he had to go. Politely, he thanked Gideon for the meal and stood.

Gideon didn't ask him any questions, but later that night wished he had. As he tried to get comfortable in his bed, Gideon wondered about his brother. Moriah seemed to take a lot of cigarette breaks and at lunchtime today, he'd wandered off and didn't return until a few hours later. *What is wrong with Moriah? Has he forgotten his hardworking roots?*

The next morning, Gideon noted that the sofa had not been slept on. Moriah usually left his blanket swung over the back of the sofa when he woke, but the blanket was still folded in a little pile on one corner of the couch.

Gideon headed out to work, hoping Moriah would be in the garage, working on Mrs. Peterson's old Ford with Luke. He entered the bays and saw Luke, but no sign of his brother.

When Kiki got to work, she placed her bike by the storage room door and then said that she'd told everyone at school to come to the shop with their bikes. "I told them eight dollars."

"Eight dollars?"

"I have to charge them something! This shop needs to make money."

Ormond chuckled from his desk. "A girl after my own heart."

"But what made you decide to come up with eight? Why not ten?" Luke asked as he washed his hands.

"Eight is what Mari said we should charge. Not as much as ten, so people will think it's a bargain."

Luke laughed. "That's what everyone wants around here, something for nothing."

"Gideon told me that eight is only the beginning."

"The beginning?" Ormond asked.

"Yeah. To look at the bicycle, that costs eight. Then if you need new tires, then I add more to it." From her pocket, she removed a folded slip of paper. "It's here. Gideon wrote it all down for me. I look at this and I know what to charge." Her smile evaporated to a frown. "It's numbers which means math. I don't have a mind for math, no mind for math."

Ormond and Luke laughed, but Gideon's somber thoughts kept him from joining in their amicable conversation. "Has anyone seen Moriah?"

"Not today," said Luke. He dried his hands and sauntered back to his bay.

Ormond busied himself with today's edition of the paper and said that he had not. He turned back a page to show Gideon a story, claiming that Ashlyn had a rather controversial column in there about local ski resorts not updating their lifts and charging too much for ski passes. "The owners won't be pleased," he said. "Jack and Mary told me that they are already losing money this season and need to increase their fees."

"Kiki, have you seen Moriah?" Gideon stood in front of her.

Kiki only moved her keepsake toolbox onto the center of the floor and sat beside it, her legs crossed. Her orange puppet friend lay beside her like a silent observer.

"Kiki?"

"What? I have to be ready. Kids are coming with their bicycles. Lots of kids."

"Have you seen Moriah today?"

"No," she said quickly and looked at her feet.

Gideon stepped closer to her. "You haven't seen Moriah?"

"I said no! For Pete's sake, I said no." Grabbing the puppet, she clutched it with both hands and buried her nose in its fur.

Gideon knelt in front of her. "Do you know where he might be?"

She looked at him then. "I can't lie. Lying is a sin. Did you know that?"

"So I have heard."

"The Ten Commandments say not to tell a lie."

Gently, he said, "Yes, I know."

Her eyes darted to the front door, the bays, and then back at her feet. Flexing her toes inside her tennis shoes, she let out a long sigh. "Angie saw him."

"Angie Smithfield? The tattletale?"

Kiki raised her voice. "She can be nice, too."

"I'm sure she can be. No one is all bad."

Kiki ran her nose over her puppet like a puppy sniffing a new toy.

"What did Angie tell you?"

"That she saw him last night."

"Angie saw Moriah?"

"She told me that today in math class. Moriah was walking down the street with Tamara, and then they got into her car."

Gideon tried to place who Tamara was. When it dawned on him, he asked, "Tamara McAlister?"

Kiki would not meet his eyes. "Reginald's girlfriend."

Gideon stood. "Thanks, Kiki." He wasn't sure how this would help him know where his brother was right now, but at least he could put two and two together. Last night when Moriah slipped out, he must have met up with Tamara. Gideon knew that his brother frequented the local pub. Perhaps he'd run into Tamara there and gone off with her. Perhaps he was still with her. Gideon wished Moriah would choose another woman. Not only was Tamara already Reginald's girlfriend, but it was common knowledge that Reginald despised minorities, including all Asians, Jews, Native Americans, blacks—and ex-Amish. When Gideon first started working for Ormond, Reginald had thrown dozens of eggs at the walls and windows of the shop. After three days of that, Ormond had called the sheriff. Henry promised to pay the man a visit. "Twin Branches is a peaceful town," Henry had emphasized over Reginald's callous injections that minorities needed to stay out of the region. "And you better not be doing anything more to show your ill feelings, or I will arrest you." The egg-depositing had stopped.

"I need a keepsake box at home for my collection!" Kiki bellowed when Gideon walked toward his office.

"I know. I know."

"I told the truth."

"And I thank you for that." He was about to say more, something his father might have said about not being rewarded every time you did the right thing, but he hesitated as a young boy with a green Schwinn bicycle walked into the shop through the front door.

When the boy saw Kiki, he said, "I brought my bike. Can you fix it?"

Kiki smiled like she'd just won an award at the state fair. Jumping to her feet, she said, "I can do it. Do you have eight dollars?"

Gideon heard Ormond laugh and felt that if there was one thing she did right, it was to bring some humor and warmth into the shop.

As usual, that evening after closing up the shop, Gideon walked home. But instead of going inside when he reached the apartment complex's parking lot, he got into his truck. With one eye on the road and the other scanning the sidewalks, he drove up and down the streets of Twin Branches. He slowed when he saw a tall blond-headed figure walking along in front of the ice cream shop. But as the man turned, he realized it was not Moriah.

Parking across from the Rusty Saddle Bar and Grille, he watched men and women enter and exit. When it grew dark and cold, the street-lights flickered on. He buttoned his jacket up to his neck and wished he was holding a hot cup of green tea. *Where could Moriah be?* He didn't know if he'd made new friends or if he already had another local hangout besides the pub.

Restless and impatient, Gideon left and drove the mile to the Piggly Wiggly. Inside he bought a pound of ground beef, a pack of hamburger buns, and some mustard. He searched for Moriah, scanning the beer aisle, but didn't see him. Remembering that he was low on bread, he added a loaf of whole wheat to his cart. He hoped his recent order of six jars of apple butter would arrive this week from the Pennsylvania Country Shoppe because he was down to his last jar at home.

At his apartment, he formed the beef into patties and fried one for himself. Placing it on a bun, he added generous squirts of mustard and ketchup, and two Mount Olive pickle slices. He would have put some Hellman's on his meal, but he was out of mayonnaise. He poured himself a glass of sweet tea and sat down to eat in front of the TV. His mind wandered as the local news played before him. He considered praying, asking God to keep Moriah safe. As he put his plate into the dishwasher, he decided that asking God for help was not a bad idea.

He woke at two-fifteen to pots clanging in the kitchen. At first, he thought he was dreaming, but then he realized that none of his dreams ever came with surround-sound effects.

Stumbling out of bed, he entered the darkened living room and made his way into the kitchen. A light was on, allowing him to see Moriah shirtless in a pair of dirt-stained jeans, standing by an opened cupboard. "What's going on?" Gideon asked, his voice raspy with sleep.

"Making some chow." Moriah had a can opener in one hand and a can of Campbell's chicken soup in the other.

"Where were you?" It was then that Gideon saw the gash above his brother's right eye. Dried blood filled it. "What happened to you?"

"Nothing." Moriah turned his back in search of a spoon.

"How did you get that cut?" Gideon skirted around him to get a better view. Not only was there a wound over his eye, but his cheek was cut, and blood was still oozing from it. Gideon grabbed a paper towel from the dispenser by the sink and reached up to wipe his brother's cheek. "What happened?"

19

Sheepishly, Moriah grinned and then gave Gideon's hand a push away from his face. Slurring his words, he said, "Some folks around here don't like me, I guess."

"Who?" He'd been here less than a month; could he really already have enemies?

"That bigot."

Gideon spoke the name of the first person who came to mind. "Reginald?"

"Is that who that idiot is?"

Gideon stepped closer, feeling small next to his brother's six-foot-two frame. "Be careful." The warning came out stronger than he'd wanted it to.

Moriah waved a hand in the air. "Don't worry about me."

Gideon smelled the Jim Beam on Moriah's breath, but there was something else that caused Gideon to worry. His brother's pupils were larger than normal, and the rims of his eyes were red.

"I said don't worry!" Moriah was yelling now.

"Shh. You'll wake the neighbors."

"Don't tell me to be quiet!" With that, Moriah let out a stream of curses and pushed Gideon against the cabinets, knocking his head against the wooden frame. Stunned, Gideon bit back anger. Something told him to go now, and he listened to that something. Turning, he bolted from the kitchen. He would get out of the way, back to his room. It was clear that Moriah was in no mood to be confronted.

In his bedroom with the door shut, Gideon sat on the edge of his bed, fear rising in his chest. Rubbing the back of his head, he felt the knot under his hair. Closing his eyes, he wondered why he'd been so anxious for Moriah to get back here.

The next morning, he was glad to see his brother sprawled out on the couch, the blanket covering his bare legs. Not wanting to wake him, Gideon showered, dressed, neglected to eat breakfast, and left the apartment. Moriah did not stir once, even when the front door to the apartment stuck and Gideon had to forcibly pry it open.

Although the sun was just coming out over the horizon, Gideon's walk to work was without its usual energetic strides. What a shame to not be able to enjoy the sound of birds and the way the clouds sprang to life as the sun lit them with its rays. It didn't help that Gideon could not stop the memories of his father's chastisement as they took over his thoughts.

Gideon pushed the shed door open. He peered into the darkness to see a figure cowering over by the bags of fertilizer. "Are you all right?"

The instructor, Judith Lane Russell, had asked the class to tell their stories in third person and then in first, just for the sake of changing the point of view. When she read Gideon's six pages told in first and then the same story recounted in third, she asked if Gideon could see it.

"See what?" he'd asked. He didn't want to confess that he hadn't had much education. He'd finished eighth grade at the Amish school and was now enrolled in mechanics training at Ormond's expense so that he could obtain his auto mechanic's certification. But reading and writing English had never been his strong suit.

"You are more honest when you write about yourself in third person."

"I am?"

She nodded. "It happens a lot. We seem to feel more freedom to write about those hard places when we write as though we are strangers looking in on the situation."

Gideon had been only a young man of seventeen then, but her words stuck in him. He would carry them with him always.

He expected that Moriah might make it to work by the afternoon, but only Kiki showed up. Setting her bicycle in its usual spot, she began chattering about school and how it had been two weeks since she'd had to pay a visit to Principal Peppers' office.

"Can you believe it, Gideon?" she asked a few times until he finally responded.

"No, I can't." He shoved Moriah's grin from his mind and looked at her. Her short hair was in two barrettes today, one was a cat's paw and the other was a cat's tail. He wondered if the set came with a third, that of a cat's face. "I bet the principal is getting bored without your visits."

He waited for her retort—something fun and teasing, but she was silent. Bracing her hands against the storage room door, she gave out a light moan. Then, with no more warning, she fell against the door like a sack of cement and slid down to the floor.

"Kiki!" Gideon shouted.

Instantly, Ormond rose to his feet. Seeing Kiki on the floor, he turned to Gideon. "What happened?"

"I don't know." Gideon knelt beside the girl, noting her closed eyes and feeling the cool skin on her forehead. "Kiki," he said. "Are you all right?"

Ormond was on the phone, and after a moment, Gideon realized he'd called the tearoom. When he hung up, he said, "She'll be right over. She said not to call 911, she knows what to do."

"Kiki." Gideon tried to rouse her. Her chalky complexion worried him, and wondering what one did in a situation like this, felt her pulse. Her eyelids fluttered when he asked, "Kiki, can you hear me?"

Minutes later, Mari was kneeling over Kiki. She'd brought a plastic cup of orange juice with a lid attached and a straw that bent like a wayward whisker. "Kiki," she said, curving a hand around her shoulders. "Sit up."

Gideon thought that making the girl sit up and drink was a bit odd, but he said nothing.

Mari must have noticed his puzzled expression. "Kiki has low blood sugar and needs the natural sugar from the juice." She placed the cup of juice by her side, and again tried to raise her sister with one arm around her shoulders.

Gideon crouched in closer and helped by letting Kiki rest against his bent knees for support.

"I might throw up." The small voice came from Kiki before she opened her eyes. "I don't want to throw up, but I might." With bleary eyes, she focused at the wall.

"Wanna go home?" asked Mari.

When Kiki shut her eyes again, Gideon nodded at Mari and gently lifted Kiki off the floor. Rising to his feet, he carried the girl out of the shop to the lot where Mari's car was parked. Mari opened the back door, and Gideon laid Kiki on the seat.

"Do you . . . ? Should I . . . ? " He fumbled for the right words.

She understood him. "We'll be fine."

He then watched Mari drive away. Taking a deep breath, he wanted more assurance that Mari had the situation under control. As he hoped Kiki was okay, he paced the floor of his bay. *For someone I didn't ever want to see again, I certainly am spending a lot of time worrying about her. And Mari.* He audibly sighed. *What if she needs some help, another adult to assist her?* Inside the shop, he emptied the lone cup still on the floor, pouring its bright orange contents into the sink. As the liquid disappeared, he knew he needed to get out of here as well.

"I'm going to Kiki and Mari's," he said to Ormond as he grabbed his jacket from the peg by the door to the bays.

"You can take my car," Ormond offered, scribbling Mari's address on a scrap of paper.

Gideon found the little house with the peeling paint on the front porch with no problem. He parked the Buick on the side of the road by the mailbox.

Once inside, Mari greeted him warmly. "You didn't have to come. I know you've got work to do."

He dismissed her concern. "How is she? I should have followed you and helped you carry her inside." He guessed he had a way to go to get the title of Mr. Chivalry.

"She's resting in her bedroom."

"Is she okay?" He wished he'd brought flowers or some treat the girl would like. "How often does this happen to her?"

"Fainting? Once or twice a month. She told me she didn't eat lunch today. That was a big mistake." Mari was clearly displeased. "She has to eat at regular intervals. The school knows she has hypoglycemia."

Mari sat on the plaid sofa, removing a lacy blue pillow from behind her back. She produced a weary smile, and Gideon was aware of the concern in her eyes.

"She'll be fine," he offered, immediately feeling stupid for the sentiment. What did he know about hypoglycemia? "How long has she had this . . . ?"

"For about three years, I think. But when she was with Mama, I didn't see her as much."

"Why didn't you see her?"

"I can't stand to be at my mother's." She spat the words out, not coating them with any form of apology. "Ugly to say, I know. But true."

Gideon recalled their conversation about her mother being a hoarder.

"Are you going to sit down?"

He grinned. When was the last time he'd been in a woman's home? He wasn't sure whether to take the spot next to her on the couch or the crimson La-Z-Boy recliner by the TV.

She patted the space beside her.

He sat as she said, "I know it sounds awful coming from such a sweet Southern gal like me, but Mama's house suffocates me."

"Sometimes honesty in sweet gals is the best."

She did smile then.

And today, he found her dimples particularly endearing.

"Right before social services came over, Mama's car was so stuffed with her cloth pets that there was no room for Kiki to ride."

He wanted to change the subject. Wasn't it enough that her sister had fainted? He didn't want her to feel badly about her mother now, too.

"The Bible refers to thinking on things that are true and praise-worthy, but I doubt it's referring to my mother and her collection of puppets."

Just as she mentioned the Bible, he saw one on the coffee table, one covered in thin leather with gold writing on the cover. "You read the Bible often?" She must; the cover was dog-eared.

"I have to. It fuels me for this massive world."

"Do you believe it?"

"You mean, do I believe that what's inside is truth?"

"Yeah, that's what I meant." Talking about God make him squirm slightly.

"I do." After a moment she raised her head to meet his eyes and asked, "What do you believe?"

Stretching out his legs, he wondered what to say to this question.

Hard work, wash your hands, go to church, live simply, respect your mother, respect your father, get up early, don't be a slacker. Why? For what? Nervously, he smiled. Mari was seated so close beside him. He could smell her hair, a fragrance of orange blossoms with a hint of something stronger like coconut.

130

"Should we make sure Kiki is okay?" He got to his feet.

"She's probably sleeping. She was up late last night working on a project for school." Patting the space he had occupied, she said, "Tell me why you don't like to talk about God."

He sat. This time he made sure that there was a little more distance between them. If he was going to have to discuss God, he didn't need to be breathing in her aromatic shampoo.

Her eyes were not teasing but serious, smooth as the pebbles he used to toss across the creek behind the farm. "So you discarded God when you left Amish land?" Her smile softened the question.

He thought that sounded like a childish thing to do. He wanted Mari to know that his decision was much more complicated and calculated than the way she made it seem. Discarding God would never be in his capacity. God was ingrained in his thoughts; he just wasn't sure that God was really for him. "Do you know anything about the Amish faith?"

"A little. I thought they were Christians."

"Do you know Reginald Smithfield?"

He saw her shudder. "What has he got to do with Amish?" she asked.

"He despises them just as he does blacks, Native Americans, you know, the Cherokees around here, Jews . . ."

"And Asians," she said, filling in his pause.

"He thinks nothing of all the minorities. We're like trash to him." Gideon hated the harshness of his words. "He makes himself feel better by cutting us down. He feels superior."

"You mean he thinks if you aren't Caucasian and born in these mountains, you are no good?"

"Exactly."

He liked the way her face looked so serious when he tried to make a point. Her brow wrinkled a little and her top lip pressed into her bottom one.

Continuing, he said, "Would you call Reginald a bigot?"

"Oh, yes. The worst kind."

"Did you know that the Amish look down on those who do not dress or live as they do?"

"Really?"

"Yes. They are close-minded. It's their way and no other."

She thought for a moment. Her brow wrinkled and she eyed him suspiciously. "What has this got to do with Christianity? You question their faith?"

"Jesus says to love everyone. He even said to think of others more highly than we think of ourselves. I don't see that in the Old Order communities at all."

"But they're Amish! Amish are like the wholesome side of America. Aren't they just about perfect?"

Gideon's eyebrows shot up, but before he could reply to Mari's outburst, a noise came from Kiki's bedroom, and Mari stood to check in on her sister.

Gideon heard faint conversation. Looking around the sparsely decorated room, he wondered if Mari was so tired of her mother's clutter that she preferred herself to deal with the bare minimum. Stretching, he yawned. Suddenly, his lack of sleep from the ordeal with Moriah early this morning was catching up with him. Taking his cell phone from his pants pocket he looked to see if there were any messages or missed calls. The screen showed there were none.

A moment later Mari returned to the sofa.

"Is she okay?"

"She's hungry."

"I can pick up something at the diner down the street."

"Or . . . I could cook."

Gideon remembered hearing Kiki talk about how her sister didn't do cooking well. "Do you really want to cook?" To soften his question, he added, "I mean, you've had a busy day."

Mari frowned. "And Kiki always complains about my food. But—"

Placing a hand on her arm, Gideon said, "What do you have? I can make us all dinner."

"Really? You cook?"

"Surprised?"

"No. Well . . . well, maybe a little." Mari stood and Gideon followed her into the kitchen.

Mari opened the fridge. "Let's see. There's some ground beef. I think I have a few chicken legs in the freezer."

"Do you have enough beef for meatloaf?"

"Two pounds," she said reading the label on the meat package.

Though excited to try his recipe for Mari, Gideon knew he had to ask one more pertinent question. "Do you like meatloaf?"

"Sure. Who doesn't like meatloaf? It's American, isn't it?"

"Does Kiki?"

"She does. She also loves mac and cheese."

He knew he had to please the little girl who was his reason for being at this house in the first place. "Do you have macaroni? Any cheese?"

Mari opened the fridge and took out a slab of cheddar cheese. From the pantry she brought out a box of elbow macaroni.

Gideon smiled as she placed it on the counter in front of him. "Looks like this is a start," he said.

20

Of course she had onions and green peppers for the meatloaf. With a slight twinge of embarrassment, she confessed that she bought those in large quantities to make her fried vegetables nearly every night. She hadn't learned to cook, which was strange since she was the manager of a food establishment. "I make pies. That's it."

"And you are good at it," he said.

She accepted the compliment and then asked what she could do to help with the meal preparation tonight. Gazing at her and then hoping he wouldn't be accused of focusing for too long on her deep dark eyes, he told her to just sit and tell him about herself.

"Talk about myself?" she asked.

"Yes. What do you like to do?" Opening a cabinet, he found the spices and retrieved the salt, pepper, and garlic powder.

Hesitantly, she said, "I sing in the church choir. I love the Beatles. But I don't sing Beatles songs in church."

As he mixed the ground beef with chopped onions, green peppers, spices, tomato paste, and an egg in a bowl, Mari sat at the kitchen table and talked. She said she liked art, but not modern; she'd once wanted to be a dancer, but she'd never had lessons. When he asked how it was being responsible for her sister, she winced. "Now how am I supposed to answer that?"

He thought of Moriah and decided that if someone asked him about what it was like being responsible for his sibling, he might have trouble coming up with an honest reply, too.

"Should we have biscuits?" she asked. "I have a few cans of Pillsbury."

"That sounds great."

Gideon popped the meatloaf onto the top rack of the oven. Adding water to a large pot, he turned on the heat and once the water boiled, he added the noodles for the mac and cheese. He'd been so concentrating on cooking and talking with Mari that he failed to realize all he was making was meatloaf, macaroni, and biscuits. Surely, the meal needed something else. "Do you have any potatoes?"

Mari pointed to a bin where there were dozens of russet potatoes.

"Mashed or baked?" he asked.

"I like them any way, but I think Kiki gets tired of them since we have them nearly every night."

"Okay. We probably don't need them anyway." He thought of his waistline and sucked in his tummy for a second. "Already have enough starch in our meal tonight." As soon as he said it, he felt like it was something his mother once said, years ago, miles away from here.

"I have carrots," she said. "Want me to peel some for steamed carrots?"

"If you'd like."

She grabbed the vegetable peeler and stood next to Gideon as he grated cheese for the macaroni and then greased a Pyrex dish. He found the strainer, drained the macaroni in it, added the pasta to the dish, tossed in the cheese and added some spices.

"Looks good," she told him as he placed the macaroni into the oven.

As the kitchen warmed with the aroma of meatloaf and a cheesy macaroni bake in the oven, Mari set the table. Pouring water over ice cubes in the glass tumblers, she asked, "Do you like ice?"

He looked at her, the oven mitt in one hand and the other lifted in mock questioning.

"You grew up without a freezer, right?"

He smiled then, catching on to her reason for asking. "Actually, we had a freezer. I know that most people think Old Order Amish don't have any modern appliances because we don't use electricity, but there are ways around that."

"Ways around it?"

"Gas-powered refrigerators are quite popular. Some Amish use kerosene ones."

"So you did grow up with ice?"

"My father allowed us to have ice trays, so we had that."

"Amos tells me that you and Moriah were raised with an iron rod."

And a stiff stick, Gideon thought, but decided to abstain from making that comment.

"I'm sorry," she said. "I have this feeling that it must have been an unhappy childhood."

Her empathy moved him. He wanted to ask her then, right then, under the fluorescent kitchen light if she'd consider going out with him. But he knew that there were times his emotions got the best of him, and this was more than likely one of those times. He thought of Moriah then. His brother knew how to charm the ladies. He wondered where Moriah had acquired that trait—certainly not from their father.

With dinner on the table, Mari went to get Kiki. Kiki's face was flushed and she walked with a slight limp. Mari asked if her leg was bothering her and the child replied that she was okay now and not to treat her like a baby.

Gideon looked over the meal. He hoped it tasted as good as it looked. When he was first learning to cook, he accidentally forgot to add sugar to a chiffon pie, and another time he'd overbaked a leg of lamb so badly that it blackened his teeth as he ate it. He was glad that both of those times he hadn't been cooking for guests.

Mari lowered her head and said, "Let me give the blessing." Her prayer was simple, thanking God for the meal and for each of them, as well as for God's faithfulness, forgiveness, and love. She asked for Kiki to regain her health. When she finished, she raised her head and taking her napkin, placed it in her lap.

"Do we pass the food?" Kiki asked eagerly, eyeing the bowls.

Gideon was still thinking about the serenity of Mari's prayer. *Thank You for Your faithfulness, forgiveness, and love.* When Mari talked to God, it was as though He was seated next to her and would soon be passing around the plate of biscuits, His knife ready to spread butter inside the flaky interior.

Kiki smiled at Gideon and cried, "You can cook here every night!" She helped herself to a large piece of meatloaf, jabbing it with a serving fork. "This looks amazing!"

Mari wanted to know where he learned to cook, and Gideon said, "I got tired of eating from cans all the time."

Mari smiled. "I guess I am just too lazy to try out new recipes."

He hardly thought her lazy. She was raising her sister and running a tearoom. Plus he knew she was fighting her own demons—things from her past—just like he was.

Kiki finished her slice of meatloaf and piped out, "Where's Moriah?"

Gideon did not want to ruin the evening with a conversation on Moriah, so he changed the subject, asking her how she was feeling.

Kiki said she was much better and Mari suggested she go to her room to do her homework.

Kiki started to protest but eyeing Gideon, simply nodded, and easing out of her chair, took her plate to the sink. She ran water from the faucet over it, opened the dishwasher, and added it with a clank into the compartment. Then she pranced out of the room, saying, "Here I go to tackle math! Wish me luck!"

"Looks like she's feeling much better," Mari said as the bang of her sister's bedroom door resounded over the hallway.

"May I ask a question?" Gideon whispered when she was gone.

"What?" Mari leaned closer to him.

"Was . . . has . . . Kiki . . ." He struggled for the right way to form his thoughts.

Mari offered, "Has Kiki always been like this?"

"What?"

"Isn't that what you were going to ask?"

"Yes." He rested his elbows on the table. "Yes, I guess it was."

"She's autistic." Mari lowered her voice as the hum of the fridge subsided. "She's always been different. As a toddler, she grew frustrated and screamed often. I hated her tantrums and there were times I wished she was normal . . . or dead." Mari avoided his eyes as she said, "I know, I'm really not proving to be that angel you once thought I was."

"I bet it was aggravating for you," Gideon said with feeling.

Mari let a sigh escape as though this action helped her maintain her serene composure. "She was slow to speak and often repeated the same word over and over. I'd go to sleep hearing her say, 'Cookie, cookie, cookie,' as she tried to settle in her bedroom. She never wanted the typical girly toys. I remember this one toy—an action figure—that she played with all the time. On its back, it had a button that caused its arms to move and it would shout, 'Super power!' Kiki hit that button again and again. I kept thinking that maybe she thought that if she hit it for the hundredth time, the figure might do something different. Kiki kept pressing the button, and each time the toy responded the same way, thrusting its arms over its head like it was going to fly and crying in that animated voice, 'Super power, super power.' " Mari's eyes glazed as she swallowed. "I was selfish. When I turned fifteen and she was two, I just wanted to get away from home and not have to put up with her."

As she talked, Gideon felt the urge to comfort her with a hug or by holding her hand. Uncertain what to do, he simply placed his own hands on the table and folded them, noting his grease-stained fingertips. At last he said, "I can't imagine."

"My mother didn't know how to handle her, and my father was out of the picture so much . . ." Mari paused as though deep in thought. Lifting her eyes to meet Gideon's, she explained, "One day—the day after Kiki turned three—a neighbor alerted Mama that Kiki needed some help. Kiki started going to a speech therapist. Then it was to a behavioral therapist every week. She was given meds to control her anxiety and aggression, as well as a mood stabilizer to keep her focused. Then we had to have these sessions with all of us to learn how to help Kiki cope."

Gideon nodded, taking it all in. Warmly he said, "She's lucky to have you."

Mari shook her head. "I don't know about that . . ." Her voice trailed off as she stared into her empty plate. "Sometimes I tell God that she's more than I can handle."

"And what is God's reply?"

"He'll show me a sky of stars or Mrs. Klass's rose garden. Mrs. Klass is our neighbor across the street, and her roses have won awards."

"So God replies by having you see creation?"

"I think He does that to remind me how vast His powers are. Anyway, it reminds me of the passage that speaks of His ways being higher than ours. His thoughts aren't ours. While I'd like for Him to make life easier, instead, He keeps supplying me with strength."

Gideon thought of all the verses from the Bible he'd been taught about God's provision and strength. Wasn't there one about God's grace being sufficient? And something about being able to do all things through Christ who strengthens me? His mind felt rusty, like a water pump left idle for years in a forgotten field riddled with weeds.

"You are strong," he said, and hoped she believed that he meant it.

She gave him a crooked smile. "I'm grateful that God helps me. I was managing Another Cup's sister store in Atlanta when I realized I needed to get a job closer to where Mama and Kiki lived in Asheville. Just then this position here opened up for me. I thought I'd move here, be on my own, and visit Kiki and Mama on a regular basis." Her smile was gone now, evaporated like a rain puddle after the summer sun dries it up. "Instead I got to bring Kiki here to live with me." After a few moments, she added, "There are times I'm so fed up with my mom. I wish God would get her mind back to a normal state. I blamed her for Kiki's autism. But in college when I took a class in psychology—you know, to figure out why my family was messed up—I learned that autism is a chemical and biological disorder." She attempted a smile. "It isn't caused by a mother who hoards puppets."

Gideon nodded.

"The day Child Protective Services took Kiki away from Mama was an all-time low for me. Kiki was crying, my mother was wailing. And I . . ." Pausing, she bit her lip.

"And you?"

"I thought I'd . . . die." She let the weight of her words slice the air for a few seconds. Pensively, she added, "But you don't get to die every time you think you could."

He reached for her hand, gently at first and then when she laced her fingers between his, he clung tighter. "You've been through a lot." Her hand was warm, soft, like clover on a summer day.

"Haven't we all?"

He was about to reveal something, just a tiny bit about his father, a question he'd pondered over the years. Did he leave Carlisle solely because of his father's relentless behavior, or was his leaving due to not wanting to participate anymore in the Amish rituals and isolation? The question that he'd rarely shared with anyone was on the tip of his tongue. He'd just opened his mouth when his cell phone rang and instead, he scrambled to remove it from his pocket.

Extending it to his ear, he heard a static voice say, "This is Sheriff Kingston."

"Henry! How are you?" Gideon's voice was cordial, glad to hear from his friend and grateful that it wasn't another one of his Amish brethren needing help. He didn't want anything to interfere with continuing his conversation with Mari.

A few lines followed, all congested with the same static so that

Gideon realized he was only getting every third word.

"What was that?"

"I have Moriah here."

"Moriah?"

"That's right," said the sheriff. "He's here at the station."

21

Clutching the cell phone, Gideon strained his ears, dreading to hear the worst. Slowly, he asked, "What's he done?"

Henry's voice, usually as cheerful as his rosy complexion, was firm. "He's been causing a ruckus. Had to bring him in."

Gideon hated the panic that surged into his veins. "What did he do? Is he all right?"

Henry's voice only buzzed, incoherent, and then Gideon realized the call had ended.

As he closed his phone, Mari's expression shifted to worry. "What's wrong?"

"It's Moriah. I need to go."

She pressed her hand into his arm, her tender fingers like little embers of heat. "What happened?"

"He's at the sheriff's. Don't tell Kiki." Kiki would worry and Mari didn't need Kiki fretting over Moriah. Pushing away from the table, Gideon looked at the kitchen counters by the stove. They were covered with dishes, utensils, and pans that needed attention. "Let me clean up first."

Mari stood. "No, just go. I can clean."

"I hate to leave you with this mess."

"You're the one with the mess."

He supposed that she meant Moriah. Pulling on his jacket, he thanked her.

"You made dinner. I want to thank you." Her eyes showed a mixture of gratitude and concern.

"You're welcome." Then he left the house, glad he still had Ormond's car and the keys to it in his pocket. As he started the Buick, he felt badly that he hadn't phoned Ormond earlier to say he would be late returning the car. Wanting to show responsibility, especially to his boss, Gideon called him, apologizing for not having phoned sooner. Ormond eased his worry, saying that he had other means of transportation. "I got a ride home with Luke and I'll drive the Oldsmobile to work tomorrow." He inquired about Kiki; Gideon said she was much better, and then before Ormond could ask any more questions, Gideon said goodbye.

It was then that he felt his heart lurch in his chest. Henry had not given any details as to why he was holding Moriah at the jail. But Gideon knew it couldn't be good. Although the drive was only three miles, Gideon hit every red light, and at each stop he wondered just what his brother was in trouble for. Causing a ruckus. Gideon visualized what that statement could mean. Moriah was most likely drunk.

Escape. At a time like this, he'd like to run from whatever it was that would soon face him at the sheriff's. His mind took him to a cozy cabin high in the Smoky Mountains, far from the reach of cell phones or visitors. He thought of Mari and imagined her seated next to him, overlooking the mountain range as the sun rose over the peaks, lighting the clouds with swirls of orange and gold, the start of a new day with promise—a day free of trouble.

Inside the small sheriff's office heavily perfumed with mildew and ant spray, Henry and his deputy, Tomlin, were discussing rifles and a recent hunting event they'd been to in a spot beyond Cove's Peak.

143

When Henry saw Gideon, his smile dissipated. Rising from his desk, he said, "Sorry to trouble you this evening." His voice was flat like he was trying to keep his composure. "But you know how it can be when folks get to complainin'. That's when I come in."

Tomlin's demeanor was not as grave. With a wry grin, he said, "And we salute when you bring order to the masses." When neither the sheriff nor Gideon smiled, he excused himself from the office.

As the door shut, Henry offered Gideon a seat across from his desk. Both men sat. "He has some warrants, Gideon."

"For what?"

Henry clicked a few buttons on his keyboard and from his findings read, "Revoked driver's license due to a DWI. Let's see, that was in Orlando. On May sixteenth, he had a fender bender in Tampa where he was cited for reckless driving on the way home from a bar. He was without a license, of course, because it had been revoked the month before. Then there are also nine unpaid parking tickets."

Gideon sighed. He was beginning to wonder if these were the real reasons his brother had left Florida. "What about now? What are you charging him with?" As soon as he asked, Gideon braced himself, certain it wouldn't be pretty.

"He was yelling and acting like a bully inside the pub. I reckon I'd call it disturbing the peace. Tomlin brought him in. He threatened to hit the bartender when he was told he couldn't have another beer."

"Disorderly conduct?"

"At a very high level."

"What else?" Gideon figured he might as well hear it all.

Henry shuffled through his desktop. A few papers fell to the floor like crinkled autumn leaves. "Says here that he was yelling something about his father being a tyrant."

Gideon's ears perked, intent to exactly what his brother had shouted. "What did he say? Do you have what he said?"

Reading from a page, Henry said, " 'I'll never be good enough for him. I'll never be worth anything.' " Pausing, Henry looked for Gideon's reaction. "I know you told me that your father is a hard man. Shame."

Gideon felt the description of *hard man* was an understatement.

"He should be okay once he sobers up. The bartender is not pressing charges, but has asked that Moriah stay clear of the Rusty Saddle Bar and Grille from now on."

Henry summoned Tomlin into the office and instructed him to bring Moriah around. Tomlin left the room.

Gideon sat slouched over, his elbows rested against his knees, hands folded. The clock on the wall hummed like a fluorescent light bulb with a short in it. After a few minutes, he wished he could unplug the annoying thing. *Calm down,* he told himself. *There's no point in me acting disorderly, too.* One Miller brother in trouble was enough for one night. Pretty soon he heard the door open and both Tomlin and Moriah appeared. Moriah's wrists were secured by handcuffs.

"What's going on?" Gideon felt anguish at seeing his brother in handcuffs. A memory from the past leapt into his mind, one he often fought to remove. The officer then had been short and agitated. His father had been equally annoyed.

Henry was calm and reassuring. "Had to cuff him to keep him safe."

"No big deal," Moriah said. His hair was free, the ponytail gone, and strands of greasy blond hair hung in his face.

"It is a big deal." Gideon's voice echoed throughout the office. "I had to come get you." He wanted to avoid his brother's bloodshot eyes, his sallow skin and the alcoholic stench that permeated his breath and clothing.

They stood face-to-face for a moment until Henry broke the silence. "Well," said the sheriff, his eyes on Gideon. "We can let him go into your custody. If that is okay with you."

Gideon knew that meant Henry expected him to keep Moriah out of trouble. At least for the rest of the night and into the day. He guessed no bail money was needed and counted that the one small blessing in the midst of the chaos. His mother had always told him to search for the blessings in everything. Nothing was ever all bad.

"Moriah," said Henry, as he hoisted his pants at the waist. "I want no more wild conduct out of you."

It was then that Gideon thought, what if he said he wanted Moriah to stay the rest of the night here? What if he left him here to sober up? It wouldn't cost anything like a hotel room would, and it'd give him a break from having to deal with his brother's behavior.

Gideon nodded at Henry, and with an, "Okay, then," Tomlin unlocked the cuffs. Rubbing his wrists, Moriah laughed.

"Like father, like son, huh?" His words came from the back of his throat. "Next thing you know I'll be shouting like him, 'Someone will pay!'"

Gideon's skin turned sticky. Now was not the time to bring up the incident that occurred in Carlisle years ago with their father who was jailed for failing to comply with the town rules of owning an outhouse.

"I guess it's in my blood to be a rebel." Moriah snickered, took a step, tripped over his shoelaces, steadied himself, and belched.

Before he could say another word, Gideon ushered him out of the office, not sure whether it was appropriate to thank Henry for letting him go or not.

In the car, Moriah muttered that it wasn't his fault. With his arms folded against his chest, he slumped into the passenger seat. His hair fell over his face, strands of it across his lips.

Gideon started the car. "Put on your seat belt."

Moriah closed his eyes.

"I said put your seat belt on. Now." Gideon waited; the car was in reverse, but his foot sat firmly on the brake.

Moriah groaned.

"What's the matter with you?" Under the streetlight, Moriah looked the color of mozzarella cheese. His stench was a mixture of sweat and fried onions.

Moriah shrugged, yawned.

"Seat belt." Gideon wished he'd listen. They needed to get home; his brother needed a shower badly.

With a grunt, Moriah roused himself, flung open the door, and scurried from the car.

"Hey, what are you doing?" Gideon shifted to park.

Moriah stumbled and then started to jog down the narrow sidewalk, lined with dispersed autumn leaves, pine needles, and a few stray pinecones.

Was he crazy? "What are you doing? Get back in here!" He saw his brother trailing away, gaining speed as he went, running from something Gideon couldn't see. Even as he drove, looking to his left and right, there was no sign of Moriah. Not even a shadow. It was as though the darkness of the November night had swallowed him.

Gideon drove Ormond's car to work the next morning, scanning both sides of the street as he cruised slowly by. He half expected to find Moriah on the side of the street, wrapped in some dark blanket—like a scene depicted in a horror movie. His back ached, as did his head. He'd only gotten about two hours of sleep after searching most of the night, and he was no good without proper rest. When he had fallen asleep, his dreams haunted him, one with that scene where Moriah was missing. He'd never given much thought to dreams and their meanings, but perhaps, with these recent frustrating dreams, he should start paying attention.

Suddenly, he saw a figure in a striped wool cap walking down a road to his left. Without hesitating, he spun into the turn lane, nearly hit a pickup, and was the recipient of a number of car horns. *Steady*, he told himself. *You can't afford an accident, especially not in Ormond's car.* He crept up to the figure, ready this time to jump out of the car and tackle Moriah to the ground if he had to. He rolled down the window and was about to shout his brother's name when the person turned, met his gaze, and glared at him. Gideon looked into the face of a weathered man, a complete stranger. Embarrassed, Gideon sped up and turned off the street.

He started to make a list in his head of what he did know about his brother. *Moriah was after a good time. He had no intention of returning to Carlisle. He liked women. He was a flirt. He liked to have his way. He drank too much, and his temper was atrocious.* Even as he acknowledged these things about Moriah, Gideon realized that his problem hadn't been solved. Moriah was still at large.

At the shop, Ormond had opened the front door, but the garage doors were still shut. He was brewing coffee. The daily paper laid out on his desktop shouted headlines about the current national economic crisis.

Gideon handed him the keys to the Buick. "Thanks."

"How is she?"

"She?" Who was Ormond talking about?

"Kiki. Is she all right?"

Kiki, but of course. Kiki had been the one in need of help yesterday. Gideon rubbed a hand over his head. In his tired state, he'd forgotten to put on his John Deere cap. It seemed weeks ago that Kiki had collapsed on the floor of the shop, ages since he'd sat talking with Mari in her house, eons since he'd felt the joy of preparing dinner for them. "Kiki is fine."

"You aren't, are you?"

"He can't live with me." Gideon let out a sigh of relief upon finally admitting it.

"You mean Moriah?"

Gideon reached for the cabinet over the sink and was grateful for the bottle of Advil. Shaking the container, he dispensed four tablets into the palm of his hand and downed them dry.

"What's he done?"

Gideon took out a bottle of Aquafina. On a normal day he would have asked why the fridge was lined with this bottled brand instead of Ormond's usual Deer Park. After two swallows, he could no longer feel the pills in his throat. Turning to Ormond, he confessed, "I don't know where he is."

"You don't know where Moriah is?"

148

"He's a lunatic." As much as he hated to hear the word describing his brother, he knew it was appropriate. Moriah was not the chubby baby boy of yesterday. He was a machine out of control.

"Maybe he got a good job somewhere. One where he actually works," Ormond said, his attempt to lighten the mood.

Gideon fought to push aside last night's scene at the sheriff's office. Gently rocking his head back, to the left and right, he tried to rid himself of a stiff neck. Staring at the coffee brewing, he considered drinking some. It just might be what he needed to help him not feel so queasy and exhausted. When was the last time he'd had a mug of coffee? The coffee was nearly ready, the hot beverage steaming and sputtering into the glass pot. He breathed in the aroma.

Ormond filled his chipped mug and set the pot back on the burner. After a slight slurp, he looked Gideon over. "Did the two of you fight or something?"

"Or something." Gideon made his way to his office. At his desk, he massaged his temples and then finished the water. He checked his cell, thinking he might have missed a call from Henry. But no one had tried to reach him.

When Luke entered the shop, Gideon asked if he knew where Moriah might be. Although he looked sympathetic, Luke claimed he had no idea.

Ashlyn came by at lunchtime, bringing her culinary specialty of homemade brown bread. Like usual, Ormond acted like he'd never seen a tube of bread before.

"Coffee can? Do you really make this in a can?" Ormond stroked his mustache. "Now how is that possible?"

Happy to explain, and in a true writer's descriptive fashion, Ashlyn launched into the tale of how she got the recipe from her grandmother who came over to this country in 1892 from Scotland.

"All my grandmother Lora Marie had with her was a tattered suitcase and the recipe for bread in a can. The recipe wasn't written on paper, for she couldn't read or write. She had it memorized." Ashlyn looked around the room at the group, making sure they were paying attention. "That was a good thing, because her first job in these mountains was as a cook. She wowed them with her bread recipe."

"So what's in this recipe of old?" asked Ormond.

Ashlyn paused to wrap her dark wavy hair into an elastic band. "It's so easy to make. You pour two kinds of flour—rye and whole wheat—into a bowl and add cornmeal, molasses, salt, baking soda, and buttermilk. Then you mix it well, add a cup of raisins, and pour it all into a greased coffee can. Make sure the lid is tight and steam it covered in a pot of water for two hours."

Luke laughed and draped an arm around his fiancée. "You know, you are the best cook in Twin Branches."

"I'm the most unusual," she clarified. "I like making recipes that are not common. Gideon's the gourmet chef."

Gideon thanked her for her vote of confidence and graciously accepted a slice of the bread. Ormond said he'd like a piece, too. When she brought Ormond's serving to him on a paper plate, he said, "This is actually something I think I'm going to like. I like anything that has to do with coffee and cans of coffee."

She laughed as he studied the slice which was the color of caramel and dotted with raisins. He took a bite. "This is delicious."

Ashlyn carried another plate into Gideon's office.

"If you hear anything about my brother, let me know," Gideon said after thanking her. He figured since she was a reporter at the *Twin Star*, she might receive a heads-up on Moriah long before he did.

Ashlyn looked worried. "What's wrong?"

"He's getting into trouble. Did your dad tell you?" Gideon figured that the sheriff shared all the antics that took place at his station with his wife and daughter.

But Ashlyn shot that theory down. "He doesn't usually carry work home with him, so I haven't heard about Moriah."

Gideon's voice sounded as lifeless as he felt. "I don't know where he is now."

Ashlyn sighed. "Is he missing? Have you filed a missing person—?"

He cut her off. "He's not missing." There was no need to file a missing person statement. Moriah wasn't kidnapped. He was just being difficult, unruly, and stubborn.

"He's a good guy, Gideon." Ashlyn's blue eyes were sincere. "He just likes attention and sometimes . . ."

Gideon knew what she meant even without her finishing her sentence. Moriah sometimes said too much and got boisterous.

"He's like all the Amish kids that have come here under your care. He doesn't want to be known as that goody two-shoes. So he plays it wild."

"Is that so?"

"Oh, you know that, Gideon. I'm not telling you anything you don't already know. My best friend was a preacher's kid. She felt she had to prove every day that she wasn't this pious good girl."

"I bet she didn't end up in jail."

"Well, no. But she did steal some bubblegum from the Walmart in Asheville once. It was that Carefree Sugarless kind."

22

Gideon didn't want Ashlyn to feel that she needed to hang around his office and console him. He knew she'd come to see Luke. So he eyed the bread on the plate before him and decided eating a second piece would do him some good. "Thanks again," he told her. "This stuff is amazing."

"You are welcome. It's healthy, so good for you. Luke calls it love in a can."

For a brief moment he envied Luke and Ashlyn's relationship. How nice to have someone to love, to want to build a life and future with. How beautiful. But the feeling lasted only for a short while; it was hard to think romantically when he was worried about his wayward brother.

After Ashlyn left to find Luke, Gideon picked up the second slice of bread. It was truly delicious. He ate another bite.

The phone rang, and he wiped his mouth with a napkin he found in his desk drawer. His heart jumped, preparing for a call from or about his brother. But the first call of the day was a lady making an appointment to have her Camry serviced and then a mother called to ask if the shop really did repair bicycles. The phone rang a few more times before Gideon said he was walking to Benson's Laundromat next door.

"Going to finally wash clothes today?" Ormond asked, his face beaming with a smile. Ormond was always good at relieving tension with a joke or a comment. He was the type of person who received all those forwarded email messages with jokes about typos in church bulletins and the funny things kids say. Often he printed them out and chuckled over them when he wasn't reading the sports page.

But today Gideon saw no humor in the shop owner's words. Stiffly he said, "No, going to get some chips from their vending machine. Want anything?" Gideon knew that chips were not as healthy as his typical breakfast of multigrain toast with apple butter, but since he'd eaten Ashlyn's bread, the raisins and whole wheat in that should balance out whatever else nonnutritious he consumed. Now that his headache was lifting, his stomach rumbled with hunger.

"Chips, huh?" Ormond looked surprised. "You are in a bad way, aren't you? I'll take a Baby Ruth bar." Ormond reached into his desk drawer where he kept change and handed Gideon three quarters. "Is that enough?"

"It is."

"I remember when a Baby Ruth was a dime."

Gideon left before Ormond could continue down memory lane.

When Kiki arrived, parking her bike with its kickstand, Gideon told her about the mother who'd called.

"When will she bring the bike in?" asked the girl. "Today?" She pulled her puppet from the basket, gave it a kiss and returned it to its compartment. "We are in business, Yoneko," she said.

Gideon realized he'd been too preoccupied with thoughts of Moriah when the mother had called. He admitted he wasn't sure.

"Did you tell her to come at three o'clock? I get here at three o'clock."

"I'm sure she knows."

From behind them a male voice rang, "Knows what?"

Gideon turned around and there stood Moriah. At first, relieved, Gideon felt the knot he'd been carrying around inside his stomach all day release. Moriah was here, no longer at large. But his relief was short-lived as he noted his brother's red eyes and dilated pupils. As Moriah sneezed, Gideon also smelled a sour stench. He wondered if his brother knew how badly he needed to bathe.

Moriah smiled down at Kiki and tenderly patted her head. "Got some bikes to fix today?"

She smiled back and energetically replied, "I will have lots of business. It's gonna happen really soon because I made more fliers."

Moriah winked at her, making Gideon wonder how Moriah could be so chummy with the girl and practically ignore Gideon. *Didn't he feel an apology or explanation regarding last night was in order?*

Not wanting to start an argument in the shop, Gideon said, "Why don't you go help Luke?" He motioned to where Luke was at his bay, prodding under the hood of a Volvo.

"Didn't come to be pestered about working," said Moriah.

Pestered! Gideon felt his blood steam. Hotly, he said, "What *do* you want, then? Everyone around here works!"

"I'm moving out," Moriah said. "I'm gonna live on my own."

"Fine!" Gideon knew the word came out the same way his father used to say it when he was angry.

"So I won't be coming by this stinkin' place no more. I'm outta here for good!" Moriah's voice was like a thunderbolt, hitting every nerve in Gideon's body.

It was Kiki's piercing look that made Gideon catch his breath and stop yelling. Gritting his teeth, he said, "Suit yourself."

Moriah flung his jacket over his shoulder and stalked out of the shop. A powerful trail of sweat and overly fried food odors lingered where he'd stood.

They all heard Moriah shout his last line across the parking lot. "Goodbye, bro! I'll see you in hell."

154

The words didn't make Gideon cringe as much as the tone. Moriah sounded like their father. Gideon let his mind spin back to that day when the police said non-Amish neighbors were complaining that the Miller outhouse was not in compliance with the town's building code regulations. Gideon's father said the law did not apply to him and cited some statement that said the Amish were entitled to build what they wanted, how they wanted.

"Not true," the cop said. "You are still under some laws."

Their father had lashed out, his temper causing him to spout words neither Gideon nor Moriah had ever heard from his lips. He was handcuffed and taken to the local jail where he'd spent a night. He promised he would not cause a ruckus again. His next act would never be punished, but it was the one that made Gideon vow to leave as soon as he turned fifteen. Forget rumspringa. He would leave before the Amish rules said he could venture out and run around freely.

As Gideon looked out at the parking lot, he only saw a few parked cars, the metal Dumpster, and the fence that ran around the perimeter of the auto shop. A catbird cried from a nearby tree, but Gideon barely heard its cry because Moriah's words were still screeching in his ears.

Kiki had just adjusted the brakes on a shiny blue bike, brought in by the caller from yesterday. Proudly, she spun the wheels and then, releasing the kickstand, pushed the Road Runner around the inside of the shop. "It's fixed! Look, I fixed it, Gideon!"

Gideon smiled, pleased that Kiki was happy about her work. He really needed to pay her for her work; he must discuss that with Ormond. However, right now Kiki seemed more interested in working than getting paid. Gideon found that both refreshing and unusual. He wondered when humans started to care more about how much they got paid instead of how well they performed a job. Had he once been more zealous than he was now? Or was he more determined to prove that Ormond had not made a mistake in entrusting Russell Brothers to him completely when Ormond eventually retired? He remembered that day the older man had set a cup of iced tea in front of Gideon and ordered, "Drink up! Hurry, before I change my mind. Or before Elma talks me out of it."

Gideon knew that Elma was Ormond's ninety-eight-year-old mother, a tiny woman who still drove a 1976 Cadillac, much to everyone in Twin Branches' dismay. Elma Russell had been known to call a blue dress, gray, and a pair of black shoes, brown. If she could no longer recognize colors, the residents wondered, then how would that help her when she came to a traffic light? The locals had all encountered at one time or another the Cadillac with the license tag that read ELMA #1. She wove in and out of the streets, made U-turns from the right lane, and stopped in the middle of the road to search for her glasses that she claimed fell off her face whenever she slammed on the brakes.

Ormond had noted Gideon's perplexed expression, so he clarified his original statement. "Congratulations! The shop is yours! When I go, it will belong to you. Elma will have to deal with it."

Gideon knew Elma had strong opinions and imagined that she had tried to talk her son out of leaving the auto shop to an outsider and non-family member. Yet, as he looked at both the cup of tea and around the shop, he wondered if Ormond was making the best decision. Feeling unworthy, Gideon had gasped, "You're leaving this place to me?"

Ormond clapped Gideon on the back. "Yep, I'm leaving it all to you. Drink up!"

Not sure what to say, Gideon had blinked. He took a sip of the tea. It was a little too sweet for his tastes. "Are you . . . sure?"

"I have rarely been more certain of anything. You just need to come with me to my attorney's and we're set in stone."

"Attorney's?"

"Don't you have those in Amish country?"

Gideon knew lawyers were everywhere, and never far, not even in Amish country.

"This is your entire headache when I go," said Ormond as he motioned a hand above his head and let it move across the office. "I've decided you would be the best owner when the time comes. You are conscientious, dedicated, and you know cars." Then he sailed out of the shop to order lunch, tossing over his shoulder as he went, "You are welcome."

Slowly realizing the impact of what Ormond had just told him, Gideon felt a smile spread over his own face. *Conscientious, dedicated, and I know cars. Well, all of that is true.* This time when he took a sip of tea, it was not too sweet at all. It was just right.

Kiki was enjoying the Baby Ruth morsels of chocolate that Gideon brought to her from his walk to the Laundromat. Flecks of chocolate smeared her mouth. Laughing, she said, "These are the best!" He'd take her some Tums later and hopefully, her stomach would be okay. Gideon had heard Mari warn the young girl not to eat too much chocolate because it did make her hyper. Kiki even claimed that chocolate gave her digestive system a bubbly feeling. "But," she cooed, "it's so delicious. No wonder they make Easter bunnies out of this stuff." She ran her tongue over her lips in an effort to enjoy every morsel.

Before Gideon could get a paper towel for her to wipe her mouth, in walked Moriah. His footsteps were heavy against the shop's floor.

Without acknowledging anyone, Moriah bellowed, "They're going to get me!"

"Get you? Who?" Moriah's tone was frightening, but Gideon strove to remain calm.

Ignoring his questions, Moriah stood inches from Gideon's face and cried, "No matter what happens to me, bury me by the weeping willow. Okay?"

Gideon wondered what his brother was up to. *Why did he always feel he needed to have all the attention?*

As Moriah faced him, demanding an answer, Gideon looked at the ground, at the wall, at Kiki—anywhere but his brother's bloodshot and crazed eyes. There were too many fears portrayed in them. Fears Gideon didn't want to see.

"Okay, bro?" Moriah repeated.

"The one by the apple orchard?" Gideon asked as evenly as he could. He was not going to get in another argument, especially not here. Not at work, again.

"That's the one. Okay? Bury me there. Only there."

Gideon recalled how Moriah loved to climb that tree and pretend he was a pirate on a ship. His younger brother's infatuation had not come from TV, videos, or books on pirates. It was a little boy who lived on York Road that had given Moriah a taste for hidden treasure and adventurous seas. This boy dressed in a black hat, brandished a toy sword, and wore a patch over one eye when he played. Moriah saw this boy when he'd ride into town with Gideon. As their horse and buggy passed the front lawn, Moriah would crane his neck to view the pirate scene. Amused by his antics, Moriah even repeated some of the boy's phrases: "Aye, yes, a pirate's life for me!" Gideon's thoughts shifted from the past to this moment. Why was his brother suddenly focused on death? "Why all this talk about burial?"

"I asked you—will you?" Moriah's shrill voice made Gideon's skin grow clammy. "That's what I'm asking!"

"Sure."

"Deal?" Moriah extended a shaky hand. Gideon took it, bothered by its lack of warmth and energy. But before he could come up with anything more to say, his brother raced out of the shop.

"He's in a big hurry," said Kiki, getting up to watch Moriah's retreat. "What did he mean about the tree?"

Gideon explained about the tree at their home place in Carlisle. As he told Kiki about the wispy tree with swaying leaves, he could almost smell the aroma of the apples in the orchard standing next to it.

"Is your home in the mountains, too?"

"There are mountains nearby."

"I want to go there. I've never been outside of North Carolina, for Pete's sake."

"Where would you like to go?"

"Some place with good food and twenty-four-hour TV shows."

Laughter shot through him. This kid could always make him laugh and feel lighthearted. One minute he was frustrated with Moriah, ready to knock some sense into his brother, and the next, Kiki had him smiling.

23

Over the next few days, Gideon found himself waking from sleep and searching the apartment for his brother—hoping to find him, and yet relieved when he was not in sight. The mixture of emotions drove him crazy with fear. If Moriah wasn't at home, where was he and what was he up to? If he did show up at home, what would he be up to and what kind of mood would he be in? The expression *walking on eggshells* crossed Gideon's mind many times throughout the week.

If it were only one ruckus, Gideon could put it behind him, but with Moriah it was clearly more. Something was causing Moriah to react in highly volatile ways—behavior that Gideon had never before experienced from anyone. Anxiety searing both his heart and mind, Gideon tried to clear his head on the next Saturday afternoon. He went for a long walk, but even after five miles, he was still anxious. He passed the Valley Ridge Apartments and wondered if he should demand that his brother move to an apartment there. *Get a backbone*, he reprimanded himself. *Tell him he has to move out today. Or else.*

Finally back at his apartment, he sat on a chair in his living room, trying to relax. He noticed a cobweb in the corner, just above the floor, so he got his mop. He decided that cleaning would be a good way to alleviate some of his pent-up aggravation.

As he dusted under the sofa with a dry Swiffer mop, he felt the edge of it hit against something. Gideon drew it out to find an aluminum-wrapped object measuring about five-by-five inches. Picking it up, he turned it over a few times and then sniffed it, wondering what it could be.

Suspicion grabbed him and he knew he would have to open it. Carefully, he pulled back the foil. Inside were five white, handmade, cigarette-like items. He heard a noise at the door and quickly stuffed the packet into his jeans pocket. As he looked at the front door, he expected it to open and for Moriah to enter. Although his brother claimed he was moving out, he had yet to make good on his promise. The sound at the door continued as Gideon faced it.

With labored breath, he waited. The noise at the entryway to his apartment ceased. Resuming normal breathing, he wondered why he felt guilty for finding whatever it was under the sofa. This was his apartment; he paid the rent. He didn't need to feel wrong for finding something, even if Moriah had tried to hide it.

He opened the foil packet again, laying it out on the coffee table. This time he noticed a small clear plastic bag underneath the cigarettes. He pulled at the edge and lifted the bag. Inside were tiny crystals, resembling rocks. Gideon's hands grew hot and he tried to swallow past the lump in his throat. Of course, he could ask Henry what these cigarette-looking items were. But as he studied the crystals, suspicion rose. He had to know now. At his computer, he typed descriptive keywords to search by until he stopped at a photo that matched what was on his table. Meth!

"Methamphetamine has a high potential for addiction and abuse," Gideon read from a website called Dangerous Drugs. "Made from household products such as lye, cold medicine, battery acid, paint thinner, and iodine, meth can be found in the form of tiny rock-like crystals, powder, or even made into cigarettes." Skimming a few paragraphs, he continued to read, "Meth is highly addictive. Symptoms include sleeplessness, paranoia." Moriah's words from yesterday shot into Gideon's memory. "They're going to get me!" That certainly sounded like what someone afraid that people were out to capture him would say.

Cautiously, Gideon unrolled one of the cigarettes and breathed in. The flaky greenish substance inside the thin paper looked like marijuana to him. *Meth and marijuana, what was Moriah doing to himself? Who supplied him with this?*

Gideon went to the kitchen and got a glass. Filling it with water from the tap, he tried to decide what to do. He'd confront his brother. He drank slowly, the liquid cool against his parched throat. Taking another sip, he walked over to the coffee table. His findings from under the sofa were still there. Drugs—here in his own apartment. Drugs that belonged to Moriah. If Mother and Father could see him now.

We've come a long way from Carlisle, he thought. But then he couldn't help but recall what Luke's sister had said to him one Christmas when she came to Twin Branches for vacation. "You can get drugs anywhere. I knew kids in Lancaster that smoked marijuana."

Could Moriah have started his habit then? Gideon tried to picture a younger Moriah in the loft of someone's barn on a warm summer night, lighting up a joint. But meth was surely not produced in some abandoned shed or barn, was it? Where had his brother picked up this habit?

When the door rattled, Gideon set his water glass down and quickly wrapped the drugs together again. He'd toss them all out, but first he needed to get them out of sight. Whoever was at the door might not believe that the substances were not his. He shoved the foil package deep under the sofa.

"Hey!" Moriah's voice boomed from the other side of the door.

Gideon stood to unlock the door.

Moriah breezed past him, a six-pack in his hand. Gideon breathed in a sour aroma.

"Where have you been?"

"Out." Moriah's ponytail hung like a knotted rope.

"You'd better not be getting into trouble."

Moriah laughed, sounding like a hyena. "In this little town? How would I get into trouble? Am I going to be caught with too much apple cider?"

"I'm warning you."

Moriah's eyes were bloodshot, the rims puffy, like he had some sort of allergy. His cheeks, like wrinkled linens, were sunk into his face. The usual color from his lips was gone; now they resembled the color of titanium white on a paint chart. "Are you warning me?" He paced toward the bathroom. "No one gets in my way."

"You can't do this to yourself." Gideon stood between his brother and the bathroom door.

"Why not?"

Why not? Gideon tried to dismiss the nausea creeping into his stomach. "It's not legal, for one thing." The minute he said it, Gideon realized that he was letting his brother know that he was aware of his drug use, even though he had not admitted to what he'd found under the sofa. For a second he feared what Moriah's reaction would be.

"So?" was all that Moriah had to say. He repeated it five times, until Gideon wanted to pull his hair out.

"I'm gonna do what I'm gonna do, so there!" Moriah sounded like a kid being told he couldn't have candy before bedtime. Not even a Snickers or Twix bar.

"It ruins your health."

"Have you ever tried it?" He opened a can of Coors.

Where was this leading to? Tried it? Why would he poison his body? Why would he— "No."

"Then don't judge. Don't be so high and mighty."

Gideon felt his blood curdle. "High and mighty?!" He was not his father. He had not come all this distance to be likened to his father.

"Just let me live my life." Moriah downed his beer and reached for another.

"Stop!" Gideon stood between him and the rest of the cans. "Stop

163

doing this to yourself." His instinct was to slap some sense into Moriah's head, but he wouldn't react as Father used to. With his hands at his side, he yelled, "Wake up!"

Moriah laughed uncontrollably. "Just stay out of my hair."

Sunday morning a week later, Gideon found himself at the door of Mari's church. He took a deep breath and crossed the threshold. Meeting Mari and Kiki at the foyer of Fifth Street Presbyterian, he greeted them and then followed the sisters to a pew lined with a long red cushion. In front of them was Angie, wearing a silky black shirt and too much makeup.

Now what did Kiki call this girl? Oh, the tattletale, Gideon remembered. He would have to refrain from calling her that name to her face. After all, she was a Smithfield, and it was likely that her relatives had donated the very pew he sat on to the church.

As Angie smiled at Kiki, Kiki smiled back, and Gideon decided that things must be okay between the girls now.

Before the service started, Mari excused herself to join the other choir members getting their music folders from the director.

Kiki sat closer to Gideon, filling the space Mari had occupied between them. "She'll be back," she said.

Gideon picked up his bulletin, a gray piece of paper, and tried to focus on the black print. He read something about a clothing drive in the announcements section. Wondering if he had any clothes to donate, he gazed around the sanctuary. The flower arrangement at the front was robust and bright. He noted the stained-glass windows, scenes of Jesus and the disciples.

As he glanced at one of a nativity scene, he became acutely aware that he was in church.

How long had it been since he was in a church? He'd attended a Christmas Eve service and one at Easter his first year in Twin Branches. Ormond had made him go. Had he been since then? He hoped this wasn't going to be one of those lengthy services. His favorite part right now would be when it ended.

The service began with a call to worship, and Gideon laid the bulletin aside. If anything, at least he'd appear interested in what was being read from the pulpit.

When the choir sang "Amazing Grace," Kiki whispered to Gideon, "This is my favorite part. This is my very favorite part. Isn't it yours?"

Gideon kept his eyes forward and let the music filter about him. For a moment, he watched Mari singing. She stood to the left, by the organ. He recalled she'd told him she sang in the choir . . . but not Beatles songs.

As the choir finished "Come Thou Fount of Every Blessing," he thought back to Thursday noon, when he'd ambled in with the paper, his head weary from thinking about Moriah. Mari had approached him with a wide smile. As he ordered a cup of green tea, she asked if he'd like to go to church with her and Kiki this Sunday. The recent events with Moriah still had him feeling dismal, and so without hesitation, he'd said to Mari, "Sure."

Now, here he was, wearing a clean, pressed, collared shirt and wondering what a good Amish man was doing in a Presbyterian church.

24

Although Gideon felt like he was from another planet, sitting in a pew at Fifth Street Presbyterian, the service was tolerable. There were even some aspects about it he felt he could get used to. Kiki was right, the choir did a stellar job as they sang "Come Thou Fount of Every Blessing" and "Amazing Grace."

After the hymns, the choir members dispersed and went to sit with friends and family. Mari squeezed between Kiki and Gideon. She and Gideon shared a Bible as the pastor read from Matthew 6. The selected passage about forgiveness seemed strangely familiar. Gideon was sure he'd heard a sermon given by a bishop at a community service years ago based on this same Scripture. Then verse fifteen jumped from the page at him like one of those windup toys where a clown popped out of a jack-in-the-box—"But if you do not forgive men their sins, your Father will not forgive your sins." Forgiveness. Of all the passages in the Bible, why did this one have to be read now? He didn't want to deal with the flood of emotions that came when he thought of words like *forgiveness* in connection to his father.

In an attempt to clear his head of the Scripture, he looked around the sanctuary. He saw a number of customers, folks who had their vehicles serviced at Russell Brothers. He returned their smiles and hoped that when they saw him next, they wouldn't ask what he was doing in church because he certainly had no answer for that question.

After the service, Kiki invited him to join the three girls, Angie, Mari, and her, for a picnic. Mari would pick some food up at the Piggly Wiggly, and they would drive out to the river. Gideon's stomach rumbled at the thought of lunch, and he agreed to join them. He followed in his truck behind Mari's car over the Smoky Mountain Parkway. Tall pines lined the winding road, their spiky tops projecting into the cloudless blue sky.

It was a warm day, unseasonably pleasant for a Sunday in mid-November. Gideon cracked his window a bit, enjoying the fresh air that flowed into his truck. They passed a small waterfall that ran out of the side of a stony embankment, and then the road curved east and the trees were not as dense. A mile later, they turned into the recreation area, and he parked his truck next to Mari's vehicle in the paved parking lot. Soon he was helping carry a cooler and grocery bags to a picnic area a short trek from the lot.

An old wooden table with benches sat by a pair of rotting logs and a holly bush laden with tiny red berries. Angie and Kiki walked over toward the edge of the picnic grounds. A few hundred yards below flowed a narrow stream with large rocks dotting the edge. The girls scampered down a dirt path, found an area that was warmed by the sun, removed their socks and shoes, and slowly tiptoed into the water. Giggles followed. Kiki splashed Angie and Angie retaliated. The giggles echoed up to where Mari and Gideon sat at the table.

"This is fun!" Kiki called up to the adults. "You should try it. You should."

"Too cold for me!" Gideon chuckled as Mari made sure that Kiki was seated safely by a mossy rock. She was, her bare feet dangling into the water. Angie joined her, and Mari turned her attention back to Gideon.

"I went to visit Mama yesterday."

"How was that?" asked Gideon.

Mari sat so that she could continue to keep an eye on her sister. "I'm worn out. She says that after she's with me, she's good for two weeks. That being with me gives her strength and courage." Mari shook her head. "But I just feel sad for two weeks afterward."

Gideon felt sorry for Mari, but he wasn't sure how to respond. After some thought he came up with, "Is her house still the same?"

"You mean still cluttered without any room to move? Yeah." Shielding her eyes from the sun, Mari let out an exasperated sigh. "Can you believe that she wanted me to take her to some secondhand store to buy more stuff? I asked her why. Why does she always need more?" Mari stood as though the action gave her the strength to confess her next feelings. "I asked her why she would let these puppets keep her from us. I asked her if she loved us. I went a little crazy with the questioning."

"Did she have answers?"

"Only the same ones she's been giving all along. She is happy surrounded by mounds of stuffed puppets. They bring her joy." Mari faced Gideon. "Joy!" she spat the word. "I dream of having a normal mother who gets joy from seeing her children happy. Not some diseased mother whose lifeless toys are more valuable than her own flesh and blood."

He wondered what to do. Should he stand and go over to her, caress her back, tell her she was strong and he admired her?

His mind was filled with questions, too. What made people hoard? Why couldn't hoarders stop their insane behavior? Pushing the questions aside, he concentrated on what he could say to Mari. But before he could come up with the right thing to say or do, the girls returned, laughing about how a fish tickled their feet as they dipped them into the chilly water.

Kiki opened the ice chest and removed a can of Sprite. She offered one to Angie. "I'm so thirsty." Surveying the containers of food stacked at the end of the picnic table, she piped, "And as hungry as five pirates."

"You're always hungry," said Mari. "Kiki can eat whatever she wants. I'm envious."

"My medicine makes me hungry. That's what Dr. Conner told me."

Gideon helped Mari spread the meal onto the table. She had packed everything they needed—plastic knives, spoons, and forks, plates and napkins with little rosebuds, even miniature shakers of pepper and salt. From the grocery store, she'd purchased turkey sandwiches, potato salad, macaroni salad, soda, and chocolate cookies.

They all gathered around the table as Mari offered a prayer. As they loaded up their plates, Kiki said she wished it was warm enough to swim.

"Where would you swim?" asked Mari.

"That stream down there." She jerked a thumb to indicate where she'd just been.

"I wouldn't let you," said Mari. "It's too shallow to swim in."

"You'd be swimming with the fishes," said Angie. "They'd be tickling you with their fins."

Kiki laughed, drank too quickly from her soda, and coughed. Sputtering, she said, "I bet I could swim faster than those fish."

Angie bit into her sandwich and then reached for a cookie. "I never get cookies at home," she said. "Mom tells me they'll make me fat."

Kiki said, "Nothing wrong with being fat, is there?" She turned to Gideon. "Are you a fisherman? Do you want to harpoon a fish for our dinner?"

Gideon laughed and was glad when the others joined him.

This was like family, he thought. He hadn't felt so connected to people, especially not to people of the opposite sex, for years. He only wished that Moriah were here. Moriah had enjoyed picnics and often took bits of food outside to eat while seated in the weeping willow tree. Once Gideon caught him with a whole loaf of oatmeal bread. As his brother sat in the tree pulling off morsels for himself to consume, every once in a while he would toss out a few for the nearby birds.

"Why did you leave Pennsylvania?" Kiki suddenly asked as she scooped potato salad onto her plate.

Gideon wiped his mouth with one of the napkins and then placed it in his lap. The question was not one he expected. He was enjoying a picnic in the Great Smoky Mountains National Park on a rare warm day in November. Did it have to be ruined by a visit from the past? He tried to let the question go unanswered by changing the subject and saying, "This food is really good. Thanks, Mari."

"Why?" Kiki was not going to let her question be pushed aside.

Gideon wiped his mouth again and said, "Lots of reasons."

The evening air was cool, the shed door cold and hard. Gideon placed his ear against it and thought he heard a whimper, like the sound of a calf when she was hungry.

"Tell us. We'll listen," said Mari.

Gideon decided that he could summarize what had caused him to go. He wouldn't need to tell every detail, just enough to give them an idea of why he knew it was time to leave. He wouldn't mention anything about the boy in the shed. Simplicity had its time and place.

Clearing his throat, he crossed his legs and then uncrossed them. "Well, I suppose I'll tell you then." He forced a smile and wondered why he felt the need to smile at all. This childhood tale was not at all humorous. His father was a rough man, demanding, and as cold and hard as the shed door.

The evening air was cool, the shed door cold and hard. It was interesting that the first line from one of his writing assignments still rang clearly into his thoughts as though he had written the words only today.

Steadying himself on the bench, Gideon placed one hand on the wooden slats beside him. It was almost as though if he let the memory plague him, he might slip off the wood. *No shed story*, he repeated in his mind. *Tell something else.*

Kiki eyed him, waiting to hear. Mari gave him her full attention as Angie said, "Is it a hard story to tell?"

His mouth was dry. He stood and reached for a can of Pepsi inside the ice chest. They all listened as he popped open the tab, the fizz the only sound that followed. He would have to start before then, before he stood outside the shed door. Gideon took a gulp of Pepsi and gave in to his audience.

"My father is a farmer. We have apple orchards, corn and wheat fields, some chickens and Jersey cows."

"Sounds peaceful," said Angie.

Gideon wished he could say something like, "It was too peaceful and calm, and I was getting bored," but for some reason, he found no ability to tease. And so he continued, telling them about how his father had a fence that surrounded the orchard across the road and how every evening, they locked the gate. "There was a shed, too, where we stored our tools." And bags of fertilizer, he wanted to add, but perhaps that wasn't so important to his audience. Those bags were, after all, not etched in this dismal memory.

Angie asked what a buggy was and Gideon explained. She said she thought she'd seen a picture of one in a history textbook. "I think they would be fun to ride."

"Me, too," said Kiki.

Continuing with his story, he wondered how much of it he could handle telling. He thought of that fateful night. Could he describe what had happened? Should he even try?

But all three faces were eagerly waiting.

"My father noticed that someone was in the apple orchard. He said he heard a noise, something that wasn't right. He had this ability to know when someone was lying or trying to pull the wool over his eyes. He took me with him to investigate. In the dark of the night, it must have been around eight o'clock, we walked from our house to the orchard as quietly as we could. The gate was open, and we went into the orchard, using the light of the moon and a small kerosene lantern as our flashlights. My father stopped at the trunk of one of the trees. He pointed up and when I looked I saw a young boy. He might have been ten or eleven years old. He was sitting in the tree eating apples. Father commanded him to come down from the tree. He did. Then my father forced the boy—he was a skinny kid—over to the shed. The whole way, the boy complained that Father was hurting him and Father kept telling him to shut up. Father had him by the scruff of the shirt."

"Like a mother cat carries her kittens?" asked Kiki.

"Exactly."

"But the kittens aren't hurt," she added.

"That's because the mother cat is gentle," said Gideon. "My father was not."

"What did he do to the boy?" asked Angie.

Gideon realized that he had to tell the rest of the story now. He'd come this far and his audience was expecting it. Well, if he was going to let them know what happened, he needed to sit. Slowly, he sat back on the bench, a piece of wood that felt just as hard and cold as the shed door. "My father locked this boy inside the shed."

"Locked him?" Kiki repeated the words three times before Mari said, "That's enough. Let Gideon continue."

"Yes," said Gideon. "My father locked him inside the shed. He told him he deserved to be punished for trespassing and for stealing apples."

"I'd be scared," said Angie. "I hate the dark with all its creepy shadows."

"Me, too. I'm scared of the dark. So scared," said Kiki.

Angie leaned in closer. "What happened next?"

Gideon looked at his hands, knowing that what he was about to reveal was grimier than any mechanic's fingernails. He hoped his voice didn't quake, although his hands were. "Father went back to the house. He ordered me to go, too. I could hear the boy crying inside the shed, but I obeyed and went back to the house with my father. I couldn't stand the thought of that boy locked inside the shed all night, though. His wails echoed in my ears. So I went back to the shed about an hour later and unlocked the door."

The scene from that night would never fade. Countless times the actions that followed played in his mind like a somber melody. And in that one writing class he'd taken, he'd recounted the entire scenario.

"Are you all right?" he asked. There was no reply, so he tried again. This time his voice was more than a whisper. "Are you all right?" The autumn wind circled his head, ruffling his mass of brown curls. He opened his mouth to ask if the lad would like a bowl of soup when he heard footsteps rounding the corner. His hands shook and his legs froze, even though he knew he must run before his father caught him.

"There was a large bolt on the door; no key was needed," Gideon said to the three as their expressions encouraged him to continue. "I pushed the door open, and there was the boy, his face stained with tears. He was so afraid. 'Run home,' I told him. Just as I said that, we heard a noise. It was my father! He must have heard me leave the house. He had a large branch in his hand." Gideon stopped. This was as far as he could go. He'd have to end the tale here.

"Did it hurt?" asked Kiki.

"What?"

"The branch."

Gideon leaned back and raised his face toward the sky. Composing himself, he waited. He said, "Yes. Father whipped the boy and then me."

Silence loomed and Gideon wished someone would say something to break it. Soon he heard his own voice. "I still have a scar."

"On your bottom?" asked Kiki.

"Yes, on my bottom."

"Did the boy run home?"

"No, Father locked him in again and took me home, yanking me by my arm. I was sent to my room and told to go to bed. I had a hard time sleeping. I was in so much pain."

"Did you tell your mama?" asked Kiki and was about to ask the question again, but Mari gave her a look that silenced her.

Gideon continued, "The next morning I woke around two because people were looking for the boy. They must have knocked at all the front doors on our street. The boy's parents had no idea where he was."

"Was he Amish?" Kiki asked.

173

"No, he wasn't."

"Did they find him?"

"Yes. Sometime after they came by to see if we had seen him, Father released the boy from the shed and told him to go home. But Father warned him that if he said a word about what happened he would tell his parents that he—the boy—stole his tools. Apparently, someone had broken into the shed and taken my father's tools the week before."

"Did you ever see the boy again?" Angie asked.

"Every day. . . . In my mind, I heard his voice and saw his frightened face every day. I still hear it some nights."

When no one spoke, he cleared his throat. "I found out later that the boy was visiting his cousins. I often wonder whether, if he had been a local boy, he would have eventually told someone what happened. I'd secretly hoped that my father would be found out, but he never was."

Mari swallowed hard, her eyes red at the rims. She brushed away tears from her chin. Clearing her throat, she said, "That's terrible, Gideon."

I hate him, he wanted to yell at the trees, at the sky, at the stream, and to anyone who would listen, but he bit his tongue and pressed his lips together instead.

"Why was he so mean?" asked Angie. "Did he have a bad father?"

Gideon shot her a surprised look. *How did she know?* "Yes," he said. "My mother told me his father—my grandfather—was abused and abusive."

"So the cycle continued," Mari said reflectively.

"I can see now," said Kiki, "why you had to get away from your family." With a glance toward her sister, she added, "We know about how parents can be, don't we, Mari?"

Mari said they certainly did. Angie said her parents fought too much. Sometimes that's why she spent so much time at her grandma's.

"We can be a family," Kiki said as she motioned toward them with a broad movement of her hand. "We can belong together, can't we?" Spontaneously, she grabbed Gideon's hand and put an arm around her sister's shoulders.

Gideon wondered if she'd belt out a verse or two of "Kumbaya," but instead Kiki dropped her embrace just as abruptly as she'd initiated it and cried, "Angie! We have to go on an arrowhead hunt! Hurry, before Mari says we have to go home." Her eyes begged permission from Mari.

Mari said, "A short hunt, Kiki. Okay?" With that the two girls darted from the picnic grounds toward a cluster of pines.

Mari started putting items into grocery bags, cleaning up from their lunch. "I hate what you went through," she said.

"I suppose he's made me the angry man I am and the one Moriah's become, too."

"Did Moriah get whipped?"

"He says he did. Told me that once he left his work boots out in the rain, and Father not only whipped him but made him milk the cows in his bare feet. It was winter about four years ago. After that, Moriah knew he had to leave home, too."

Mari sighed. "I hope you'll find some forgiveness somehow, Gideon. But who am I to talk? Look at me, I'm so aggravated with my own parents."

"Both of them? Even your dad?" He knew she was disturbed by her mother's hoarding and choosing a lifestyle that kept her from her own children.

"Yes," she breathed, stuffing the leftover cookies into a bag. "I always felt he should have stepped in and helped. Instead he stepped out, and away from Kiki and me."

"I guess you and I have something in common," he said, not sure if the ability to share dysfunctional family stories was ever a good thing to have in common. "I always thought adults could forget their childhoods. You know, grow up and leave them behind. But childhoods are what we grapple with even as adults."

When a wind picked up and the sun dropped in the sky, he helped her carry the paper grocery bags that contained the remains of their lunch to her car. He wished he had some magic words to say to alleviate her pain—and his, too.

175

As she summoned Kiki and Angie, he waited for words of hope, of promise. All he could come up with was from one of today's congregational songs, "I Am with You Always." The song spoke of how there is trial and turmoil in this life, but Jesus promises to be with you no matter what. Did he believe those words? As the tune played in his head, he thought, *I want to. I want to believe. I need to.*

Although they hadn't found any arrowheads, Kiki and Angie each had a bird's feather when they rounded the bend and joined Mari and Gideon at the parking lot. Kiki waved hers like a flag. "I think it's a hawk feather," she said. "I'm going to add it to my pirate's hat."

All the way home, as Gideon followed Mari's car out of the park, he let Kiki's suggestion of being a family together push away the visions of his past. Belonging, that's what he wanted. To be cared for, to belong, to be accepted.

At his apartment, he checked for any sign of Moriah. As he made a bologna sandwich for dinner, he thought he heard his cell phone ring, but when he checked, there were no missed calls or messages.

25

Thanksgiving came like it did every year in the Smokies, a canopy of deep blue mountains framed by bare maple, beech, and pin cherry trees. Rotund firs, still green, dotted the mountainsides.

Gideon spent the holiday with the Kingstons at their house nestled in the forest away from the Parkway. He and Luke were their two guests, spoiled by Mebane as she made sure their dinner plates were abundant with turkey, gravy, and chestnut stuffing. Although they talked of hunting season and a recent forest fire, wedding planning took precedence. Luke and Ashlyn discussed what kind of cake to have at their reception. They'd be sending out invitations to their May wedding in March. Luke then asked if Gideon would be his best man.

"Me?" Gideon pushed back from the dining room table, admitted he was honored. In Amish country, friends were asked to be witnesses— similar, he guessed, to being bridesmaids or groomsmen. He'd been a witness for a cousin's wedding when he'd just turned thirteen, but in all of his years away from the farm, he'd never been asked to be a groomsman or a best man. He'd have to ask Ormond was what expected of him.

From photos he'd seen, he knew he'd have to dress the part. "I guess that means I'll have to put on a tux and take off my ball cap," he said.

Both Luke and Ashlyn said they were grateful he agreed to be in their wedding party. "I'd like to ask Moriah, too," Luke said later in the evening as Henry snored in his recliner and ESPN blared on the plasma TV. "But I don't know if I should—"

Gideon motioned the suggestion away with the flick of his wrist. "He's not reliable," he said.

"But will he be offended if I don't?" Luke's eyes softened.

"No," lied Gideon. He knew his brother could let his emotions get bent out of shape because Moriah was like that. He wanted to be the center of attention, he craved the limelight. But Moriah was not well, and expecting him to perform as part of the wedding party was neither a feasible nor wise expectation.

Nights later, Gideon brought his eight-foot artificial tree out of the cardboard box in his closet and, since none of the lights he'd bought last year still worked, found some lights on sale at the local Kmart. After decorating the tree with two strands, he strung a multicolored strand up around the doorway to his kitchen. He turned off the overhead lights and plugged in the Christmas lights. He added fifty ornaments Mebane had given him over the years. There were bells, baubles, a glass angel, a star made of porcelain, and a dozen reindeer with red bows. His favorite was the wooden manger scene with Mary, Joseph, and Baby Jesus. Perhaps he liked it because it was made of wood, or perhaps because it was simple without any commercial fanfare, the way he imagined the birth of God's son had been so many years ago, aside from the angels singing glory to God and that star that led the magi across the country. Admiring the tree, he thought, *now, this is warm and cozy*. This was the kind of atmosphere that made him want to invite Mari over to watch *It's a Wonderful Life*.

He was determined to ask her, but the next day at the tearoom, Mari seemed preoccupied. He learned she was going to have to visit her mother for a few days during Kiki's Christmas break. Pondering the visit made her anxious. She didn't mind the drive, as long as the weather wasn't icy—she wasn't good at driving in inclement weather—but she wasn't sure what to do about the nights she'd stay in Asheville. "I don't think I can sleep in Mama's house," she confessed. "It's covered in puppets and hard to find the furniture. I think I'll tell her that Kiki and I are staying in a hotel."

Something about the way she said it, Gideon knew the choice to do this was not going to bring any favor with her mother. "Tell her you don't want to put her out."

"Put her out?"

"You know, have to clean and get the house ready for you."

Mari sighed. "She doesn't. I mean she doesn't clean for anyone, so that line won't work."

Gideon wasn't sure what to say next. In this one way he wished he was like Moriah, freely able to make conversation.

"I could say we have allergies. That might work," Mari said. "I have been sneezing more lately."

Gideon felt sorry for Mari and her obligations. He could see that the holidays were a chore, and he wanted to make them merrier for her. But his own heart felt loaded with uncertainty. He wondered why Christmas now couldn't be as it was for him his first Christmas in his apartment. That first Christmas, he'd been eager to decorate a tree and invite his new friends over.

Even last Christmas Eve, he'd hosted a small party, made a new recipe for lobster soufflé he saw in an issue of *Cooking Light*. The soufflé was rich in color and texture, reminding him of sunflowers back home. Also to the menu he'd added a hot cheese dip with artichokes and had sliced French bread to create bruschetta with mozzarella and a mild salsa topping. But the dish he was most proud of was his own creation. Using what he had in his pantry and fridge, he'd concocted a salad with avocados and Roma tomatoes. Preparing it had been easy; he created the recipe as he was inspired. First, he took out a box of acini di pepe pasta he'd purchased on sale months ago, and dumped half of the contents into a pan of boiling water. Nine minutes later when the tiny gel-like pasta was ready, he drained it and then tossed it with sour cream, seasonings, chopped onions, tomatoes, and a ripe avocado. The red and green mixture looked festive, and after a taste, he added more salt and garlic powder and named it Gideon's Southwestern Christmas Salad. Everyone who stopped by last Christmas Eve had enjoyed it.

Ormond, Luke, and Ashlyn had arrived at seven and stayed for hours. Ashlyn brought a key lime pie she'd made, and later, when her parents stopped by for a few moments, they added homemade sugar cookies and apple cider to the spread on the kitchen table.

Beside his festive tree, they'd sung Christmas carols together and between selections, Luke had played his banjo. When Bruce, in town visiting family, came over, they were on the sixth stanza of "The Twelve Days of Christmas." Bruce encouraged Luke to play along as they sang the rest of the verses, and both instrument and vocals joined together harmoniously. They all agreed Luke sounded more like a true southern mountaineer than any northern Amish lad.

This year, with Moriah . . . Gideon was not at all certain what would happen.

His first Christmas card arrived two days later—a glittery card of heavy blues and reds with a church bell on the front. It was from Josiah, one of the first Amish kids he'd helped "cross over into civilization," as the then sixteen-year-old had put it. Josiah left Indiana during his rumspringa, when he was allowed to venture out of his Amish community. He worked at Russell Brothers for three years and then went to Appalachian State University. At twenty-two, he graduated with a business degree and married a third-grade teacher who encouraged him to open his own computer business. The two moved to her coastal hometown of Beaufort, North Carolina, and raised their family of three boys. Five years ago, they'd stopped by for a visit, Josiah praising Gideon for all he'd done for him over the years. With fond memories, Gideon placed Josiah's card on the shelf under the TV stand. As more cards arrived, he'd do what he did each Christmas—string them along his living room wall, a display for him to view every day.

On Christmas Eve, Gideon returned home from a small party at Henry and Mebane's to find Moriah waiting for him with a turkey and an armful of potatoes. Ignoring the fact he hadn't even said hi in over a month, Moriah asked his brother if he could come in and if Gideon would cook a meal for them on Christmas. "You know, a nice dinner like they have in the movies."

"I can do that," said Gideon as he took the groceries from his brother.

"Great." Moriah entered the room like he had never left. He sprawled out on the couch and within minutes, was asleep.

Gideon defrosted the turkey that night in a pan of warm water and at eight in the morning, as Moriah slept, he put it in the oven. While the turkey cooked, he planned what else to serve with it, continually keeping an eye on his brother as he quietly moved about the apartment.

At two in the afternoon, the brothers sat down to a meal of roasted turkey, mashed potatoes, gravy from the giblets, green beans, and Gideon's Southwestern Christmas Salad. For dessert, Gideon had whipped up the traditional Amish shoofly pie. Cooking for his brother had been a delight; he was grateful for the opportunity to serve him a real Christmas dinner.

As the local radio station's selection of Christmas carols filtered through the apartment, Gideon kept the conversation on a light note, talking about the weather, Christmas mornings in Carlisle, and sprinkled in a few mentions about the auto shop. He didn't comment on what he saw—a skinny Moriah with circles under his eyes, enlarged pupils, sallow skin, and hair as dull as the hay from the bales on the farm.

As each carried their dishes into the kitchen—Moriah's plate still half full with untouched turkey and potatoes—Gideon contemplated what to say. He knew that he couldn't keep up the placid front any longer. Bravely, he asked what Moriah's plans were. Moriah shrugged.

"Okay then, where have you been keeping yourself?"

Moriah looked him in the eye but said nothing.

Annoyed, Gideon said, "I asked you questions. I'd like some answers."

"What does it matter? I'm living *la vida loca*. And it's great!" He hummed a few lines of the song by Ricky Martin. "Sure beats plowing fields and being watched by old Beasty Eyes."

"I know about this halfway house—"

"I don't need any help! If only everyone would leave me alone!" As Moriah spit the words out, Gideon noted that his lisp was more pronounced than when he was calmer. Moriah muttered a few phrases and Gideon realized he didn't comprehend them at all.

"Moriah," he pleaded. "Why don't you rest?"

Moriah's arms flailed, jerking to the right and left. "I don't need to be told what to do!"

Gideon struggled with what to say next. Perhaps letting his brother know that he was aware of his drug usage would break Moriah of his relentless mood. Gently, Gideon said, "Kiki told me about the guy who brought you packages to the shop. I know meth is inside. I found some under the sofa." For emphasis, he pointed to the couch, the throw pillows still indented from where his brother had earlier laid his head.

"You're snooping on me? You?! I thought you were my friend. I thought we were brothers." Moriah's arm closest to the Christmas tree twitched, knocking a silver angel off the branch and onto the hardwood floor. The sound of shattering glass echoed through the living room.

He left after that. In fact, he took Gideon's truck when Gideon went into the kitchen to retrieve the broom and dustpan. The tires squealed over the pavement as Moriah backed it out of the apartment complex's parking lot.

Gideon watched from his kitchen window. The proverbial red flags of danger were all around Moriah. As he made a hasty left turn and swerved to miss a gray Subaru, Gideon knew his truck and brother were not going to be together for long. The way Gideon saw it, Moriah would either have an accident or, due to reckless driving, be stopped by the police and placed in jail once law enforcement realized he had no license. Gideon felt helplessness cover him like a cloak, darker than any his mother or father wore.

He cleaned up the broken ornament with his bare hands. Blood oozed as a jagged shard cut his index finger. There was something symbolic in the crushed angel, the blood, and his feelings of despair. Perhaps an angel like Gabriel would come to his aid now, assuring him that there was no need for fear.

He hated to interrupt anyone's Christmas festivities; nevertheless, he was desperate. As night settled over his apartment, he mulled over the day with a glass of iced tea, a fresh Band-Aid wrapped around his finger. Where could Moriah be? Who would know what he was up to? At 8:30, he called Luke. "Have you seen Moriah?"

Luke said he hadn't seen even his shadow in days.

"I thought he might have come over to your place," Gideon explained. "He came here and we had a nice meal, and then he just walked out." He wondered what else he should tell Luke. Should he let his coworker know that Moriah had taken his truck? That he, the Getaway Savior, was at the end of his rope, frustrated over what to do about a brother he couldn't keep in line?

In a low voice, so low it was almost a whisper, Luke said, "I think he's into drugs."

Gideon sighed. So Luke knew. Here he'd been trying to hide, to cover up who Moriah had become, and Luke was already aware of Moriah's illegal behavior. Letting his guard down, Gideon moaned, "What can we do? What can I do?"

"I don't know."

"Where does he go when he leaves my place? Where does he sleep? Or eat?" Gideon didn't expect Luke to have the answers; he just wanted to voice his concerns.

"I'm not sure."

183

"If you see him, give me a call, will you?"

Luke said he would be sure to do that. "Gideon, you know meth makes you paranoid and crazy."

"Yes," said Gideon. "I've researched it on the Internet many times, each time hating what I read." Remembering that it was still Christmas, Gideon said, "Sorry to bother you. I hope you're having a Merry Christmas." He assumed Luke would want to get back to spending time with Ashlyn, so he wrapped up the call. "Bye—"

"Wait!" Luke's voice was sharp in his ear. "I did see him two weeks ago at Walmart. He was so hungover and out of his mind, he didn't even recognize me."

"He's in a bad way," agreed Gideon.

"Skinny and he smelled like . . ."

After a few seconds Gideon supplied the description. "Beer, sweat, and moldy onions."

"That would be about right. That's when he told me he was snorting meth."

"He admitted that? Because today he said he's fine."

"Of course—he thinks he's fine and that it's others who have the problem."

Gideon felt his stomach twist as the horror of Moriah's condition became more real to him. When he hung up the phone, he sat on the sofa, staring at the Christmas tree with its blinking lights and dangling baubles. His Christmas cards, strung along his wall, announced their seasonal messages of joy and peace, but he felt none of those blessings.

At midnight he wanted to go out and search for Moriah, but he had no vehicle to drive and he was too tired to walk.

26

Gideon wondered if he'd ever see Moriah again. Their last exchange of words on Christmas day still rang in his head like a resounding gong. He was sweeping the shop for the fifth time when Ormond said, "Are you looking for buried treasure?"

Gideon rested his hand on the broom handle. "Am I overdoing it?" Although temperatures had dropped this January day, sweat glistened on his brow and neck.

"This place has never been cleaner. Take a break," Ormond advised.

His words reminded Gideon of his first year at the auto shop when Gideon was fresh from Amish country. Gideon pushed himself to work as hard as he could, dedicated to sweeping and dusting in addition to helping with carting quarts of oil from the storage room. Desperate to please, Gideon had hoped Ormond would praise his long hours of labor. But after careful observation, Ormond did not offer any compliments about the fifteen-year-old's work ethic. Instead he said, "Take it easy, boy. You work too hard."

"Really?" His father had never told him that; he'd always made

185

Gideon believe he had so far to go, he'd never achieve any accolades.

"Yes, you are making my head spin. A boy your age ought to be enjoying life. Go have fun." At the time, Gideon wondered if he knew how.

Today Gideon's mind was racing, wondering where Moriah was and calculating how long it had been since he'd seen him. Had it really been twenty-five days? There had been no call from Henry to say that Moriah had wrecked his truck or been caught without a proper driver's license. In the restroom, Gideon studied the bags under his eyes. He felt a cold coming on; his throat was scratchy. He'd better buy some DayQuil. Silently, he prayed, *God, let me find him. Wherever he is.*

When he walked to the Laundromat, he was sure his prayer was answered. A large black sedan raced past him and in the passenger's seat was a man with long blond hair. Gideon's steps halted; his heart quickened. *Could it be Moriah?* But before he could catch the license plate's numbers, the sedan took a left at the corner and sped away. Gideon sprinted, hoping to catch a glimpse of his brother again. If he could just get his attention, he'd ask if he was okay and beg him to go to the Narcotics Anonymous group that met at the Episcopalian church on Third Street. He'd get him a sponsor, get him cleaned up, get him whatever it took. Then they'd go hunting together, play pool. But there was no sign of the car anywhere now.

Gideon stood motionless on the sidewalk. A woman pushed past him with a child bundled in her stroller. He apologized for not moving out of her way. He'd been caught up in some sort of trance, unaware of his surroundings. Recalling that he'd been on the way to the Laundromat, he turned and headed in that direction, eyeing the street as he walked. A car slowed, but it was a dark blue Ford, and inside sat an old man in a tweed hat. Gideon continued to watch the road. Suddenly, he stumbled into an electric pole; the pain of the impact seared his forehead. Feeling foolish, he concentrated on walking carefully, ignoring the street and its vehicles.

He'd seen Moriah. Wasn't that enough for today?

At the Laundromat, he bought four Baby Ruth bars to take back to the shop. He knew Kiki was fond of chocolate, even if it did make her stomach gurgle. She'd be coming to work in about an hour, and a chocolate bar would surely add to her spirits.

When he looked at his reflection again in the shop restroom mirror, he noted the swollen bump on his forehead. Seated at his desk, he placed a cold bottle of soda against it, hoping to alleviate the nagging pain.

Kiki breezed in, chattering about how she'd heard it was going to snow. She wanted to make sure that everyone had gloves. "Do you have a nice warm pair?" she asked Luke. "I got a red pair for Christmas."

Luke, who was under the hood of Hiber Summers's Volvo, said he had gloves, but from the way he said it, Gideon felt he was just trying to appease the girl.

"What color are they?" Kiki stood beside the car.

"What? Uh, um . . . orange."

"You have orange gloves? Orange?" Kiki's insistence made Gideon wonder if she denied that Luke actually owned a pair of that color.

"No, um . . . yeah, black." It seemed Luke doubted the orange pair, too. Taking out the dipstick and wiping it with a tattered cloth, he said, "Yeah, my gloves are leather and black."

"Black, now that's more like it for a man. For a man. A man shouldn't have orange gloves or pink ones. And never bright green gloves. Unless he's an elf."

"I wish they made gloves that wouldn't bother my fingers," said Ormond as he flexed the fingers on his right hand. "I have a couple of pairs somewhere in my house, but the truth is, I don't like the feel of gloves against my fingers."

"What's wrong with your fingers?" asked Kiki.

"Arthritis."

Kiki followed him to the coffeepot. "Angie said that her grandma rubs her fingers with IcyHot every night."

"Really? Is that what Luva does?"

"Every night. She wears gloves to bed, too."

"Gloves, now why would she do that?" He poured a mug of coffee.

187

"I think it keeps the IcyHot from getting all over her sheets. Angie said that her grandmother's arthritis pain has gone away."

Ormond looked doubtful. "Never did like the smell of IcyHot. I don't think anything that foul smelling could bring any relief."

As Ormond stirred sugar into his coffee, Kiki asked if he wanted her to cart the pile of accumulating cardboard boxes to the Dumpster. The stack was against the storage room door, some flattened and others still in their square forms.

"Gideon usually does that," said Ormond. "But he's in another world today."

"I heard that," said Gideon as he pressed the bottle onto his head, hopeful that the pain would eventually lessen.

Kiki chimed in, "If you put a cold compress on each temple and then massage your forehead, headaches disappear . . ."

"I heard that four ibuprofen taken with water would do the trick, too," Gideon said as he stood to look for some medicine.

Kiki clutched at two of the flattened boxes with her gloved hands. Immediately, she dropped one. Sighing, she secured the cardboard pieces under her arm. "I'm going to take these boxes out of here for you, Gideon." Slowly and awkwardly—looking like she was walking barefoot over a bed of pinecones—she made her way outside the bay doors toward the Dumpster.

Gideon was going over some paperwork at Ormond's desk when Kiki rushed into the shop through the open bay, her steps hard against the floor. He heard her gasp and Luke cry, "Kiki, you okay?"

As she raced toward Gideon, something about her expression made him jump to his feet. "What's the matter?"

"I—I saw—saw . . ."

He reached out for her, fearful that she might fall.

But she turned, making her way once again toward the bays.

He followed her, Ormond close behind him.

She only got to Luke's bay, her face pale. She steadied herself at the trunk of the Volvo.

188

Seeing her wild eyes, Ormond took off for the fridge, bringing back a bottle of orange juice. "What is it?" he asked, approaching her with caution. He uncapped the bottle, handing it to her.

But Kiki wanted nothing to do with the orange juice, turning from Ormond to lean against Gideon, her breathing labored.

Gideon put an arm around her waist. If she fainted, at least he would catch her and keep her from falling to the floor. "What's wrong?" he asked. "What did you see?"

But her breath only came out in guttural spurts.

Luke said, "Do you want us to call your sister?"

Kiki managed to shake her head. "Don't . . ." Clutching Gideon's arm with both of her hands she said, "I saw . . . I saw . . . a . . ."

"What did you see?"

"Was it a mouse?" Luke asked. "They love living inside the Dumpster. We used to put rat poisoning around."

Kiki's fingers pressed into the fibers of Gideon's shirt. "Oh, tell me it isn't so."

"What is it?" Gideon took her by the shoulders and tried to make eye contact. "Tell me."

She avoided his eyes.

Gideon tried again. "Kiki, what did you see?"

"A finger."

"A what? Where?"

"At . . . at . . ." She covered her mouth, choked. "Dumpster."

"Where did you see the finger?"

"I said at the Dumpster."

Ormond and Luke exchanged confused looks. Ormond muttered, "What in the Sam Hill is she talking about?"

Gideon ushered Kiki into his office and helped her to his chair. "Wait here. I'll go check it out."

Beside the Dumpster were the two cardboard boxes Kiki had gone to throw away. The dirty green metal sliding door was partially opened, something leaning near it. Gideon stepped closer. What could she have meant? A finger? Is that what she'd said? Once he'd seen a mouse climbing over the opening and was embarrassed that it scared him so much that he hated going to toss anything in the Dumpster after that. About that time he'd suggested mousetraps, and when they didn't work, Ormond bought d-CON baits. Gideon inched closer so that his face was parallel with the door.

Immediately, he saw it. Resting against a stack of flattened boxes, barely visible due to the sunless day, was a human hand, an index finger sticking out of the sliding door.

He yanked the door to open it completely so that he could get a better view. Then he stopped, paralyzed for a moment. Bile rose in his throat. *No, no, this couldn't be!* With a sprint to the garage, he rushed to the storage room. He grabbed the ladder and carried it outside. Propping it against the Dumpster, he climbed until he was higher than the metal compartment. He made himself cast his eyes downward.

Moriah's eyes were open, hollow with fear. Crusted blood stained his army-green cotton shirt.

Gripping the ladder, Gideon fought to stay on the middle rung.

Kiki was now behind him. "Do you see it? Who does it belong to?"

"Take her inside!" Gideon shouted as both Luke and Ormond came after her.

He couldn't look any longer. His stomach twisted and jerked like a car sputtering out of gas on a rocky road. Stepping off the ladder, he turned from the Dumpster as his last meal spewed from his mouth.

"What is it?" Kiki demanded. "Who does that finger belong to?" Quickly, before anyone could stop her, she bolted up the ladder. "No! No! No!"

Wiping his wet mouth with his hand, Gideon tried to stand straight. "Take her inside!"

He wished that Ormond would listen, would take her inside, away from this horror. "It's not him! Say it's not him!" Her voice escalated as Luke lifted her up and carried her into the shop.

But Gideon couldn't lie, as much as he wanted to. For inside the

190

Dumpster lay a dead body, stiff as a board and caked with blood. Every inch of him seemed to be bloody. Bruises—the color of moldy cheese—spread across his chin and sunken cheeks.

"I'll call the police," Ormond said.

Gideon wiped his mouth again. For a second, he thought of climbing the ladder again and letting himself fall off, onto the hedges by the fence. When he came to after that, surely this scene would be erased. He'd be in bed, grateful that this day had only been a nightmare.

Gideon made himself look at the body again. The wide, lifeless eyes ... searing his mind like a hot iron ... the mouth that broke so easily into a smile ... clamped shut. Upon closer observation, he saw that the jeans and shirt were torn in places and soiled with not only blood but dirt. "Moriah," he cried, agony draining his voice. "Moriah," he repeated. "Please, wake up."

Surely this was a nightmare. Gideon pinched the skin on his arm. He squeezed harder and felt the pain. Taking a swallow of water, he waited. Any minute now, he'd awaken. He'd be in his bed and all would be fine. He'd enter the living room and find his brother on the sofa, sleeping like a baby, a light snore escaping from his nose.

He saw his mother, dressed in one of her dark dresses, her hair bound inside her bonnet. He saw her face when she was distressed and imagined how destroyed she'd be to know that her youngest child was dead.

When he thought of his father, all he heard were the words he had been trying to escape all his life. *Can't you ever do anything right? You can't even keep your brother safe.*

Slumping onto the floor, Gideon felt his chest expand into his throat. He muffled his first sob, but let the next ones out in loud, escalating cries.

The sensation to throw up again evaporated, and a new one took its place. Guilt.

He was at fault. He'd let Moriah die.

191

27

How could he be dead? It is a lie! Even though she'd seen the body, cold and lifeless, Kiki wanted to believe that it had not been Moriah's. She clutched Yoneko until her nose itched from the puppet's fur. She wanted to go home, to her real home, with Mama. Mama would rub her shoulders and buy her ice cream. Mama would—

Kiki tugged at Yoneko's red collar. Mama was ill. Mama was not able to care for her. Why couldn't she get that through her head?

Gideon said Moriah was ill, too. He had an addiction. Mama's is hoarding stuffed animals, but Moriah's was drugs. She'd heard of cocaine and marijuana but did not know as much about this drug called meth. And she—she, Kiki Yanagi—thinking she was doing Moriah a favor, had hidden a package of this drug for him.

Kiki didn't feel like watching *Rescue Animals* this afternoon. Her mind kept going back to tidbits of conversations she'd had with Moriah. Sure, he could be irritable—the way she got sometimes—but most of the time, he'd been nice to her. She remembered how his hand

felt on top of her head, the way he smiled at her. "I love him," she had said to the mirror in her room.

He was dead.

Was it okay to still love someone who was dead? Was it acceptable to say, *I love you, Moriah?*

Kiki stood slowly and was glad that the blood did not run from her head and make her dizzy. She looked out the window where she'd seen Angie and others playing in the shadows in the yard next door. She wished Angie was outside now. She'd join her. Angie was not to be feared because she was a friend now.

Moriah is dead, and Angie is a friend. She wondered why the two thoughts kept bumping around together in her mind.

And people in town were saying that Gideon might have been the one to end Moriah's life. *That is crazy. Gideon wouldn't kill. Gideon is kind. Sure, he fought with Moriah. But I fight with Mari, too.* She'd never harm her sister, just as she was sure that Gideon would never do anything bad to Moriah.

Sheriff Kingston had arrived immediately when Ormond called his office. He and Tomlin took turns standing on the ladder to look into the Dumpster. An ambulance blared through town, its tires shrieking to a stop in the parking lot. Kiki expected men with a stretcher to immediately lift Moriah's body from the Dumpster into the vehicle. But they didn't. Instead, other vehicles followed, even a fire truck. Soon a bunch of people Kiki had never seen before filled the lot. Ormond said that some of them were here to investigate the scene. Rolls of yellow tape were stretched across orange cones just like Kiki had seen on TV shows, keeping those that were just nosy out of the way. Mari arrived, and Mr. Kingston allowed her to slip under the tape. When she saw Kiki, she squeezed her tightly, but after a moment, Kiki pushed away. She didn't want to be coddled; she wanted to watch everything that was happening.

The owner of Benson's Laundromat said he'd overheard Moriah yelling at Gideon over the fence that separated the auto shop from the

Laundromat. "I heard Gideon say he'd kill Moriah," Mr. Benson said to the sheriff. "I heard it one afternoon about three weeks ago, plain as day."

Others were now suspicious, and even though they'd been closed for three days, business had been slow at the shop ever since. Seemed people weren't sure whether having a car serviced at Russell Brothers was safe since a corpse had been pulled out of the Dumpster. *Sheesh*, thought Kiki. *Doesn't everyone know that Gideon is like a big teddy bear underneath his John Deere cap?*

She knew she had to get out. This house was too stuffy, too cramped. Although it was dark, she got her bike from the garage and hopped on. She would ride and ride. She would ride until she got blisters on her feet from pedaling and until her back was sore. She would ride to Heaven if she could and ask God to please bring Moriah back to earth.

Gideon rubbed his eyes and then tried to ease the tension in his neck. If his desk phone rang now, he wouldn't answer. He'd let Ormond or the answering machine take the call. What if the caller was another Amish, wanting to leave home? Here he'd been the Getaway Savior and now, the most important person he'd ever wanted to help was dead. What kind of savior does that? *I couldn't even keep my own brother alive. This is it, never again.* As much as he enjoyed helping dissatisfied people from his community and others around the country find fulfillment in the Western side of life, he could do it no more. *I'm a farce; I am no savior.*

Mechanically, he walked outside, leaving the shop, calling out that he was heading to the tearoom. He wasn't sure if anyone heard him, and he didn't care. *What mattered now? Who cared about life and morals and all of those other things I once held dear?* He cringed at how determined he'd been on keeping the auto shop clean, on making sure everyone came to work on time and left when they were supposed to. What a crock it all was. Where was the meaning in any of it?

Mari filled a customer's water glass quickly when she saw Gideon

194

enter Another Cup. Without a word, she poured green tea into a large mug and handed it to Gideon.

He thanked her, took a sip, burned his tongue.

"It's hot."

"I know. Guess I'm not thinking today."

She reached over the counter and took his empty hand.

He tried to smile, but his mouth wouldn't move. He took another taste of tea. It seemed bland this afternoon.

Customers came and went, and he tried not to notice those who spent too much time glancing at him. He purposely ignored the whispers from a table behind him. Seated at it were three elderly women sharing a plate of club sandwiches. Was it all hearsay or had the *Twin Star* printed a story about the incident? He didn't want to know if there was a news story. He would avoid the newspaper and every other form of media connected to this town. Gideon drank the tea, now cool against his tongue, as his mind hosted a mass of noisy thoughts.

Who killed his brother? Did Henry have a list of suspects? The autopsy report revealed that Moriah was shot in the chest with a handgun, the point of penetration just half an inch from his right ventricle.

Suddenly Kiki was at his side at the counter. She must have slipped in without him noticing her footsteps. "We have to take his body to be buried," she announced.

"What?" Gideon ran a hand over his face.

"He asked you." Kiki climbed onto the barstool beside him.

"He asked me what?"

"If he died, to take his body to the weeping willow tree by the apple orchard. Don't you remember anything?"

Gideon felt the weariness ache behind his eyes. He would bury his brother here. There was no way he was going to take a body to Carlisle. Besides, Moriah would never know where he was or wasn't buried.

But Kiki's eyes were pleading, and when Gideon looked at Mari for some sort of help in explaining to the child that driving all the way to Pennsylvania was not necessary, he got none. Mari's eyes were hopeful.

195

"I can't go." His words sounded hollow and hoarse.

"You can," said Mari.

"We will be with you," said Kiki.

"Yes," whispered Mari. "We will help you." Gently, she put her hand over Gideon's.

Gideon would rather have Angie's family's funeral home take care of the arrangements. He told the two this, knowing that it was his last attempt to get them to see that a trip to the homeland would not be necessary. Moriah could be buried in the plot beside the wooded lot he passed on his walks to work. He'd come up with a eulogy; Angie's family could take care of everything else. Moriah would never know that his body didn't lie under the weeping willow.

"You can get the funeral home to give you a coffin, but then you need to take it to your parents' house." Kiki's hand was firm on his sleeve.

What was it about this child? Even when he stretched his arms onto the countertop and lowered his head on them, Kiki's fingers were still attached to his sleeve.

"You have to live up to expectations," she said. "Sheesh, didn't they teach you that in school?"

"No."

"You say no too much," said Kiki. "You should go home, Gideon."

"Yes," agreed Mari. "Go get some sleep. Kiki and I will take care of what needs to be done."

Even though he thought he'd made clear his refusal to take Moriah's body to Pennsylvania, no one seemed to hear him. Kiki and Mari were determined to assist him with what was *expected* of him.

28

But Gideon didn't go home. When his cell rang minutes later, he was summoned to the sheriff's department. He walked there, even though it was over a mile. He didn't trust himself behind the wheel of a car right now. Besides, he still had no idea where his truck was, but even with that excuse, he was not about to ask Ormond if he could borrow the Buick.

The air was crisp, typical January weather in the mountains. The stark tree limbs housed a few bird nests. Smoke curled from stout chimneys as he passed three homes adjacent to the local playground. He wondered what the residents were doing this afternoon and what was on the stove for dinner. He wished he felt hungry, but he didn't seem to have that luxury. His stomach knotted like a ball of yarn he'd seen Mebane knit a scarf from at Thanksgiving. He wondered if it was too late to pray.

"God . . ." He recalled the bedtime prayers he'd offered to God as a child, back when his parents taught him that he should talk to God every night before sleep. He wondered where the concept of prayers before bed evolved. Was it biblical? "God." He sighed. "Help."

The steps up to the station were covered in salt to compensate for the patches of ice that shone on their bricks. Gideon felt the soles of his shoes slick against the moisture of the ice. He recalled the frozen pond on the farm, at the corner of the apple orchard, visible when you turned down Pike Level Road. That pond was a marker for telling his friends which orchard belonged to his family. "Our house is right across the road," he always said and pretty soon the kids were saying, "I know where you live. By that pond on Pike Level, right?" He wondered how many times ice had crusted over its surface this winter. Once he and Moriah had tried their hand at ice fishing until their father told them to get back to work.

Inside the warm building, he caught a whiff of beef soup, and the distinct aroma reminded him he hadn't eaten today. There was no sign of any food at the station though; he supposed that the soup had long been consumed. Tomlin greeted him and offered a chair. Gideon took it and sat waiting for Sheriff Henry. Before excusing himself, Tomlin said he'd be right along.

As Gideon stared at the plaques on the walls, his eyes blurred. He recalled the last time he'd been here . . . when Moriah had been picked up for disorderly conduct.

The door sprang open and in walked Henry. "I just need to ask you some questions." He held a clipboard with papers attached.

His tone made Gideon stiffen. If it was just questions, why had he needed to come all the way down to the station? Why couldn't they have discussed this over the phone? The first series of questions had taken place when Moriah's body had been found in the Dumpster. Later there had been questions asked of Luke, Ormond, and Gideon, as well as the store owners who shared the street with the auto shop. Gideon needed to be at work now. He'd already taken too much time off over the last couple of days. What kind of example was he setting for Luke and Kiki? What if Ormond changed his mind and reneged on his previous desire to have Gideon take over the shop once he retired?

Henry placed the clipboard on his desk and rubbed the buckle on his belt. Without making eye contact, he said, "I just have to ask these questions as a matter of protocol. Just need to know where you were the night of January seventeenth."

"Where I was? I told you."

"We have to cover all our bases."

Nausea coated Gideon's stomach. "You think I—I did it?" He couldn't bring himself to use the word *killed*. It was one thing to hear rumors at Another Cup but to now have Henry even consider that Gideon could have . . . murdered . . . his own brother. . . . It was incomprehensible.

Henry looked like he might throw up, himself. "I have to question you, Gideon. I'm sorry, but I have to. . . . Procedures, you know how it is . . ."

Gideon found his voice. "Am I guilty?"

"I didn't say that." The sheriff avoided eye contact, causing Gideon to squirm in his seat.

"Do you think I am?" He wondered why he asked. Right now he didn't care to know if the answer was yes.

Henry adjusted his glasses. "You said you were at home?" His focus was now on his desk with its many piles of paper. Lifting one stack that sat by his elbow, crowding the framed photo of Mebane, he found a pen.

Gideon tried to remain calm, but the blood was pulsating throughout his head. *We've eaten meals together,* he thought. *We've even watched the Super Bowl together for the past ten years.* Is this what their friendship had come to? A session of accusations? Gideon tried to remember the question.

"Yes," he said, "I was home all night long."

"Alone?" Henry scribbled, his eyes on the sheet of paper.

"I don't have any pets."

Henry's confusion cleared to understanding after a moment. He cleared his throat. "What I mean is, is there anyone who can vouch for the fact that you were at home all night?"

"Me."

"What?" Henry's face showed puzzlement.

"My word, Henry. I said I was at home all night from the time I got off work, and that's all I got."

Henry looked like he might cry. Scratching his bald head, he said, "I want to believe you, Gideon." For a moment silence passed between them. Then Henry lowered his voice. "I *do* believe you. Of course I do. You have always been an honest man."

With that out in the air, Gideon stood to leave.

Henry cleared his throat again. "The fact is, I need more than that."

"More than my word?"

"Yes. Folks around here are a little antsy."

"Antsy?"

Solemnly, he said, "Worried. We've always been a peaceful town."

With Reginald and his boisterous antics? With those rednecks from Gatlinburg who came into town to harass waitresses at Another Cup just because they could? Gideon wanted to argue but decided now was not the right time to disagree with the sheriff.

"The body was found at your shop. Who found it?"

"I told you before. I found it." Technically, Kiki had discovered it first, but Gideon wanted to keep the child out of this.

Henry wrote a few lines and, as his pen skittered across the paper, Gideon felt the clickety-clack of his own heart in his ears.

"And your truck? Where is it?"

What does my truck have to do with my brother's death? Gideon had seen a few episodes of *The Twilight Zone*, and now he was certain he'd been cast in one of them. "What do you mean?"

"Your truck isn't parked at the auto shop or at your apartment. Where is it?"

Gideon felt it was odd that he was being watched and someone had come up with the fact that his truck was missing. "Moriah took it on Christmas Day."

Henry made a note of that and then without raising his eyes from his paper said, "We'll get back to you, Gideon. Just stick around."

"Where would I go?" asked Gideon. "I hope those antsy people realize that Twin Branches is my home."

"They do."

Gideon knew that some in this small town recognized him as one of their own, but others would never feel that way about him. He was one of those Amish; his roots were not Scots-Irish. He was a transplant; his parents did not believe in electricity to light a home or in telling children stories of Santa Claus. Like those foreign men who had come into the tearoom the other week, he was an outsider.

Gideon could not remember a time he had felt more alone. As he left the station, his mind spun back to when he was seven. Some English boys at the little grocery store in town had teased him about his suspenders and straw hat. They'd called him a freak. At home, he'd cried. His mother had cuddled him for a minute, and then she'd pushed him off her lap.

"You are a strong lad," she'd said, "and this will only make you stronger. The Millers are God-fearing, and those boys will get their justice. Nothing goes unnoticed from God's eyes."

At the time, Gideon had felt reassured, plotting ways that God could borrow from him to show vengeance to those boys. God could zap them with a bolt of lightning in the next storm; he could infest their bedrooms with termites. Mother was right; those boys were going to suffer for what they did. At last, Gideon dried his eyes and was glad that nothing escaped God's vision.

On this evening, he couldn't gauge how he felt. The word *outsider* raced across his brain and lodged in it like the nagging yelp of a dog. He'd always been good at diagnosing his emotions. But now he wasn't sure if he was tired or just sad or hungry or restless. To think that folks here could even think that he'd be the type to pull a gun on his own flesh and blood made his chest constrict. Reaching for the bottle of Tums, he took two. Chewing, he closed his eyes, only to see Moriah . . . Moriah, tall and broad-shouldered, handsome and healthy. How could he have let his brother waste away into a wispy shadow of that creature? Why couldn't he have made him go to rehab, forced him to stop his antics and get clean?

Opening his eyes, he expected to see Moriah seated before him. But there was only an empty chair.

When his cell phone rang, he grabbed it like it was a lifeline, a respite from his heavy thoughts. "Hello." His own voice scared him, sounding dull, foreign.

"Hello," said the female voice on the other end. "I've been thinking about you."

"Mari." Her voice was a soothing lullaby, familiar and serene. He took in a breath and before any other words could form, he let out a sob. And then another.

"I'm on my way over."

"No . . . no . . ." He tried to stop, but his chest was like a heaving wave, pounding out of control.

"Gideon, stay there. I'll be right over." The phone clicked, and he listened to a voluminous wailing that filled all of the spaces in his apartment. Covering his ears, he hoped to block it out until he realized the loud noise was from his very throat.

29

"What if they put me in jail?" Gideon swallowed hard as the severity of the situation hit him. "What if they lock me up?" If only he had a solid alibi for the night of January seventeenth. "Can they do that? Until they find the real killer?"

Mari, seated next to him on the sofa, tried to ease his worries. "They have no proof."

"Are you sure?"

When she arrived at his apartment ten minutes ago, he'd been wiping his face with a dish towel. Although he tried to hide his tears, he knew she knew.

As he thought of Moriah lying cold in the morgue, he choked up again. Turning from her, he stood and walked toward the farthest living-room wall. With his back to her, he said, "Don't look at me." The words sounded like that of a child. Father never allowed him to cry. Especially not in front of a woman. That was weak, uncalled for. "You can't see me cry." It was not only Father's rule that boys and men didn't cry; according to him, neither should women. "We came here from religious oppression," Father was known for saying. "We fought for the freedom of religion so we could openly be Amish. We didn't get here by giving up and crying."

"Gideon." She was at his side.

"No." Abruptly he turned away. "You just can't. Don't."

"Why not?" She resumed her spot on the sofa.

Blinking back tears, he waited a moment, sniffed, wiped his nose with a balled-up tissue he found inside his pants pocket. He had no recollection of how it got there. Did he even own a box of tissues? He wasn't sure.

"Is it . . . ?" She tried again. "Is it because of your dad and the whip?"

Gideon wished she wasn't so good at remembering things. He wondered if he should have ever told her in the first place. After that picnic in November, she'd never mentioned his father to him again. He hoped then that she wouldn't look at him with pity and that she'd eventually forget that he had told her the whole story of the boy and the shed. Now she was bringing it up as though she could see through him, as though she knew more about him than he might even admit to himself.

When he didn't reply, she prompted him. "Gideon . . . ?"

"Tears are a sign of weakness. I hate them." He was relieved when he gained his composure and was able to rejoin her at the sofa.

"Tears show you have heart. There's nothing wrong with them." Gently, she said, "In Japanese, *kokoro* is the word for heart. But it can also translate into spirit, soul, and even mind. Mama told me from the *kokoro* come tears."

Gideon wanted to listen to Mari's explanation, but years of bitterness and hard, fast stubbornness seemed to crowd his desire to change and let tears be all that she claimed they were. He did not want to cry now. He didn't want to show heart because once he did, who knew where it could lead? He could cry and never stop. Besides, if he was headed to jail, this was not the time to suddenly develop the freedom to cry. He needed to construct a heart of steel. Bleakly, he said, "Maybe I deserve jail."

"What?"

"I didn't protect him well. I should have done more."

"Look at me, Gideon."

He met her eyes.

"Trust me," she said softly. "I trust you."

"What do you mean?"

"I know you're innocent."

Am I? He watched shadows, cast by a single lamplight, play across his living room floor as Mari used her hands to emphasize her point. "Am I?" The words came out weak, like a cup of tea that hadn't brewed long enough.

"Of course you are innocent! And if no one else agrees, we'll get you a good lawyer to prove in court that you are."

He appreciated her confidence, her boldness. Still, he doubted. "I wanted him to find another place to live. I wanted him out." And if asked if he was accused of harboring ill thoughts toward his brother, he could not deny that he had.

Mari ran a hand over Gideon's back. "It won't be much longer, Gideon. They'll find who killed him." She leaned her face against his shoulder. "Trust God."

As Kiki rode her bike home from the garage, tears clouded her vision. She hated that every bone of hers was filled with sadness. Dr. Conner told her yesterday that if she was feeling angry, it was best to call him and not to take it out on any wall, teacher, math book, or student at school.

"Make sure you take your medicine now," he'd said before she stood up to leave his office.

For Pete's sake, does he have to remind me like I'm five? Just because Moriah was dead did not mean she was going to forget to take care of herself. In fact, Kiki knew she had to be extra strong now. Gideon certainly needed lots of help. He hadn't even swept out the bays like he always did. He was slipping. She would have to watch him. She sure hoped he got the letter she'd placed on his desk. Before leaving, she'd told Ormond that there was a white envelope for her boss and to make sure he saw it when he got back from whatever he was doing. "It's very important," she'd reminded Ormond a zillion times until he said, "I heard you, Kiki. I might be old, but my ears still work."

When she reached her porch, there was a creaky sound, and as she stepped off her bike, she peered at her house to see what caused it. In the movies, people always said things like, "Hello? Is anyone there?" but as soon as they did that, the killer attacked. Kiki felt her cell phone in her jacket pocket. She'd push the emergency button if she had to.

Just then, from behind one of the plastic chairs, Angie stepped forward.

Relief filled her, it was only Angie! "Oh! You scared me! What are you doing here?" asked Kiki.

"Shh." Angie put a finger to her lips.

"What's going on?"

Kiki rested her bicycle beside the oak tree near a pile of moldy leaves and was about to pull Yoneko from the basket when Angie said, "We need to talk. But inside."

Kiki had tried to talk with Angie many times at school yesterday and today, but the girl had avoided her. At lunch yesterday, Kiki had squeezed in to sit by Angie at one of the round tables in the cafeteria. Kiki complained about how hard that math test was. Angie had barely eaten her bologna sandwich, and Kiki knew Angie loved bologna almost as much as she loved talking about boys. *Fine*, she'd thought. *Be that way. Just when I thought you were my friend, you're acting weird.* And now, Angie was acting weird as well. She wanted to talk, but she was acting jumpy like she had marbles inside her sneakers.

Kiki jiggled the front door until it popped open. Mari used to never lock the doors to the house, but ever since Moriah's death, she'd found the keys and given one to Kiki. Kiki had forgotten to carry the key to school with her today and wondered how she'd get inside the house. Watching criminal shows paid off—she wiggled the doorknob and lifted it a bit until it opened.

Angie stuck behind her as Kiki led the way into her bedroom.

206

She thought Angie might say something about her room, like how drab the paint on the wall was, or how silly it was that the bedspread was a bunch of kittens with pink ribbons. But Angie didn't seem to notice anything about the room at all. She closed the door. Leaning against it, she blurted, "I have something to tell you, but you have to swear you won't tell anyone!"

Certain this was going to be about Robert Jefferson, the kid Angie was always asking to borrow sheets of notebook paper from, Kiki got ready to hear her friend pour from her love-stricken heart. She sat on her bed, drawing her legs up so that her knees were by her face. "What is it?" She tipped her cheek to rest on top of her knee. Depending on what Angie said, she just might tell her that she'd overheard Robert telling Jeremy that he thought Angie was cute. Perhaps, she would.

"You have to promise. Promise?" Angie's voice had an urgency to it.

"Sure."

"Really promise!"

"I said I promise. Sheesh!" Kiki held her breath, hoping it would keep her from saying anything about how annoyed she was right now with Angie. *What is up with this girl?*

Again, Angie nervously scanned the room. "I know how Moriah died."

"What?" Kiki's legs shot out from under her chin.

"I know."

"How?"

"I saw it. I saw who killed him."

"For real?"

"I was at my grandma's house. I couldn't sleep and went into the kitchen to get some milk."

"And...?"

"I heard lots of noises, people talking. I recognized a voice, so I snuck outside."

"You did not! You're afraid of the dark!"

"Shh! I'm not lying."

207

"So what did you see outside?"

"I saw him."

"Who?" Kiki had a feeling that Angie was really going to tell her a secret, so she sat up straight because Mari told her she listened better in that position.

Angie's voice was low. "Reginald. And two other guys."

"Your uncle?"

"It was him."

"Well?" Kiki wondered why Angie couldn't just spit it out. She seemed to have no trouble in school getting to the point. *"Miss Stevenson, Kiki is being annoying!"*

"They were by his car and saying that Moriah was dead. I heard my uncle say that, I really did." Angie drew in a gulp of air and continued. "They talked really quietly and then they argued, and so I heard everything they said. I swear. You have to believe me."

"What did you hear them say?"

"They said that they were going to put his body in the Dumpster at the repair shop." Angie stepped away from the door, as though she no longer needed its support. Now her words came out like water from a pressure washer, freely, unrestrained, and quickly. "They wrapped his body in a quilt. That quilt isn't on my grandma's sofa anymore. I looked for it everywhere, but it's gone."

Kiki's skin burned as though that quilt was now tightly encasing her body. She stood, almost too quickly. *Be careful*, she scolded herself. Now was not the time to faint. She saw Reginald's broad face, looming in her mind like the monster she knew he was. Fear gripped her; she fought to push it aside. "We have to go to see Henry," she said.

"The police, right?" Angie's face was the color of chalk.

"Yes. Sheriff Kingston." Kiki brushed past her, opened the bedroom door. "Come on."

"What will we say?"

"What you just told me. What you saw. Hurry."

Angie seemed unable to move. Kiki pulled at her arm. The tattletale was afraid, Kiki knew this, and it somehow gave her the power she needed to carry through with the plan. Kiki had never felt so scared herself, nor yet so bold, in all her life.

"What do we do?" asked Angie, her breath now hardly audible.

"I already told you. We go to the police." She hoped her words registered to Angie this time so that she'd get that dazed look off her face. To emphasize her point, Kiki added, "That's what people do on TV shows."

At last, Angie found her feet and let them move her out the door, trailing behind Kiki, who wondered where the TV crew was now. This was Kiki's moment, and she was going to be a star.

"Do we ride over there?" asked Angie.

"Yes," said Kiki. "Get your bike."

30

What is taking him so long?" Gideon heard Kiki say just as he entered Henry's office and saw the assembled group. The room was stuffy, like the heating system was overworked and no one knew how to lower the thermostat. He wished he'd brought a bottle of water.

Angie and Kiki sat on straight-back chairs against the wall, their postures erect, their hands in their laps. Standing to Kiki's left was Mari, still in her frilly tearoom apron, her face flushed like she'd run all the way here in the cold.

Henry sat at his desk, a pen in his hand and a finger across his chin. When he saw Gideon, he stood, shook his hand. "Seems we have some more to the story." He motioned to an empty chair, but Gideon declined and kept standing.

"Reginald did it," Kiki blurted, her voice loud. Then she glanced at Henry to make sure her outburst was acceptable.

Gideon searched the sheriff's eyes. "Reginald?"

"Yes," said Kiki. "Angie saw him. She was in the front yard."

Gideon steadied himself.

"They got into a fight. Reginald shot him!" Kiki screamed both sentences before anyone could stop her.

But it seemed that no one was trying to shut her up. Angie was nodding like a bobblehead, and Henry cleared his throat in a raspy way that took a minute. With that out of the way, he said, "The girls came in to tell me what Angie saw take place the other night. They've given their statements." He pointed to sheets of paper in a stack on his desk by his phone.

Gideon slumped into the chair then. Trying to calm his breathing, he was aware of the ticking of the wall clock, the same one that had bothered him when he'd been here to pick up Moriah. "Has he been arrested?"

"We found him at the meth cabin," Henry said in his marbled-voice sort of way.

"Meth cabin?"

"Same one Moriah was involved with. Evidence has come about. The cabin was a small operation, making meth for the locals." Henry put a hand on his belt before pulling up his trousers at the waist, his signature gesture. "Moriah was heavy into meth. That's what we were told. Seems Tamara spent her time at this cabin up on Cove's Peak, too. Reginald didn't like Moriah fooling around with his woman."

"Tamara is Reginald's girlfriend," said Kiki, an attempt to clarify.

The sheriff nodded and continued. "We brought her in for questioning early this morning. She was there when Reginald shot Gideon at the cabin. Now the rest of what happened . . . we dragged Reginald down here. After hours of denial, he admitted that he and two others— Jack Northern and Linwood Michelson—hauled Moriah's body to the repair shop. On the way, they stopped at Reginald's mother's to dig around in the garage and get blankets and towels to wipe up the blood out of the trunk and to wipe away fingerprints."

Gideon thought of all the times he'd warned his brother about Reginald. *Didn't Moriah know that pests like Reginald were not folks he should associate with? They were bad news. But had Moriah listened?* Gideon swallowed; his throat felt dry, like he'd eaten a whole sleeve of

211

saltine crackers. He knew Henry kept bottled water and cans of Pepsi in the little fridge in the adjacent kitchen, but Gideon was at a loss for how to ask for any beverage. Leaning his head forward, he closed his eyes. When he opened them, he hoped to see his brother. Instead, he felt a hand on his back.

Mari stood behind him, her fingers lightly rubbing his shoulder. "Can I get you anything?"

"No, thanks."

"We are going home, Kiki," she said to her sister. To the other girl, she said, "Angie, you are welcome to come over to our house if you would like."

Kiki's face brightened. "Really? She is?" Kiki nudged Angie. "You want to?"

Angie gave a small nod and stood up to go.

"You can put your bicycles in the trunk of my car." Mari's eyes were grave. Even so, she squeezed Gideon's arm and said, "Call me. Anytime."

Gideon watched the three leave. Suddenly, Kiki turned at the door and broke from the group. Toppling onto Gideon's chest, with one arm around his shoulder, she cried, "It will be okay."

Mari told her to hurry along, and with that, the girl obeyed.

Sheriff Henry made his way across the room and sat beside Gideon in the chair Kiki had occupied. "Your truck is at the cabin. You told me Moriah took it, but you never filed a stolen vehicle report, did you?"

Images from Christmas night when Moriah left in his truck sped through Gideon's mind. He hadn't minded not having a vehicle; he preferred to walk, and the town was small enough to get anywhere by foot. "I didn't want to bother you on Christmas day," Gideon said softly. He hoped the sheriff wasn't going to say that if Gideon had reported the vehicle, Moriah might still be alive. He didn't want to hear that, so he changed the subject. "Where is Moriah's body now?"

Henry wiped his brow with a thick crumpled handkerchief he seemed to pull out of thin air. "At the morgue. Do you want to see it?"

"No. No."

"It can be released to you now. The autopsy has been performed. I'll get a copy of that report to you. Do you know where—where—?" Pausing, he shifted in his seat. "Do you have funeral plans?"

Gideon wasn't sure how to answer that question, so he merely shrugged.

Henry coughed into his handkerchief. "The town is in a state of confusion. Reginald was liked. Not sure why, since he was such a hell-raiser at times. But he was born here, raised here."

Gideon groaned. *What was it about belonging? Don't I belong here just as much as Reginald?*

As though reading his mind, Henry explained. "Reginald is the son of Luva Smithfield. You know Luva, don't you?"

"Everyone knows Luva."

"She's a prominent citizen here. Her late husband donated money to every charity in this area. Benches at the local park have his name on them in memory."

Gideon knew where the sheriff was headed with this talk. The Smithfields were the cornerstone of Twin Branches. Reginald was a Smithfield. It was going to be tough to put a member of such a renowned family behind bars for life.

"Everybody likes the Smithfields." Henry drew a deep breath and ran a beefy hand over his chin.

"No," Gideon interjected. "Everyone likes their money."

Henry coughed a few more times and when his throat was cleared, stood. Using both hands, he pulled his pants up at the waist. "Well. Well." After that, he seemed uncertain as to what else to say.

"Justice still prevails, even among the Smithfields, doesn't it?" Gideon searched the sheriff's face.

"Yes, of course. He will be tried by a jury. Just like anybody else would be and is."

Minutes later when Gideon stood to leave his office, Henry bit his lip and then murmured a few lines which Gideon found inaudible. Finally, as he walked Gideon out the door, he looked him in the eye.

"Things really got out of hand up there at that cabin. I wish it could have gone down differently." Fingering his glasses, he added, "Reginald's in custody now. He will have to answer for this."

Gideon guessed he should feel some comfort in knowing that the loud-talking Reginald was off the streets. But he felt none.

His brother was still dead.

Gideon's apartment was cold, damp, and smelled of lost causes. Weary from the day's events, he sat at the kitchen table and thought of the apple orchard and the weeping willow Moriah had enjoyed as a boy. He'd only seen his mother cry twice in her life. Once, when her father died. The other time was when Moriah had been bitten by one of the pigs on the farm. After that, she hated pigs and didn't want to have any.

He drank two glasses of water from the kitchen faucet and then downed another. The ringing phone pierced his thoughts and he debated whether or not to pick up. He was glad that he did; it was Mari.

"I just wanted to make sure you're all right."

"Thanks."

"Henry said that his body has been released."

"I guess so."

"Is it at the funeral home now?"

Was he supposed to call to arrange for this? He rubbed his temple and wondered why death was so complicated. "I think so."

"Kiki and I will be glad to go up to Pennsylvania with you for the funeral."

At her words, Gideon's eyes clouded. "Thank you."

"Have you told your parents?"

"I will."

"They need to know, Gideon."

"I suppose they do."

Tentatively, she asked, "Do you want me to come over there now? I could help you."

He was a Miller. Millers were strong, capable, born with fortitude. "Yes," he murmured. "Yes, please."

Before she arrived, he knew he had to make the inevitable phone call. Seated on the edge of the sofa, he pulled his laptop onto the coffee table. He did a Google search for the church Moriah had mentioned and found the number. Covenant Church in Harrisburg. Maybe now he knew why Moriah had brought it up.

Pastor Nate Mitchell's secretary answered the phone at the third ring. She said the preacher was busy until Gideon cried, "My brother was murdered." After a moment of silence, Gideon had the pastor on the line.

"Hello, Gideon," the pastor said. "My secretary told me your awful news. I am so sorry to hear this. What happened?"

"Moriah was killed. Moriah Miller, my younger brother." Gideon choked back the fear that came from hearing his own voice speak those words.

"I remember Moriah, Gideon. How did this happen?"

"He was twenty-one. He was only twenty-one—" Suddenly, Gideon halted, as though he couldn't form any more words. Although he opened his mouth, his vocal cords would not produce a sound.

"I'm so sorry to hear this. That is young."

Gideon, sapped of energy, sat speechless. This was embarrassing.

"What would you like me to do?" Nate's voice gently asked.

"His wish was to be buried on our farm in Carlisle. It's there, east of Carlisle, just before you get to . . ." Gideon's mind went blank. The names for all of the old landmarks escaped him today. Finally, "Could you perform the service?" He hoped the pastor wouldn't shoot off a bunch of questions, beginning with, "Why do you want me to conduct a funeral for an Amish man? Wouldn't an Amish bishop be the one to do that?" Gideon didn't want to have to explain that since Moriah had broken from the community, he doubted a bishop would be willing.

Pastor Nate only asked, "Are you in Carlisle now?"

"Moriah and I are in North Carolina. But I'll be in Carlisle soon."

"Which funeral home will you be using? Do you want to have the service at our church?"

"No. Just a graveside service. That's all." Gideon did not see the need for a formal service inside a building like the English held. Perhaps his Amish roots weren't so far from him after all. "He wanted to be buried on our property," he repeated. "At the orchard." In his mind, Gideon saw the rows of fourteen graves on the grassy spot to the left of the orchard. By now, he was certain more graves had been added to the number.

"Okay. I'll be glad to do that."

"Thank you. It will probably be about a week from now." Gideon knew if he could, he would prolong the service till next year. "I was thinking at two." He hoped he wasn't being too demanding, so to soften his words he added, "If that works for you."

"Which day would you like the funeral to take place?"

Gideon felt silly. He'd been so adamant about having the service around two when the day might be warmer, that he'd neglected to suggest a day first. "Uh, well, what day is today?"

"Today is Thursday."

"Saturday?" Didn't people have funerals on Saturdays? Would that be enough time for the local funeral home to prepare the body? Thoughts collided through his mind. He wished there was some manual on what he was expected to do. Of course, he had to buy a coffin. The reality of that hit him hard. What kind of coffins did the Smithfield Funeral Home sell? *Reginald Smithfield killed my brother. He supplied the bullet; his family should supply the coffin.*

"Which Saturday? This one?"

"Yes. No. No." He rose to check the calendar on his wall. "The Saturday after this one."

"Saturday, the second of February at two," said the pastor. "I'm making a note of that. When will you be arriving? If you could stop by and see me before the service, we can go over any last-minute details."

Gideon felt the weight of the day pressing over his shoulders. "I'll call you when we get into town."

With those arrangements taken care of, Gideon knew he had one more phone call to make. Mari had insisted that he call his parents. While many Amish had phones in their barns—well apart from their living quarters—he knew his father would own no such *device of the devil*. With the help of the Internet, he found the number to the furniture store just two miles from their farm. He punched in the area code and then stopped. He needed a glass of water first.

He noted the time on the kitchen clock and wondered where Mari was. She'd said she'd be right over, or had she? Perhaps she had to make dinner for Kiki first. Suddenly, panic seared his skin. What if something had happened to her? What if she had been in an accident? Gripping the side of the sink, he tried to push aside his mounting fear. "God," he said, "I promise to never be selfish again. I will be nicer to everyone and I won't get so angry about everything. I'll go to church. I'll cut back on those Twix bars. Just don't let anything happen to her." *Silly*, he scolded himself. *You have never been one to bargain with God.* He felt low, embarrassed, grateful that no one but God had heard his prayer.

He wondered if the furniture store was still open at five-fifteen on a Wednesday. He forgot the hours Joseph Swartz kept. But the old man's voice was still the same when he answered the phone.

"Gideon Miller! You have blessed me today. How good to hear from you."

His tone changed when Gideon asked if Mr. Swartz would tell his parents about the funeral.

"Moriah? Young Moriah Miller?"

"Yes," breathed Gideon and as he admitted it, once again he had a hard time believing it himself.

"He's dead?" Mr. Swartz's accented voice had a faraway tone to it.

"He was murdered."

"Murdered?"

Gideon wished he hadn't provided the manner in which Moriah died. It wasn't any of Mr. Swartz's business.

"I will let your parents know. I'll go over there right now."

Gideon didn't want to trouble the old gentleman. He looked out the window and knew that if it was dark in Twin Branches, it was even darker in a region where electricity was scarce. "It can wait till morning."

"No, no," said Mr. Swartz. "Not this, son. This is something you can't wait till morning to tell parents."

31

Mari was a lifesaver. When he saw her standing at his door, he quelled the urge to wrap his arms around her and do what he had only done so far in his dreams—plant a kiss on her beautiful lips. The very thought of kissing her brought him joy. Quickly, he brushed aside his emotions. Moriah was dead. How could he feel anything but sadness right now?

"Sorry I'm late. Kiki had math troubles."

He took her coat and led her to the living room sofa. "You should have brought her along," he said as they sat down.

She shook her head. "I had to bribe her to stay put and do her homework."

"What did you bribe her with?"

"A pizza from Dominoes. They were slow in delivering it. That's why it took me so long to get here."

"I'm just glad you're here. Have you eaten?"

"Don't worry about me. How about you?"

He tried to remember if he had eaten today. "I think I had something earlier."

"I want you to come to the tearoom and eat tomorrow. The meal will be on me."

"Thank you." He lowered his eyes from her face to his nails. It had been days since he'd worked on a car and yet the skin on his fingertips still held that mechanic's perpetual mark of grease. Moriah had said no woman would want a man with so much grime. Yet Moriah had been terribly dirty, and Tamara, for whatever reason, was attracted to him. "He took Reginald's girlfriend. Why?"

"She must have liked him. She had a choice and she chose him over Reginald."

"And because of that, everyone is against Moriah."

"No one blames Moriah," she said gently.

"They don't think Reginald's at fault either," said Gideon.

"I think they do. He killed Moriah. The evidence is there."

"Have they really proved that it was Reginald's gun that killed him?"

"Angie saw him from the front yard and overheard him and the other two talk about getting rid of a body. You were there when she told Henry that."

He had been there, and yet, he wondered if the verdict would stick. Reginald was a Smithfield, one of Luva's children. What if she bribed Henry to make it look like Moriah was at fault. Gideon leaned against the back of the sofa and let his eyes close.

"You need sleep."

He forced his eyes opened. "No, no. I want to hear you tell me what happened. Again."

"Okay. This is what I know. Tamara admits that both Reginald and Moriah were at the cabin where the meth lab was. She said there was an argument over her. Moriah stood up to Reginald, claiming that he was dating Tamara and that Reginald needed to get out of the cabin. Reginald told him to get lost. Moriah—much too high from meth, accord-

220

ing to Tamara—punched Reginald in the jaw. Reginald hit him back, called him a bunch of derogatory names. There was a big fight, and then Reginald just pulled his gun out of his back pocket and shot Moriah in the chest. Tamara is a witness, and two others who were at the cabin said pretty much the same thing. Reginald's been brought in and he confessed he killed Moriah."

Gideon felt the heat rise in his face. "But they think Moriah deserved it. You know, he was with Reginald's girlfriend."

"I don't think so at all. Deep down they know Reginald let his temper get the best of him. He's guilty. They've all seen how he can be. It's just hard because at one point, Reginald was well thought of."

"Why?" Gideon had never seen any good in the loud man who flung around racial slurs.

"Well, he's one of them. He's raised here. I told you that before."

"Are you getting exasperated, Mari?"

"What do you mean?"

"You've had to repeat yourself a lot over the last few days."

"That's okay. I know your brain has to be fuzzy."

He sighed. *Yes, it was.* His brain seemed to be covered with a heavy morning fog similar to the kind that shadowed mountain peaks.

Hours later, when he laid down to rest his eyes, he finally fell into a deep sleep. In his dreams, Moriah was alive, healthy, whole.

When Angie Smithfield's father told him that there was such a thing as a particle board coffin, Gideon said he'd take it. The coffin weighed sixty pounds when empty and was held together with hinges and a plastic clasp. The inside was laid with a blue cotton cloth, not silk or satin. A coffin like this was more like what he'd seen used on the farm to bury family members. Nothing fancy, nothing ornate. A plain box for plain people. This coffin resonated with him, with those roots he thought he had long buried.

On Friday morning, before the sun had a chance to peek over the Smoky Mountains, they set out. Seated in a black hearse, rented from Angie's parents' funeral home, Kiki, Mari, and Gideon headed to Carlisle, Pennsylvania.

As Kiki said, "A promise is a promise." That weeping willow was calling Moriah's name.

Mari had asked Amos and Della to run the tearoom for a few days, and willingly they agreed they could handle the job. When Gideon asked Ormond if he could have some time off, Ormond said, "Well, it's about time you realize you need to take a break from the shop. Of course!" Then he handed Gideon some folded bills. "For gas and food and whatever else you need," he said. Lifting his arms to encircle Gideon, he gave him a tight hug and muttered into his shoulder, "I hate this for you. Hurry back."

When Gideon counted the bills, the total came to eight hundred dollars.

As planned, Mari had picked up the hearse last evening and parked it in front of her house. In the morning, she drove to Gideon's apartment complex to pick him up. Gideon opened the door to the black shiny vehicle as Kiki greeted him from the backseat, her left hand holding Yoneko. "Good morning. Hurry inside. It's cold."

Formal drapes made from a tan velvet-like material hung in arches around the back windows of the hearse, reminding Gideon of old movie theater décor. The words to an obscure children's song sprang into his thoughts. *Did you ever think when a hearse goes by that you might be the next to die?*

Mari said, "We put our bags in the back. You can open it."

Gideon walked to the rear of the hearse and opened the back. He tried to avoid looking at the coffin that was lying on the right side. Seeing Kiki and Mari's luggage, he placed his duffel bag by them. He had a sudden image of that bag. He'd carried his things inside it the last time he'd been in Pennsylvania. That had been fifteen years ago when he was determined to leave his life there . . . for good.

222

Gideon shut the door to the back of the vehicle and made his way to the passenger seat. "I never realized hearses have backseats," he said.

"They usually don't," said Mari, the streetlights casting their orange glow to her face. "I asked for this one. It's a little longer than the other two the Smithfields have. Angie's mom said it is a one-of-a-kind vehicle."

Kiki waved a box of blackberry Nutri-Grain bars at Gideon, asking if he'd like one. "They're blackberry, which is your favorite, right?"

Gideon said, "No, thanks." His stomach was queasy, and the thought of a sweet fruit bar was not enticing to him right now.

Mari waited for him to put on his seat belt. As she pulled away from his apartment, he wished it was any other day. He remembered the day he got his wisdom teeth out, just two months after his nineteenth birthday. The pain had been agonizing once the Novocain wore off. He'd take that day again, over today.

"This car is cool," said Kiki as she pressed a button to lower her window. "And Moriah is in the very back. Did you see the coffin, Gideon?"

"Yes."

"He's riding with us." She pressed the button to close the window and then stretched out on the backseat. "Did you see him?"

"Kiki, that's enough." Mari's voice was stern.

"I'm just asking a question. Sheesh!" With that she curled into a ball, cuddling Yoneko. She'd brought a light blanket, and she pulled it over herself, muttering until she got it the way she wanted it.

"She doesn't get out much," Mari said. "She's a bit excited about the trip."

It's not every day you get to ride in a hearse, thought Gideon. *I suppose that could constitute a reason for being excited.* In Carlisle, when a horse-drawn carriage with a pine coffin in the back rode by, he never knew how to feel. Other children must have had trouble knowing how to react as well, and many decided that a silly rhyme was the best way to express the morbidity of the moment. As he thought of black carriages and a world that had been removed from him for over a decade, the words to the children's song rehearsed themselves through his mind.

Did you ever think when a hearse goes by that you might be the next to die? And the worms crawl in and the worms crawl out . . . He'd belted that song out once after first learning it, and his mother, appalled, asked where he'd heard it. "From the English, of course," said Father, not waiting for Gideon to explain. For Father, the English represented all that was uncouth. The truth was, Gideon had heard it from Esther, his older sister. But he knew better than to squeal on her.

Leaning back in the passenger seat, Gideon closed his eyes as the heat from the vent flowed throughout the vehicle. He tried to block out all thoughts and just concentrate on the lull of the car's engine. Yet his mind went back, way back, to the writing course he had taken at the community college. He had written about the lyrics to the ditty and about his father's reaction. The assignment had been to write about a memory of a song from childhood and the one about the worms crawling in and out had been his choice. "My sister liked poetry," he'd written. "She had an ear for picking up lyrics. One day, when in town on family business, a hearse rolled by and two young boys started to chant. Later I guess she felt safe sharing the song with me. From early on, she knew I could keep my mouth shut, and so I was often privy to things she said she would never tell our parents." At the time he wrote the piece, recalling his relationship with Esther had made him nostalgic, but he brushed that away and instead thought of his father. The image of the man always kept him from the feel-good memories of hearth and home.

By six-thirty, the first ray of sunlight lit the highway. Hours later, he watched the sky turn dark with clouds and felt that the sky mirrored his mood. The hearse rose and fell on the road as one mile turned into hundreds and questions circled through his mind. *How could I have let it come to this? What am I going to do the rest of my life, knowing I was not able to stop my brother from his demise? How can Moriah be dead?*

Each time Mari stopped for a bathroom break or to get juice so Kiki could take her meds, Gideon wanted to believe that the three of them were just headed on a little trip together. Happy and having fun, just like other people did. Perhaps when they passed a McDonald's he'd buy them all milkshakes. Or a slice of apple pie. Then they could slurp and laugh and play a game like finding license plates from each state. Mari sang in the choir; maybe she could sing one of her favorite hymns.

But each time he stepped back into the hearse, he knew he couldn't escape the truth. He was going home to bury his brother.

And he kept reminding himself that he'd never planned on going back home. Ever.

32

At the BP station where he pumped gas into the hearse, he saw his first windmill towering to the left of a nearby winding road. As he strained his eyes, he saw a white barn. The scene flooded his senses with emotion—his thoughts raced back to what seemed like yesterday. He recalled the birth of Moriah as he had huddled animatedly with his sisters, waiting to hear whether Mother had delivered a girl or a boy. He'd prayed for a boy. Three sisters were enough.

He jumped when he felt a hand on his arm.

Mari was unmoved by his reaction. Like a pillar of strength, like the courage that he needed, she stood beside him. Her hand stayed on his arm, warm in spite of the breeze that had picked up and was ruffling his hair.

"Need anything?" she asked.

He shook his head, swallowing the lump that had lodged into his throat.

"I'm getting some coffee. Want me to see if they have green tea?"

He wondered if he'd ever be able to drink a cup of green tea at Another Cup again, if he'd ever laugh again with Mari. He wondered if he'd be able to get through another Christmas without thinking about the gift Moriah gave him when Gideon was eleven. Moriah had wrapped a piece of wood in a handkerchief. The wood was to be used to build a pirate ship.

It was at the BP station that he looked through the backseat window and saw the day's edition of the *Twin Star*. Mari watched as he opened the door, bent over, picked up the paper, and then placed it back on the floor by Kiki's discarded green-laced shoes. Kiki, wrapped in her blanket, didn't notice; she just continued to sleep and snore.

"You should read it," Mari encouraged.

"Is there anything in there about Moriah?" He didn't want to read about how Reginald and two others were involved in his brother's death. Whoever had written that article from a few days ago had gotten so many of the facts wrong; they'd made it sound like Moriah was such a lowlife that his death was welcomed, even justified.

Mari gingerly took his hand. "It's okay. The piece is a good one. Ashlyn wrote it."

Gideon knew that Luke thought the world of Ashlyn, but she was the sheriff's daughter, and Gideon wondered if she was influenced by her father and what he said about the town's politics and ideology around the dining room table. Part of Gideon still felt that the majority of the town wanted to believe that he, Gideon Miller of Carlisle, Pennsylvania, was guilty of Moriah's death.

Mari handed him the paper, but he brushed it away. "I can't. Not today."

"Well, it's here when you are ready." Folding it, she put it by her sister's shoes and shut the door.

It was five when Mari drove slowly past the Welcome to Carlisle sign. He asked her to stop and when she did, he scrambled out of the car, stood to the side of it, and waited. He could taste the sour juices of his stomach inside his mouth. Clutching the top of the hearse, he waited some more, hoping that the late-afternoon wind would calm his nerves. The muscles in his torso contracted, the pressure sharp throughout his abdomen. He exhaled slowly, his knuckles white and rigid.

Nothing seemed to help. No amount of breathing in and out or even casting an eye toward the sky relieved him of his pain or the face that kept plaguing his vision. He saw his father's face, anger lining each surface. He couldn't do it. There was no way he could face his father after this. "Let's leave. Let's get out of here!" he said to Mari as he stumbled back to his seat.

"Leave? We can't." With empathy in her eyes, she said evenly, "We are supposed to be here, Gideon. This land, this town, it's yours as much as it is anyone's. Moriah wants to rest here."

He shivered and drew a breath. He was glad that Kiki was still asleep in the back. He watched her curled body, covered in her coat, the blanket slipping to the floor. Her head rested against a pillow; her puppet-cat peeked out near her face, like a guard on duty. Although she was sleeping, he knew just what she'd say to him had she been awake. "You have an obligation." She would add, "Moriah trusted that you would bury him by that tree. You have to."

Have to. Have to. He let the two words rumble inside his head.

"Close the door," Mari said and when he finally, reluctantly did, she said quickly, "We've got to find the hotel." She'd made the reservations, again taking over because he could not make the phone call to book the two rooms. Ever since he'd found the body in the Dumpster, he'd had trouble making decisions. It was as though his brain had turned to sand. Mari was the one who borrowed the GPS from Della so that the trip here could be without error.

With her eyes ahead and obeying the directions of the voice on the GPS, Mari drove. Her jaw was set, and although she didn't speak, Gideon felt she must be disgusted with his antics.

At last he said, "I'm sorry."

"For what?"

"Being difficult."

228

A moment later she said with conviction, "I'm so glad he's in jail." He guessed she'd been thinking about Reginald.

Kiki stirred and asked, "Are we there yet?" Her voice was sleepy, but once roused, she looked out the window and cried, "This must be it! This is it! It looks just like the picture."

"What picture?" asked Gideon.

"The one Moriah showed me. He showed me one like this with pastures and the mountains way in the background." With her nose against the windowpane, she cried, "Oh, wow! Hey, there's one of those buggies."

On a side street stood a black buggy with a gray horse. The horse had one charcoal ear. Gideon thought he knew that horse; it belonged to the Benders. He turned away and placed a hand over his face. He didn't want to be recognized, not now, not yet. Lowering his hand, he felt silly. The Bender horse with the gray ear had been ten years old back when Gideon was a boy. There was no way that this could be that same horse now, so many years later.

A white sedan pulled beside the buggy and a camera snapped a photo from the opened window.

Tourists, thought Gideon. *Just like in Twin Branches, always wanting to catch the local scenes and townsfolk for their photo albums.*

As the car sped away, a memory of Moriah flashed into his mind. Moriah in the high chair with his fist grasping a piece of apple-buttered toast. And he was laughing because Moriah was a happy toddler. Mother had said, "If only every baby was as sweet as Moriah." Now her sweet boy was dead.

He steadied himself, closed his eyes and didn't open them until Mari said, "This is it. The Old Carlisle Country Inn."

"Do they have a pool?" asked Kiki.

Mari slipped the hearse into a parking space. "It's much too cold to go swimming."

"An inside pool," said Kiki. "Do they have one?" She was looking at Gideon; he guessed she assumed he would know.

Choking back emotion, Gideon said, "No, Kiki. No pool, no room service, none of what you see on TV. This is a quaint inn and it comes with a bed." He hoped the owners wouldn't recognize him. When he'd lived in Carlisle, the place had been run by a couple by the name of Guttenberg. From the old country, they spoke English with guttural accents.

"Ah, they had a pool at the hotel where Mari and I stayed in Asheville when we went to see Mama at Christmas. But it was outside. What good did that do? What good was that?"

Mari opened the rear of the hearse and removed all three of their bags. "We aren't here to swim," she said to her sister as Kiki exited the hearse. She patted Moriah's coffin. "We'll be back soon," she said, as though talking to a child.

Gideon ambled to her side. For a moment he thought of telling the others to go inside the inn before him. He hadn't seen Moriah in the coffin, and perhaps he needed to look at him one last time and pay his respects. Isn't that what people said, *I came to pay my respects.*

Seeing his sad expression, Mari tried to console him. "It will be okay."

Taking the bags from her hands, he nodded. Somehow, some way, he wanted so much to believe her.

33

The inn held three floors, a lobby with a bushy Christmas tree, and one elevator. Kiki made a comment that Christmas had ended over a month ago and wondered why the tree was still up. Mari told her to lower her voice.

The woman at the front desk was short and had graying hair. Gideon waited for her to speak, tugging his John Deere cap over his head, hoping she would not know who he was.

Her accent was not German and, relieved, he relaxed his shoulders. He wouldn't have to worry about being recognized and having to make small talk.

Mari checked them in as Kiki observed the large Broken Star quilt hanging on the powder-blue wall to the left of the front door. Sure enough, Kiki asked Gideon about the quilt, what it was used for, and why it was on the wall.

Gideon gave a short response. He knew she didn't care to know all he did about quilts and quilting. Mother and his sister Esther were excellent quilters, so he'd grown up being privy to all the patterns. He'd even cut a few squares for the Stars Log Cabin design one winter. Helping Esther had been a nice change from his usual task of collecting eggs from their seventeen hens and milking the twenty Jersey cows.

Mari conversed with the woman at the check-in desk. Gideon admired her for making the effort to be chatty and interested in all the woman had to say about the region. When she handed Mari the keys to their two rooms, Mari thanked her and, taking the opportunity, quickly moved away from the desk.

"Hungry?" Mari then asked him as Gideon watched the tree lights twinkling on and off.

He felt he could just stand there all evening, as though he was in some sort of stupor.

When he said nothing, she repeated, "Are you hungry?"

"I am!" Kiki grinned at them. "Where do we eat?"

"Sure," said Gideon, moving from the tree, trying to move from that gift of the wood Moriah had given him back when the kid had been just four. *What did I do with that block of wood?* He tried to think back to that time, but it was so long ago, back when he himself was just a boy wanting to leave the farm, and yet uncertain how to do it.

"Hey," Kiki was nudging him, her fingers jabbing at his hands like woodpeckers do to the trunks of pines.

Gideon forced himself back to the present. "We can get something to eat."

W hat is it?" Mari asked after they'd taken the elevator up to the second floor, found their adjoining rooms, and Kiki had run about both of them, claiming she loved being in hotels. "I know you'd rather not be here in Carlisle, but Gideon, come on, don't be so silent."

Staring out the window into a dark night, he let the numbness of the past week take over. He hadn't been aware that he'd been silent, as she put it. The noise in his head was so loud, he couldn't believe she couldn't hear it. He wished for silence.

Mari observed the view from the window as the streetlamps glowed against the buildings. "This is a cute town. How far is your house from here?"

"Seven miles east," he said. "Once you get out of the city limits, you'll see farmland." He could curl up and sleep, as Kiki had. Perhaps he shouldn't bother with dinner.

But Kiki was at his jacket sleeve, tugging on it like a small child. "Come on, Gideon, let's go get some grub."

He did have the wherewithal to guide them to a small restaurant on the edge of town, hopeful that it would be fairly vacant and void of anyone he might know. The place was the Daily Bread Diner, and although he'd never eaten at it, he'd passed it when riding in a buggy on the way to the Yoder farm to deliver cartons of eggs. The diner's sign was painted to look like a pinwheel, with narrow strips of light blue, metallic green, and sunflower yellow painted from the center. In the middle of the narrow strips was an orange dot and the words on it were "Best chicken and biscuits in the whole world."

Inside the dimly lit restaurant, a waitress showed them to a booth. Kiki said she wanted macaroni until she saw that the menu didn't have it listed. Mari said she should try the chicken and biscuits and she agreed she would. Gideon ordered toast with apple butter. He was glad that no one commented on his small selection.

Mari tried to make conversation, and he was appreciative of her attempts. She noted the décor on the wall, two identical photos of a lopsided black buggy and one of a loaf of bread in a wicker basket. On the bread photo was the caption, "Give us our daily bread."

Kiki yawned and said that once she finished eating, she wanted to go to bed. "Which bed do you want?" she asked her sister. "The one by the door or the window?"

"It doesn't matter."

"Great! I want the one by the window. I want to see the sun come up over the mountains." Slurping her Coke, her mood changed to pensive. "When do we bury Moriah? Do we really have to stand outside? It's cold here. It's like, going to snow."

233

Gideon thought of the phone call he'd received nights ago regarding the burial. "A friend from here called me," he said. "Jeremiah heard about Moriah and called the auto shop. I wasn't there, so Ormond took a message."

From the looks on both Mari's and Kiki's faces, Gideon could tell that he had yet to tell them about this incident. These days he had a hard time being aware of what he said and what he thought he'd said.

"How'd he get the number?" asked Kiki.

"Oh, you know, it's painted on every fencepost."

"I know why! You're famous. You help people when they want to try another kind of life."

"What did Jeremiah say?" Mari asked, after telling Kiki she needed to sit up and stop slurping.

"He said he and some others would be by to dig the grave. He said not to worry about that." Sheepishly, Gideon said, "I hadn't been worried. I hadn't thought that far ahead."

Their orders arrived shortly after that, the waitress carefully placing their meals in front of each of them.

The apple butter was tasty. Gideon dipped his finger in the little dish that came with his plate of toast and was pleased. Then he spread it lavishly onto the three pieces of toast and took a bite.

Kiki dug into her chicken, using both a knife and fork. "Watch me eat with my best manners," she said.

Mari simply sipped from her water glass.

"You must be exhausted," he said, realizing that she had driven most of the way.

"A little. What time do we need to be up tomorrow?"

Gideon hoped tomorrow never came. He knew he needed to call the pastor of Covenant Church in Harrisburg just to make sure he was still able to come to Carlisle to perform the funeral. And if he'd forgotten? What would it matter?

"I want to buy some flowers," said Mari after taking a bite of food and chewing it. "Who sells them around here?"

Gideon realized he'd never purchased flowers here. Growing up, Mother had a small garden where she grew daisies in the spring, roses in the summer, and chrysanthemums in the early autumn. Whenever his family wanted flowers, they just picked out of the garden. "I think there's a florist a few miles from here."

Kiki wanted to order dessert, saying the apple pie looked good, but Mari told her that they needed to get back to the hotel.

Gideon shot Mari a grateful smile, and with that, she asked the waitress for the check.

Gideon took bills from his wallet and laid them on the table. Mari folded them and handed them back. He protested, but she said, "My treat tonight." He read her eyes, certain they spoke the words: *Let me help you because I want to do all I can under these circumstances.*

Gideon wanted to say that she already had helped immensely, that her presence during the trip up here was more than he could ask for, more than he deserved. But his mouth felt rubbery and so instead, he just said, "I appreciate it."

At the inn, Kiki and Mari headed toward the elevator. Gideon said he'd sit on the sofa in the lobby for a minute and make a phone call. But once they'd left, he couldn't recall the pastor's name. He searched his cell phone for recently made calls. Finding a Pennsylvania area code in front of a set of numbers, he decided that one must be it and hit dial.

He had just disconnected when Mari pulled up a chair beside him. He smiled wearily at her. "Hey."

"How are you?" she asked.

He rubbed the back of his neck. "Okay, I guess. Is Kiki tucked in?"

"Already asleep. And you? Aren't you going to your room?" Her voice was laced with concern and for that, he was grateful. He wanted to thank her for all she'd done, but he felt so unworthy at the moment. Difficult. He knew he was not the easiest person to deal with even during normal circumstances. Moriah had told him more than once to chill and not be so worried about cleaning and working so hard all the time.

Gideon put his phone into his shirt pocket. "Soon. I just can't seem to turn off my mind."

"It seems surreal."

"It does."

"I've wanted to come to Amish country, but not like this." He was aware of her hand reaching over to rest on his.

"I never wanted to return," he confessed.

"Did you get to talk to Pastor Nate?" She removed her hand, but the warmth from it lingered.

"Once I recalled that was his name." He grinned and then leaned back into the fabric of the sofa. "He wants me to stop by his office first thing tomorrow. I hope it doesn't rain."

"Rain? Is it predicted? I think it's cold enough to snow."

"No, but it always rains during graveside services in movies. You know, they all stand with black umbrellas as the minister says something about ashes to ashes—"

"Good night," she said.

He wondered why she interrupted him; it was not like her.

Gently she whispered, "You need sleep, Gideon. I could talk all night, but I think it's best we get some rest."

Gideon swallowed, noting the tightness in his chest had not decreased, but had, in fact, expanded into his shoulders. He wasn't ready to rest quite yet. In addition to coming back to Pennsylvania, something else was troubling him. "Do you think that it would be okay if I opened the coffin and looked at him?" He didn't tell her that he'd almost pushed the lid back when they first arrived at the inn. He didn't admit that he had been contemplating this and trying to muster the courage. "Is that an acceptable thing to do?"

"Of course, if you want."

"I might go do that then."

"You should sleep first. You can view his body in the morning."

"Did they clean him up well?" He hoped the Smithfield Funeral

Home had done a thorough job of making Moriah's body look like the cleaned-up corpses in the movies.

"They made him look attractive. Morticians are great at fixing people up. He's not like when you saw him in the Dumpster. He's handsome."

"Handsome." Yes, Moriah had been the one with the good looks and now what did it matter? His good looks had not been able to save him from Reginald's bullet. Perhaps he should just take Mari's word for it and call it a night. He rubbed a throbbing neck with fingers that felt numb. Or should he actually go outside and open the hearse to take one last look at Moriah? Would he regret it if he never touched his brother's face and said goodbye in that fashion?

"Good night." This time when Mari spoke the words, she stood and made her way to the elevator. When he did not move, she asked, "You coming?"

He rose, made his way to her side.

She pushed the button for the elevator. "I'm glad you got up. If not, I was going to ask the lady at the front desk to drag you to your room."

He looked over at the lady at the desk, a short, thin, frail-looking creature with a ponytail. "It's good I stood up. I don't think she'd be much help."

Mari snickered and covered her mouth. When the elevator door creaked open, she made sure Gideon entered first.

As they rode up, he saw an image of Moriah. Moriah, as a child, climbing the apple tree, making his way up to branches that seemed to float into the sky. Where was he now? Heaven? Hell?

The hotel room's double bed was lumpy. The sheets smelled of bleach and scratched his skin. He turned to his left and then his right, pulling the blankets over his shoulders. Closing his eyes, he tried to black out this day, wanting again to pretend that he was on a trip somewhere fun. As he listened to the hiss of the central heat blowing through the air vent above his head, he relived the horrible afternoon when Tomlin had driven him up to the cabin near the cove on the Tennessee border.

The rustic cabin was isolated in a dense forest, its frame cracking at the foundation. Inside, a table crammed with glass bottles, pans, pots, and burners sat in the middle of a room. Cartons of bleach, lye, and cough medication filled a tabletop. The cabin had a foul odor, and Gideon had covered his nose several times. Tomlin told him how law enforcement, borrowing police from a neighboring county, had burst into the lab shortly after Tamara confessed that she'd been there and witnessed Reginald shoot Moriah.

The horror from that afternoon suffocated him. Gideon sat up and concentrated on breathing before lying down again. The digital clock showed 11:25. Why was it that every muscle ached, but his eyes would not close? He moved his pillow closer to the headboard and then back to the center of the bed. The pillow was the problem, he concluded, so to make it more voluminous, he stacked two on top of each other and tried again. Staring at the ceiling, he wondered why he let Kiki and Mari persuade him to make this trip. What if he'd put his foot down, as Father always had? Pushing his father's voice out of his mind, he turned over. It was now 11:42. Was this how this night was going to be, each minute falling into the past, as he lay restless?

If he could stop time, stop tomorrow from ever coming . . . Then he'd never have to bury Moriah. It would always be this day, the day before the funeral. He recalled the first movie he'd ever seen in a movie theater. *Groundhog Day*, starring Bill Murray, had played at the discount theater on Fifth Street. Gideon had entered the theater alone that evening, found a seat, and then left to buy a bucket of buttered popcorn. Something reminded him that a movie at a theater had to be enjoyed with popcorn. It was, after all, the American Way. Back in the theater with his popcorn, Gideon tried to relax. God was not going to zap him for going to see a movie.

He thought of the movie now. Until Bill's character got the day's actions right, he kept having to repeat the same day over and over. Yet, though tedious, Bill continued to live over the same twenty-four hours until he changed into someone who was much more likeable to those around him.

If only real life had second, third, and sixth chances. If only real life were a movie with scenes that could be cut and re-created.

34

The sun shone across the acres of fields like a beacon, illuminating the rustic barns with their matching silos, two-story homes, and white fences. The air was cool, yet refreshing, with only a light wind. If it weren't the day of the funeral, Gideon would have called it great weather, a day for a picnic by the stream, a hike in the woods, a perfect day to climb trees like he had as a kid. But today was the day he was to bury his brother, and he wasn't sure it was appropriate to comment on the unseasonably good weather when one was in mourning.

The inn's airy breakfast room was decorated in wicker baskets, prints of buggies, and quilts. A tempting buffet of cinnamon buns, chipped beef over toast, scrambled eggs, bacon, a variety of juices, and coffee and tea beckoned them in.

Kiki was delighted, going back for seconds and thirds.

"Look at it this way," said Mari as Kiki downed a slice of bacon and then stood to refill her plate. "We won't have to feed her again until much later today." She stirred a Styrofoam cup of coffee and added some creamer from a white packet.

Gideon wanted to smile but couldn't. He even wanted to laugh because Kiki was stacking her plate with three cinnamon buns and balancing a cup of orange juice in the other hand.

"I love this breakfast!" she cried after she made it safely to their table. "I'm sad about Moriah. Really, really sad." Picking up a bun she asked, "But is it okay to want to eat, too?"

Gideon finally managed a smile. "Yes," he said. "It's okay."

When Mari handed him a cup of hot tea, he thanked her, but only stared at the contents.

"Drink," she encouraged. "It's okay to drink."

Kiki said, "Hey, Gideon, when you come to my school, don't tell them how much I eat, okay? Kids already make fun of me enough."

"When am I coming to your school?" he asked, his eyes focusing on the framed picture on the wall. He thought of going over to straighten it; it was lopsided. In his apartment, he only had two framed pictures on the wall, but he was constantly making sure they hung straight.

"For Role Model Day." Kiki chewed on a generous strip of bacon.

"What's that?" asked Mari.

"I told you. Sheesh!"

Gideon looked at Kiki, the crooked picture no longer holding his attention. "Did you tell me?" he asked.

"I gave you an invitation. I put it on your desk!" Kiki was getting agitated, and he wondered why.

"An invitation to what?" Gideon's eyes went back to the picture. The simple scene of a gray barn beneath an azure sky was pulling him in. He studied two bulky cows standing to the left of a barbed-wire fence. Now Gideon knew why the painting was riveting to him. The boy painted on a swing by the fence looked like Moriah as a child.

Kiki took two more bites from her bacon, began to say something more, saw her sister's disapproving look, and decided to chew a few more times. Finally, with her mouth free of food, she cried, "The invitation is to Role Model Day. I invited you, so you have to come. You have to . . . *have to*. I get to tell everyone why you are my role model."

Mari smiled. "Wow, Gideon. What an honor."

Gideon tried to shrug it off. "I don't think you need me there," he said. He certainly wasn't anyone for a kid to look up to.

"I do!" cried the girl. "Lots of people will be there. I picked you."

He saw her smile, happy, delighted even, that she had chosen him to come to her school for a function. He started to protest, but she interrupted.

"And besides, I already told Mr. Lincoln you were coming. When you tell my teacher something, then you have to do it." She downed a glass of orange juice, wiped her mouth. "At least he's not as bad as Mrs. Bloodhound."

"Mrs. Bloodhound?" Gideon asked.

Mari let a light laugh escape. "That's the name Kiki's given to the social worker who comes in to check on us every month. Kiki calls her Bloodhound because—"

"She can sniff out anything." Kiki grinned. "She's like Santa Claus."

"Santa Claus?" Gideon let his puzzlement show.

"She knows if you've been bad or good. 'Course, I'm always good, aren't I? Aren't I?" Kiki nudged her sister with a bony elbow.

Before Mari could reply, a hotel guest turned the volume up on the TV that sat between two artificial peace lilies.

Listening to the news commentator for a moment, Mari said, "Oh! Today's Groundhog Day."

Groundhog Day, thought Gideon as he watched the screen where a man in a black top hat raised the infamous Punxsutawney Phil for all to see. Three other men in coats and hats stood by, each offering comments. Gideon wondered if there was any significance to having a funeral on a day when everyone was preoccupied with a furry creature who could predict whether winter would end in six weeks or if spring would come early. Moriah was dead, and grown men were acting giddy over a fat rodent. The severity of his own circumstances kept Gideon from hearing whether Phil saw his shadow or not. And to be honest, he really didn't care.

Gideon entered the Covenant Community Church located in the outskirts of Harrisburg. It was already quarter after nine, and he'd told Pastor Mitchell he'd be there by nine to go over the graveside funeral ceremony. Late, he hated being late. All these years of working at Russell Brothers, and he'd never been late. He wore his ability to be on time like a medal of honor, like a symbol of courtesy and respect. And now, he had broken his own cardinal rule.

Pastor Nate Mitchell, a burly man with a head of thick red hair sprinkled with a little gray, didn't mind what time it was. He hugged Gideon, recalling when he'd first met him. "You came to our youth group when you were about thirteen, didn't you?"

"Snuck out of the house to do it." The memory, for some reason, made Gideon smile. There had been an attractive girl in the group who piqued his interest. He was ashamed to admit that studying the Bible had not been his first desire.

Nate sat at his desk, an oversized mahogany piece of furniture that glistened under the overhead light. Taking out a memo pad, he searched for a pen. "Now Moriah was quite a bit younger than you, correct?"

"Ten years." Gideon tried to decipher some of the titles of books the pastor had in the long bookshelves behind him. *There must be ten editions of the Bible,* he thought. There were books on marriage, on sin, on the power of the Holy Spirit, and one called *How to Forgive.* The title of the last one seemed to bore a hole into his soul: *Forgive us our debts as we forgive our debtors.*

Nate crossed his legs and balanced the pad on one knee. "I wanted to go over some characteristics about your brother to say in my sermon. I know he was comical and loving." He poised his pen over the paper, ready to jot down more characteristics.

Gideon sat in a leather chair across from the desk. His lower back pulsated with pain and somehow the chair alleviated some of the throbbing.

"What else can you tell me about him?" Nate's eyes looked into Gideon's.

"He's in hell, so you don't have to preach about him being safe in heaven," he said.

Nate cocked his head, his lips tightly pressed, puzzlement lining his middle-aged face. "Hell?"

"You know that if you leave the Amish communities, hell is your only friend."

"I have heard that."

Of course he had. He was in Harrisburg, home to hundreds of Amish. He had to know their beliefs.

"Do you really believe that God came to save only the Amish?"

"What?" Gideon wondered what Nate was getting at.

"Does God care only about the Amish?"

"Well, no . . ."

"So if I were to die—as an Episcopalian or Presbyterian or Methodist or even someone without a denomination—God wouldn't consider me for heaven?"

Gideon wondered where this conversation was headed. He rubbed his temple. A headache was about to brew; he could feel it.

"I think we have to avoid denominations. We find security in them. Some prefer the way the Baptists worship, some the services of the Methodist. Others, especially around here, the Amish. But the real key is when we look to the Bible."

"It is?"

Nate opened a Bible that was next to his phone and flipped through a few pages. When he stopped searching, he read, "Go into all the world and preach the good news to all creation. Whoever believes and is baptized will be saved."

Gideon cleared his throat. Was this some sort of code?

Seeing his confusion, Nate smiled. "Whoever. Whoever believes will be saved. There are no denominations or communities described within Jesus' words to His disciples." He read another passage. "For God so loved the world that he gave his one and only Son, that whoever believes in him shall not perish but have eternal life."

"But Moriah wasn't living a life of belief. He was out of his mind." Gideon hated to have to admit this, but it was true.

"And from what you told me on the phone last night, at the time of his death, he'd let drugs steal from him. But when he came here as a boy, he was seeking God."

Gideon wanted to believe that his brother had looked to God because, at this point, that thought gave him comfort.

Nate closed his Bible and laid it back on his desk. "Now," he said, picking up the pen and pad of paper. Easing out of his chair, he stood and walked over to Gideon. He pulled up a chair and sat. "What are some of the characteristics about Moriah that you want me to say?"

Gideon realized he'd been slouching. He was in a pastor's office; he supposed protocol was to at least sit up straight. He looked at the blank paper, crisp and white. What positive traits did he have to share about Moriah with Nate? His mind clouded with words like womanizer, thief, deceiver, and addict. He should have let Kiki and Mari attend this meeting with him. They would be able to supply some decent characteristics about Moriah.

Nate broke into his thoughts. "Was he funny? I think I recall his laughter. He seemed to be easygoing. Would you agree with that?"

Gideon ignored the question and quickly asked, "How often did he come here?"

"He attended our youth group a number of times. Apparently he arranged for someone to pick him up at the convenience store a mile from your house, and then when the meeting was over, he got a ride back to your house."

"My parents?"

"I don't suppose they ever knew."

Gideon let a smile escape from his puzzled expression. The next thing he knew, he was laughing. He had snuck out to come to the youth group meetings here, too. Moriah was so much like him.

"He looked up to you."

"I let him down." A shadow now brushed across Gideon's eyes. No more laughter. Guilt had him clenching his hands together, and a shot of remorse rippled through his veins.

Gently, Nate said, "Moriah was responsible for Moriah."

Gideon lifted an unsteady hand near the pastor's face, fingers erect, a hand that spoke the language of "Say no more. Stop." He wanted the pastor to cease his spiel. What did he know of his and Moriah's relationship? Let him, Gideon, feel the guilt. He needed to be the guilty one—someone had to—and he would take the blame.

The pastor saw Gideon's hand and nodded.

Grateful to have won this battle, Gideon rose to his feet. There was nothing else to discuss. Suddenly, he just wanted to get this day over with and head back to Twin Branches. He reached out to shake Nate's hand. "I'll see you soon," he called over his shoulder as he made his way to the office door. "Two o'clock. It's the orchard on Pike Level Road. A mile from the Stop and Serve convenience store, two miles from the Swartz's Furniture Store."

"I'll find it, don't worry. Oh, and I hope you don't mind, but I did two things."

Gideon stopped. Turning to face Nate, he asked, "What did you do?"

"First, I called."

"Called?"

"I asked around for help to dig the grave. Interesting thing is, seems your people have beat me to the punch."

Confused, Gideon asked, "My people?"

"Your friends. Moriah's friends. Always amazes me how fast the Amish grapevine works. I made a call and the next thing I knew, some man had arranged for a group to dig the grave."

"Jeremiah," said Gideon, certain it must be him. "I grew up with him."

"And the other thing I did . . ." Once again, the preacher paused. "Well, I knew you'd most likely forgotten how solid the earth gets in these parts in the dead of winter."

Gideon felt defeat spread over him, certain the next words from

246

the pastor's mouth wouldn't be anything he wanted to hear. How could he have forgotten how the snow made the ground as hard as bricks? How would the men be able to dig a grave?

"Don't worry, Gideon. It's all taken care of."

"How?"

"There's this thing called a frost dome. One of my church members works at a cemetery in town. When I told him about your coming up here to bury your brother, he said you would need a backhoe to break the ground. I didn't think the Amish would approve of machinery like that."

Gideon knew his father wouldn't. Graves were to be dug by the sweat of the brow.

"Three days ago he took that frost dome to a spot by the weeping willow—with your mother's permission. Not sure how your father felt about it, but . . . well, anyway, this contraption is a tin structure heated by propane. It heated the earth and made digging possible."

"A dome? Those things people put over plants?" Gideon had seen one of these on his walk to work.

"Yes, but a propane tank is attached so that it warms the ground." Nate smiled. "It was the perfect solution."

Amazed by this kindness, Gideon tried to find words. "You thought of everything."

The Amish grapevine. The phrase made Gideon smile as he pulled in at the inn where Mari and Kiki waited to ride with him to the orchard. There was an ongoing joke that even though Amish were without modern devices like the Internet and phones, they still managed to get messages across the communities to each other. He hadn't even wondered how he would dig a grave under the weeping willow—he hadn't thought that far ahead—and yet, his community had come to his rescue. When Mari and Kiki hopped into the hearse, Gideon teased, "Kiki, you won't have to dig Moriah's grave by yourself after all. I heard Moriah's friends did that for us."

"I want to meet his friends," said Kiki. "I bet some of them are pirates."

"Please don't ask them if they are," pleaded Mari, turning to the backseat to give her sister one of her be-careful-now looks. "Just observe, okay?"

"Sheesh! Yes, ma'am, I will be good."

As they drove east of Carlisle toward Pike Level Road, Gideon felt his stomach churn as it often had before a test in school. He passed the Brenneman home, noting three rocking chairs on the porch as well as a stack of firewood, bundled like a present. Next was the Baumbergers' large two-story and then an English farm, clearly still English, for in the front yard was a satellite dish. The farmlands in-between looked just as they had when he'd left them, the pastures dotted with cows. Fifteen years and nothing had changed here.

He parked the hearse parallel to the fence around the orchard.

"Is this it?" asked Kiki, her face pressed against the window. "Where's the weeping willow tree?"

He couldn't help but look across the road at his own childhood home. The barn and silo seemed smaller than they had when he was a boy. Briefly, he watched for movement from the house, expecting to see a family member. The house was still.

When they got out of the car, a man made his way briskly toward them. Gideon recognized him immediately as Jeremiah. He'd grown into a man of over six feet and yet still had those same rosy cheeks from boyhood. Gideon wondered if he still cried often. As a kid, he was teased for being a crybaby.

"Gideon," breathed Jeremiah. He embraced him tightly. "Gideon."

Gideon tried to avoid the tears in his friend's eyes. He introduced Mari and Kiki to him and then opened the gate to the orchard. Anxious to see whether or not the ground had been dug for the coffin, he made his way toward the weeping willow. The others followed him.

The tree had grown into a large gangly presence. Its bare branches rose up and out like the ribs of an umbrella. As the lower limbs swayed,

Gideon noted a shovel with a wooden handle propped against the trunk.

To the left of the tree were simple white stones, blemished from time. These were Miller graves. Gideon expected to see a hole dug for Moriah's coffin in front of the tree, facing the homestead. But the grave was behind the tree, looking out over the pond. *It doesn't matter*, he thought, as he surveyed the deep crevice and the mounds of dirt cast over to its side. *What's dug is dug.* Even so, he'd pictured burying his brother closer to the other markers, not behind them.

As though noting his puzzlement, Jeremiah started to speak. But right then, Kiki, with her gloved hand on the tree trunk, cried, "His name is here! Moriah's name is here!"

Jeremiah nodded, gave Gideon a slight smile, and said, "We saw that. We felt his grave should be on the side of the tree where he carved his name."

About four feet up from the base of the tree, crudely itched, was Moriah's name.

Gideon ran a finger over the bumpy letters. He wondered how old his brother had been when he'd done that and which tool he'd used. Somehow, touching Moriah's name now made him feel closer to him.

With Jeremiah's help, Gideon lowered the brown coffin out of the hearse and placed it on the ground. The words to the old tune, "He ain't heavy, he's my brother," sprang into Gideon's mind. They weren't appropriate for today, Gideon told himself. Moriah had been heavy, wearing on him, causing him sleepless nights and worry. But how he wished Moriah was still capable of doing those things. I'll take his antics, he wanted to say to God. Just give him back to me. Please.

Although Kiki insisted that she could help carry the coffin, too, Mari simply told her to trail behind the men. Gideon and Jeremiah then hoisted the coffin and carefully walked it into the orchard until they reached the foot of the weeping willow. Gideon pulled a muscle in his left arm. He massaged the spot while Mari left to park the hearse a little closer to the side of the road. The road was narrow, and she was afraid an oncoming car would have trouble getting around it. Gideon wanted to tell her that cars rarely passed by. Carriages drawn by horses were much more common in this town, and he doubted they would have any difficulty getting around the hearse.

"We miss you," Jeremiah said to Gideon, his voice as somber as his dark coat. "I have eight children now. How about you?"

"Not married."

"You will one day."

Mari buttoned her coat against the wind that had picked up and was moving brooding clouds across a violet sky. It seemed the sun was losing its strength, and real winter temperatures were taking over.

"What time is it?" asked Gideon, shoving his hands into his coat pockets. Surely Pastor Nate should be here soon.

"Ten till," said Mari with a glance at her watch.

Looking up, they saw a young man cutting through the field toward the orchard. As he opened the gate, he waved at them.

"Is he one of Moriah's friends?" Kiki asked.

He approached them, his strides quick and purposeful. Without any introduction, he made his way to Gideon who was studying a worn marker, uneven in the ground. Waiting until Gideon acknowledged him, he then stood with his back to the others and whispered, "I heard."

"What have you heard?"

With a glance over his shoulder, he stepped closer. "You help others."

"Yeah, well, my brother died." So much for helping him.

"I knew your brother." He said the *th* like a *d*, like many Amish when they spoke in English. "We were friends. We used to smoke together behind the mini-mart." His expression showed that he wasn't sure whether or not this was the proper place to make such a statement.

Kiki and Mari huddled together while Jeremiah joined the men, greeting the young man. "Good afternoon, Lowell. Nice to see you today." To Gideon, he explained, "Lowell helped dig the grave." He shivered beneath his coat. "There were about six of us out here working from Thursday on."

Gideon wondered if he'd thanked them for their thoughtfulness. "I appreciate that. I heard someone brought a frost dome."

Jeremiah grinned. "I got the task of asking your parents if it would be all right for the man from Covenant Church to set up the dome and two propane tanks. Your mother told me we had her permission."

Gideon didn't ask what his father had said about the situation. He had no idea if his regulations permitted such a device.

As Gideon shifted his glance from those around him toward the landscape a distance in front of him, he nearly gasped. Over by the edge of the field on the other side of the fence that surrounded the orchard, stood his mother. She was wearing a long black dress, and a black cloak. The hood to the cloak covered her bonnet and hair. Beside her stood his three sisters. He searched for their spouses; he'd heard all of them were married and that each had children. But no men or children were gathered with them. At the sight of his family, Gideon's heart pounded like the engine of a car. He felt the urge to race over to them, but his legs were like pillars, stiff, grounded.

Kiki tugged at Jeremiah's sleeve, asking why his coat held no pockets and where his gloves were. Jeremiah explained that the people in his community didn't wear gloves due to their plain dress code.

"We have a dress code at my school," said Kiki. "We can't wear spaghetti straps."

As the two talked, Lowell once again vied for Gideon's attention. This time he stood in front of him, blocking the view of his family. "Can I go with you?"

Not sure he'd heard the young man's words over his own heart, Gideon asked, "What was that?"

Lowell looked Gideon in the eye. "I want to go with you."

Gideon noted his clean-shaven face, the freckles across the bridge of his nose, the blue of his eyes.

Intensity filling his voice, Lowell said, "You could pick me up behind the mini-mart on your way back to your home. North Carolina, right? Are you leaving today? I can meet you anytime."

"What's your surname?"

"Baumberger." He paused to adjust his straw hat that had become lopsided on his head. "I could leave with you tomorrow if you aren't going back until then. Mr. Miller, I want to go with you. Please, sir."

"Lowell, what do you like to do? What are you good at?" Surely this man had some ambition besides just wanting to escape this countryside. Gideon thought of the safety that lay within this community. When there was no risk, how much easier life could be. If only Moriah had stayed here and had had no desire to see what was on the other side of bonnets and buggies.

"I want to work in a grocery store and run the electric cash register." He smiled. "Eventually, I'd like to go to college and teach."

When Jeremiah came over, Lowell resumed silence. His face seemed to plead, *Please don't mention a word of what I said to anyone.*

Gideon nodded at Lowell, his way of indicating that he knew how to keep silent.

As the wind rattled the bare limbs of the weeping willow and the surrounding apple trees, Gideon once more cast his view across the field. Who was that man now beside his sisters and mother? Oh! He'd know that stoic stance anywhere. There was no *demut* or humility in his posture; he was as arrogant as he'd always been. *Cry,* Gideon wanted to yell out at him. *Cry, or at least come over here!*

He'd always thought that seeing Father again would make him succumb to a crime, one where he'd beat the tar out of him. But he had no desire to lift a hand to him now. His anger toward the man he'd known as his father somehow, today, only made him want to beg him to soften his heart and show some compassion.

35

When Pastor Nate Mitchell arrived in a thick overcoat, woolen cap, and leather gloves, the sky was a mass of shifting clouds. Kiki and Mari wrapped woolen scarves around their necks and huddled, shivering together.

"What about your family?" Nate motioned toward Gideon's sisters, father, and mother. "Shall we invite them over?"

"They don't need to be asked," said Gideon, the words harsh like sharpened arrows.

"Perhaps they do." The pastor waved at them, beckoning them to come over the orchard to this side by the willow.

Gideon muttered, "They won't come. Just start the service. Please." From the corner of his eye, he could see that no one across the rows of trees was making any attempt to traipse over to the grave. "Let's just start."

Nate acknowledged Gideon's request, drawing Kiki, Mari, Gideon, Jeremiah, and Lowell around him. "Dearly beloved," he said. "We have come together to remember a man we loved. He was a brother, a son, a friend, and a child of God. He was loved and cherished, and his death has broken our hearts."

Upon hearing those words, Gideon fell to his knees. He waited for the sobs to form, for wailing to rush out from his chest like a waterfall along a mountainous trail, but nothing came forth. *It's okay,* he said to himself, *cry right here, right before Father. Show him it is all right to cry.* Inching forward on his knees toward the opened grave, he felt the dirt rub into his pant legs. *Are we formed from dirt, only to return to dirt? What is life, but a passing shadow, at times only brief enough to say hello. What was the purpose? Was it to serve God? Why couldn't Moriah have made more of his years?*

With his head between his hands, Gideon felt anguish and agony lodge themselves on each of his shoulders as the limbs of the willow nearby swayed back and forth, rocking like a mother cradling her child to sleep. "Moriah," he moaned. "Moriah, I'm so sorry."

Mari knelt to his left, and Kiki followed, bending beside him.

"I'm sorry, too," Kiki cried. Although tears moistened the girl's cheeks, Gideon's eyes were dry.

He's broken me, he thought. *He's made me believe that I can't cry in front of him.* Gideon wanted to lift his head and glare across the orchard at his father, but he wouldn't. He would let this be a ceremony for Moriah, not a clash against a man he had come to despise.

Before ending the service, Nate asked for all to join hands. As a shadow fell across the orchard, he offered a prayer. "Dear Lord, we commit Moriah's spirit into Your care. Amen."

"And please take care of Gideon here," Kiki said, her voice rising above the sound of sniffing back tears. "He needs a whole lot of help."

Gideon looked up at the heavy, dark sky. Just like in the movies at graveside services, it looked like rain.

When it was time to lower the coffin into the ground, Lowell studied the particle board box for a moment and then looking at Gideon asked, "Are you sure Moriah's body is inside?"

Was he joking?

"I heard this story once where the family was burying a body and when they opened the casket, it was empty."

With that, Kiki tugged at the hinges. "He's in here," she said. "I know it."

"Kiki," said Mari, "that's not how to go about opening it." She walked over to the right side and, within seconds had the coffin lid raised.

And there, resting against a cotton lining was Moriah, dressed in jeans and a periwinkle shirt. His eyes were closed, his mouth serene. Gideon forced himself to look, made himself see Moriah's arms, crossed over his chest, his broad hands, his fingers, his blond hair combed into a ponytail. Beige makeup covered his facial bruises. It seemed every effort had been made to make Moriah look like Moriah. Even his feet were encased in a pair of leather boots.

Gideon felt tears sting his eyes, but he lifted his head so they couldn't flow down his cheeks. What had he expected? That he could experience this embalmed body that belonged to his brother and not feel excruciating pain and remorse? Unable to suppress the sudden urge, Gideon lifted his brother's shirt, pulling the hem from where it was tucked inside his jeans. He wasn't sure why he felt the need to view this portion of Moriah now, perhaps it was to make sure that it was really him. Or perhaps it was because he knew he'd never again be able to observe this work of art that Moriah had been so proud of. And as he expected, the tattoo was there—a pirate ship on a stormy sea, seeking treasures—a metaphor of Moriah's short life. With a clenched jaw, Gideon demanded, "Close it. Please."

"It's okay, it's okay," said Kiki as she rocked back and forth on the balls of her feet, one of her hands on Gideon's back. "That's not him, that's just his body." Looking into the sky, she cried out as though delivering her own sermon, "Moriah is on a beautiful heavenly ocean right now. He's God's very special treasure."

Jeremiah blew his nose into a handkerchief as Pastor Nate repeated, "Amen."

When the casket was firmly in the grave, Gideon picked up the shovel and flung some dirt onto the smooth top.

Kiki asked if she could help and when Mari affirmed that she could, Kiki took handfuls of dirt and dropped them against the casket. "It's too sad," she said, watching the dirt land and scatter. "I miss him so much." With that, she rushed over to the hearse.

"What's she doing?" asked Gideon, watching her run and fumble with the door to the vehicle.

In a minute he knew. Kiki returned with a bouquet of flowers. This morning they'd found a florist and purchased an assortment of flowers because none of them knew which were Moriah's favorites.

The arrangement had white daisies, three red roses, a dozen sprigs of baby's breath and six pale yellow carnations. Gideon remembered how his brother had once picked weeds and put them in a dish of water. Upon hearing that story, Kiki grabbed a cluster of dried brown grass from under the tree. She sprinkled the pieces onto the bouquet and said, "There, now we have everything Moriah could have liked and did like."

Gideon shoveled dirt into the hole until he'd rubbed a large blister on the palm of his hand. Lowell took the shovel from him and continued filling the massive hole.

When Gideon looked up, what he saw surprised him. Esther, his oldest sister, was making the trek around the perimeter of the orchard toward him. She opened the gate and entered.

Approaching her brother, she nodded, the black bonnet on her head bobbing with her movements. As she stood beside him she said, "Mother wants to invite you to the house."

Gideon ignored her, bending over to grab soil with his hands, joining Kiki and Lowell in covering the casket.

"Gideon."

He looked at her then. Her plain face looked like so many others. He wanted to tell her that a light pink shade of lipstick and some mascara would enhance her looks, bring out the sparkle in her hazel eyes.

But he kept scooping the dirt into the grave.

"Mother invites you to come to the house."

Perhaps she'd go away. Maybe she'd get the hint and leave him alone. He was an outcast; he'd left the community. A shunned son should not enter his parents' home.

"Gideon. Did you hear me?"

Something made him freeze inside. For a moment he wasn't sure what he would do. He was aware that Kiki was about to speak, and he didn't want her to. Because knowing Kiki, she'd probably say something like, "Yes, Gideon, let's go inside. I'm cold." If Kiki said that, how could he deny her a warm place to sit? Quickly, before Kiki could utter a word, Gideon faced his sister. "Why? Why should I go to her house?"

"She has some food."

Gideon knew it was customary to have food after a funeral. But why did his mother want him to come over now? Why hadn't she joined him at the graveside? "No, we have to get back to North Carolina." He and Mari had discussed that they needed to leave once the service was over. They would drive all night, taking turns.

"Please, Gideon." She pulled her dark shawl around her thin shoulders. Gideon wondered why Esther didn't don a cloak as her other sisters had, as Mother had. Then he recalled how warm-natured she was. Esther was the one who never seemed to feel the cold. Once, while Father was still asleep, she'd even walked outside barefoot after a light snow. "Please, come to the house."

36

Gideon stopped filling in the grave. He looked at his blistered hands and shook his head. "Why, Esther?"

"Why?" Esther repeated. "Is that all you can say?"

"Why can't he come over here?"

Esther shot a glance at their father and then quickly turned to face her brother. Gently, she said, "He can only handle Ordnung."

Trapped by Ordnung. *Of course*, thought Gideon. *We must follow the Amish way of life, strict rules and regulations.* Father was stubborn, not able to participate in anything unless it was according to the rules. Having a non-Amish give the service at his own son's burial probably had Father wanting to claw at his skin. Well, if Father was sticking to his precious way that he felt things were to be done, he, Gideon, would be just as obstinate. "You tell him to come here or we're going home." With that, he grabbed the shovel back from Lowell and began tossing soil into the hole as though he wasn't tired. Truth was, he suddenly had new strength and determination fueled by anger. "My home," he reiterated. "We are going to my home in just a few minutes. Not his."

"He's not well. Please." When he didn't respond, she fervently said, "Please. I'm begging."

Mari was at Gideon's side, standing between him and his sister. "Gideon," she said softly. "What if we stopped in for just a few minutes?"

He would have declined even her suggestion, but she put her hand on his arm, just below where his biceps ached from the physical strain of shoveling. From her fingers, warmth spread over him, like a blanket, like a memory. This was not about him. He looked up at the weeping willow and could almost see a young boy on one of the lower limbs. A boy calling out, "Gideon, take it easy, bro. A stop in his house isn't going to kill you." Lowell reached over and took the shovel from him again.

"Hey," Kiki said, her hands clutching the bouquet for the grave. She pulled out a daisy and handed it to Mari, a rose to Gideon, and a stalk of baby's breath to Esther. The adults took the flowers, holding onto their thin stems. "Let's lay them on top of the grave one by one," Kiki instructed. "One by one by one by—"

"Okay, Kiki," reprimanded her sister. "That's enough."

"I just wanted to make sure that everyone got the rules right."

For a moment the group stood speechless, looking at one another as Lowell continued to shovel dirt into the hole. It was almost full; the dirt was beginning to form a mound now.

At last, Kiki said, "Who is going first?" When no one said anything, she looked at Gideon. "Gideon, you go first."

Gideon gently tossed the red rose onto the dirt Lowell had begun to smooth over the top of the grave. Mari followed suit, and in a whisper said, "Moriah, you were fun to be around."

"Amen to that," Kiki said. With a finger pointed at Esther, she said, "You are next."

Esther stepped closer to the grave and threw her sprig of baby's breath next to Gideon's rose. When Gideon saw her face, this time, two tears curved down her cheeks.

Kiki plucked another daisy from the arrangement and waved it in front of Lowell's face. "Your turn," she said.

He paused from his task, reached for the flower, and seeing the other flowers, laid his beside the baby's breath. "Rest in peace, Moriah," he said.

Jeremiah, blubbering, refused the daisy Kiki handed him. With his back to the group, he tried to compose himself.

Allowing him space, Kiki lifted the rest of the bouquet over her head. As she closed her eyes, she said, "These are for you, Moriah. You're in God's heavenly garden now and don't care about measly flowers from earth, but hey, we got you some anyway." With a light flick of her wrist, the rest of the flowers landed on the center of the grave like an offering.

Gideon wondered how in the world Kiki was always able to make him smile even at the most sentimental times. Sometimes people looked at her and muttered that she wasn't *right*. But they were incorrect because most of the time, Kiki was the only one who *was* right. Her honesty, her openness, her ability to forgive, and her freedom to be Kiki and no one else was what she offered to all she met. And to Gideon, that seemed like the right way to live.

As rain splashed against the farms of Carlisle, inside the Miller home, a fire crackled in the stone fireplace. Father, who'd removed his cloak and hat, sat in a chair to the left of the hearth, adding logs to it from a stack of hardwood. Up close, his beard seem sparse, no longer the thick mass of whiskers that had prickled Gideon's face when, as a boy, he'd tried to hug him. He even moved slowly; the agile body of yesteryear was no longer his companion.

Straight-back wooden chairs were pulled across the bare floor, creating a circle. As the fire spurted with flames of red and violet, Mother and Gideon's sisters laid food out on the dining room table. Mother claimed that once word had gotten around, neighbors had begun bringing over dishes this morning. There was an assortment of tasty looking platters and bowls with potato salad, red cabbage salad, beef soup with dumplings, schnitzel, apple butter and molasses bread, chess pie, apple pie, and even blackberry pie.

Kiki and Mari sat like statues on sack-back chairs, the very chairs Gideon had built to go around the dining room table. He'd used an English neighbor's workshop because the neighbor had a high-powered lathe, and Gideon wanted the legs of each of the Windsor chairs to be carved like he'd seen on the flier at the furniture store. He knew at the time that Father would disapprove of him using an electric tool and especially one borrowed from someone who was not Amish, but he didn't care. His mother's excitement over the set was matched by his sisters', making Gideon's chest swell with pride. His father had merely refused any comment.

Kiki took in the sparsely decorated living room; Gideon knew by the way her eyes went from wall to ceiling to floor and back again that she was finding the room unusual.

Esther joined them and the minute she sat, Kiki spouted, "Hey, why don't you have any pictures of Moriah on the walls? I want to see what he looked like as a baby."

Father, Mother, Esther, Yolanda, and Irene all turned to look at Kiki as though she'd just uttered a string of obscenities. Mari muttered, "Kiki, behave."

Upon hearing her sister's reprimand, Kiki said, "What's wrong? Gideon said Moriah was a cute kid, and I want to know if it's true. Just show me a picture."

Gideon moved from the dining table to Kiki. Standing behind her chair, he said, "Kiki, Amish don't believe that photographs should be taken. You know how some people don't believe it's right to . . . to . . ." All eyes were on him, and Gideon felt discomfort surrounding him. "Um . . . Well, what I mean is . . ."

"I know!" Kiki piped up. With sudden revelation, she said, "You didn't have money for a camera! Sheesh! I know money doesn't grow on trees."

And with that explanation, the others gave small smiles, nodded, and let that be that.

Quickly, Yolanda asked Mari some questions about where she was born, and what she did in North Carolina. Mari answered with short, polite sentences. Gideon noted she was uncomfortable, and Esther must have picked up on this too, for she then encouraged everyone to eat. Irene handed both Mari and Kiki plates.

Kiki stood, excited to partake in the feast she'd been eyeing. With her plate against her chest, she rounded the table and said, "This looks wonderful. Mari, you should see this." To Gideon, Kiki said under her breath, "No fried potatoes like Mari always makes. Not one fried any-thing. Yum!"

With the focus on the women and the food, Mother rose from her chair by the fireplace. She cast a glance at her husband who was looking off into the distance, unaware of the conversation around him. Gideon wondered if what Esther had said was true—that Father was not well.

Mother made her way toward the kitchen and motioned for Gideon to come with her. Gideon followed her into the kitchen and watched as she opened the heavy cellar door. He followed her down a set of concrete steps. As he remembered, the cool cellar was crammed with shelves of canned goods. Mother's forte was pickling vegetables and canning jellies and fruit concoctions. The racks of shelves reached from floor to ceiling. As a child, Gideon had helped her with the sum-mer squash when it was time to cook and can them. His job had also been to carefully bring the jars down the cellar stairs and place them gently on the shelves. He'd always been fearful that he'd trip coming down and that the broken jars would give his father a reason to beat him.

"You've been busy," Gideon observed as nostalgia filled him. It seemed only yesterday he had been down here, dreaming about his fu-ture, a future he hoped was far away from this confined place.

She removed her black bonnet from her head, exposing a headful of hair secured in a tight bun. "When I heard the news from Mr. Swartz about Moriah, I came down here. There was nothing to can, so I went to the store and bought tomatoes and pumpkin and squash. After cook-ing them in the kitchen, I filled the jars. I ran out of jars."

Gideon recognized much of the food she'd canned. When he saw three jars of apple butter, involuntarily his eyes closed as though he couldn't bear to see or feel any more.

"I can cry down here," his mother said.

He opened his eyes and looked into hers. How she'd aged over the long years since he'd last seen her. For some reason, he'd still pictured her as a woman of forty, the age she'd been when he left home. "Why can't you cry upstairs?"

At first she wasn't going to reply. He could tell by the way she touched a quart jar of canned butterbeans and changed the subject. "We had a good crop last year."

Persistently, he asked again, "Why can't you cry upstairs?" He knew he was being dogged about it, but he wanted to hear her reply.

Reluctantly, she responded, "You know he doesn't like to see me cry."

Her words evoked a lump in his throat. The old Gideon would have let it go, but the new Gideon, the one who'd left the old lifestyle, was more determined to show that the Amish way was not the only way to live a life of wholesomeness and faith. "Sometimes tears are okay, Mother. They show that we have heart."

She wouldn't look at him. She only lifted a hand to her forehead and pretended to be studying the shiny bottles of pickled beets.

"Were Esther, Yolanda, and Irene's husbands and children not invited to be here?" Gideon had to know the answer.

"He thought it was best—"

"Is it really best that the entire family not be here for a son's funeral?" Gideon felt the saliva thick and hot in his mouth.

Quietly, she said, "He has his rules, his ways."

"Yeah, Ordnung mixed with his own pride." Gideon rammed a clenched fist against the wall. The jars rattled on the shelves. "There have been more compassionate Nazi guards than him." He'd actually written that line for his creative writing class and felt that now, it was time to let those words skip off the page and be heard.

263

A shadow hovered at the top of the stairs and immediately after seeing it, Gideon heard a gruff, "Are you coming back upstairs? We do have guests here, you know."

Gideon wanted to shout up at his father, "Stop trying to control everything!" But he would not give in to that retort. Not now when his mother had already suffered enough.

She was bent over a small pine table, one where she often sat to view her shelves full of harvested goods and make inventory in a little notebook she kept. There were sections for each variety of canned good. The cellar was clearly her place, her sanctuary, her respite. Now her face was covered by her narrow hands.

He drew her to his chest, feeling her sobs against his heart. "It's okay," he repeated, for he knew nothing else to say, no words of comfort that were fitting for her at a time like this. "It's all going to be okay."

As Father started down the stairs, his shoes clicking against the concrete, she sniffed, pulled from Gideon and called out, "We are on our way up."

Father hesitated on the third step as Gideon waited for his angry words. But none were spoken. Turning, Father started his climb up the stairs, his shadow not large and impressive, but thin and wary.

After rubbing her nose with the back of her hand, Mother said, "You cannot change others, Gideon. You can change yourself." With that, she followed her husband.

Gideon guessed he'd better head upstairs as well and resume the chitchat with the others. At the first step he halted—the respite of the cellar was inviting. No wonder this dark and hidden storage space was his favorite part of the house, as well as his mother's. This underground place almost seemed free from the restraints of Ordnung.

Back in the living room, Kiki and his sisters were eating. Mari held only a glass of water without ice. Gideon guessed she'd either already eaten or was not going to. As she gave him a weak smile, he felt she had not eaten. She'd once said that funerals and food made her uncomfortable, and when her grandfather died, she had dished out the prepared-by-friends-and-neighbors-meals, but had not touched a bite.

Gideon acknowledged her smile and watched her until she turned from him to Esther who was asking her yet another question.

"Do you like working in the tearoom?" Esther's voice had a monosyllabic quality to it, and Gideon remembered how he had once spoken in the traditional faltering Amish tone.

"We have all missed you, Gideon," Mother said, her voice low, as she pulled out a box of matches. Gideon followed her as she lit various kerosene lanterns to offer light to the living and dining rooms.

"I see you still have some of the furniture I made."

The oak table by the dining room entrance was one he'd built the winter he turned thirteen. He'd hit his fingernail with a hammer and it'd turned purple and eventually came off. To the left was the hutch that held a shelf where his mother's royal teacups sat. Each one was like a soldier holding a trophy over the lone battle she'd won with her spouse. The teacups were not too fancy for a proper Old Order Amish house. They were permanent, part of the landscape, like her bonnets and unadorned clothing.

"I'm glad to see the furniture," he added. For some reason, he had envisioned that they'd thrown out everything that he'd touched the minute he left them.

"Of course—we keep it and use it every day." She blew out a match. Shadows fell across her face. "Did you know that ever since you went away, Moriah was ready to follow in your footsteps? Five years old and he wanted to be just like his big brother."

"He had his own mind."

"Oh, I'm not blaming you."

"I think everyone else does."

"There is so much we don't understand." She quoted a few lines in the German dialect that to the world was called Pennsylvania Dutch. He was amazed that he understood most of it, the meaning of the words coming back to him like a familiar melody.

Then with a smile she said, "Do you remember the day you asked me what this means? *We grow too soon old and too late smart.* Do you remember?"

He forced a smile. He'd seen those words cross-stitched in cobalt blue on a throw pillow at an old Amish souvenir shop when he was about six. He repeated the saying during the whole buggy ride home with Father and then entered the kitchen to ask his mother what it meant and if in fact, it was an Amish quote. "They said it was Pennsylvania Dutch," he quipped.

"That's what they call what we speak," Mother said.

"But we speak German."

"Yes, we do. But someone made a mistake." She used the German word *fylschlicherweise.* "They called our language Pennsylvania Dutch and that stuck as its name. But you and I know our language is not at all any form of Dutch. Someone thought the word sounded like *Dutch.* Really what was being said was *Deutsch,* the German word for *German.*" She'd smiled at him. "Do you remember?"

"I do. I remember how you taught me the Twenty-third Psalm in German. I often think of all those songs that great-grandmother used to sing. There was that silly one about cabbage salad."

"I'm glad you remember the good things, Gideon. We must always hold on to the good." He had the feeling she wanted to say more, perhaps even hum a few lines of the familiar tune. Instead she ran her hand through his curls and down the side of his face. He felt her love in each fingertip. Her love was giving and free, and he hoped he could love like that one day.

At 7:15, just before leaving the house, Kiki followed Gideon into Moriah's bedroom. The simple room held only a twin-sized wooden bed and one cedar dresser. Gideon opened the top drawer of the dresser and sure enough, as though time had not forgotten, there was the keepsake box he'd made for his brother. Taking it out of the drawer, he admired the cedar wood. He'd sanded it for days and then with a chisel had carved Moriah's name into the lid. Once, he had been

266

a good craftsman. But since then he'd given up wood and nails for Pennzoil and engines.

Gideon handed the keepsake box to Kiki. "For you."

"Me?"

"Moriah would have wanted you to have it."

"Is this one you made?" She clasped it in her hands. "It says Moriah on it. Wow, he was right. He told me you made him a box." Then she set the item on the foot of the bed and lifted the lid. "What's inside?" she asked.

Gideon peered into the box. Inside was a piece of gray cloth, a scrap from a quilt, perhaps, and as Kiki removed the material, there lay a block of wood. Gideon knew then. The wood was the gift Moriah had given to him. He must have put it aside, and Moriah had added it to his box.

Quickly, Gideon shut the box, handed it to Kiki, and ushered her from the room before memories of Moriah could take over and squeeze him into a ball of emotions.

"He told me you made him a beautiful keepsake box," she said with feeling as they walked into the living room.

"He called it beautiful?"

Kiki pressed the box to her chest and merely smiled. To his father, she said, "I got a box. It's very special. Gideon says I can have it."

Father glanced at her and then took a look at his son. "Gideon is a skilled builder." Gideon thought he almost smiled, but no, it was probably just the way the lanterns in the room flickered their light against his face.

As Kiki ran her fingertips over the box, admiring it over and over, Father's face grew more sullen than it had been before. Awkwardly, Father stood from his chair, opened the front door, and walked outside onto the porch—as though he had shown too much heart.

37

The weather was gloomy in Twin Branches the following Friday, and as she listened to the rain beat against the roof above her room, Kiki spread her arrowheads out on her kitten-patterned bedspread, one on the head of each of the kittens. Admiring the treasures, she felt each one's soft surface, letting her fingers gently glide over every smooth stone. The keepsake box lay opened by the lines of arrowheads. One by one, she laid the arrowheads inside the box. They fit like they belonged, like this box and they were meant to be, made for each other. She thought of her grandpa and the way he got a twinkle in his eyes when he was about to share a secret or a story about the early days of living in the mountains. He'd take a puff on his pipe, lean back in his worn recliner, and close his eyes. Kiki knew a good tale was about to begin then. Now she swallowed back the tears that sprang to her eyes.

She would not cry. She was not a baby.

She went to the shop to work her shift. She was grateful when Ormond said a man had dropped off his kid's bicycle with a broken chain. She labored, concentrating on getting the chain repaired until it was time to go home. As she washed oil from her hands, she asked where Gideon was, but Ormond just said that Gideon would be back to the shop tomorrow. He was getting the new guy situated into an apartment.

"Fresno," said Kiki.

"What?" asked Ormond, lifting his head from the sports section of the paper.

"The new guy wants to be called Fresno. He met us at a gas station after we left Gideon's parents' house and rode with us all the way back here. He wants to start a new life and doesn't like his old name. So he chose Fresno."

When Ormond chuckled, Kiki didn't mind. He wasn't laughing at her, he was showing that he could laugh. Gideon hadn't in weeks, and Mari was worried, she knew. But some people, like Ormond, just seemed to spring back to their normal selves, and the world was better for it.

She, on the other hand, was aware that she wasn't one of those types of people. She couldn't laugh and although she wanted to slam her hand against the wall, she knew she couldn't get angry. Look at what being angry did to Moriah. She wanted to be able to smile and feel happy about important things like macaroni and cheese, pirate hats, and oatmeal cookies.

When Luke finished working on a black Nissan, he entered the shop to wash his hands. Kiki remembered when Luke and Moriah had a water fight at this very sink. Moriah had started it, splashing water onto Luke. Luke had splashed back until Moriah had droplets dripping off his chin. Laughing, they each got a few more splashes in until Gideon came along and told them to wipe up the floor. If customers slipped on the wet floor, they might get hurt and sue. Suing was, after all, the American Way. Recalling the water fight, Kiki felt her eyes burn from tears. She hugged Luke. "I'm sorry your friend is gone," she said.

Luke's eyes watered. For a few seconds he was silent until he was able to speak. "I'm sorry, too."

269

Kiki left the shop after that, tears nearly blinding her bike ride home.

"Now if you need someone to talk to, don't hesitate." The words Principal Peppers had spoken to her earlier today were fresh in her mind. "You can come talk to me or any of your teachers." She figured he knew about Moriah because this was a small town and word got around fast. Mari had also had to write her a "please excuse Kiki" note when she'd returned to school on Monday. Angie said Mr. Peppers had invited her inside his office, too, to make sure she was "handling the situation." Handling? What a funny word to use at a time like this.

At her house, she placed her bicycle inside the garage. She remembered to turn off the overhead light and shut the door. She was trying to remember to be more responsible these days. Mari didn't need any more stress. Dr. Conner reminded Kiki that she could be very helpful if she just thought about other people more.

Seated on her front porch step, Kiki thought of her sister, of Gideon and Luke and Ormond. Could she really make their lives better? She supposed she could go inside and start by cleaning her room like Mari had asked her to do yesterday. But she didn't want to go inside the cramped house. Although she shivered in the evening wind, she preferred to be cold and stay outside.

January was over. She was glad she wasn't born in January. No one would have remembered her birthday. It had been a terrible month. February had to be better. Blowing on her hands, she tried to warm them. Looking up to the sky, she wished she could see heaven and the warm sea she was certain Moriah must be enjoying. Mari said she trusted that Moriah was at peace, not having to run anymore, with a new body, free from addiction. It was these creatures still on earth who needed so much help, and Kiki so wanted to be a help to Gideon.

As Kiki zipped up her coat, Angie walked across the lawn from her grandma's. Stuffing her hands inside her coat pockets, Angie made her way up the steps to sit beside her.

"I haven't done any homework," Kiki said. Seeing her classmate made her well aware of the three math pages Miss Stevenson had assigned. Math would never matter to her, and now with Moriah gone, she doubted she'd ever have the strength to figure out another pointless word problem about miles, rates of speed, and cost per ounce again.

"Me neither." Within moments of her own confession, Angie's arm was tight around Kiki's shoulders. Kiki could fight it no longer. Burying her face in her friend's neck, she let the tears come. "It is okay to cry, Kiki," she heard Dr. Conner's voice from her last session with him. "Tears serve their purpose." These were making her nose run. She wiped her nose with the lone mitten she found in her pocket.

"The new guy is cute," said Angie. "I like his name."

Not as handsome as Moriah, thought Kiki. No one would ever be as good looking as Moriah. She stuck the mitten into her pocket and for some reason, the action made her think of Moriah's coffin, how it fit so perfectly in the grave and how she'd sprinkled dirt over the top of it.

Angie looped her scarf around her neck. It was orange, the color of the Tennessee Volunteers, and Kiki knew it had been a Christmas gift. "Uncle Reginald is locked away for the rest of his life."

"I know. He did a bad thing."

She bit her lower lip. "He did."

"But you were brave."

"Brave?"

"You shed light on the truth. That's what my sister told me. You shed light. The truth is supposed to always win out."

"My grandma says she'd like you to come over for dinner sometime."

"Really? That's cool." She'd heard that Luva was a good cook. Hopefully that meant that she could make more than fried potatoes, onions, and green peppers.

Angie leaned against Kiki's arm. "Wanna watch *True Stories of Rescue Animals*?"

"Yes," said Kiki as she dried her eyes with the edge of her jacket sleeve. She sniffed and cleared her throat. "Yeah, I'd like to do that." Mari wouldn't be home for another hour; she'd called earlier to say that she needed to make three pies because the tearoom was low on black-berry. Kiki knew she was making them for Gideon.

"We can make hot chocolate," suggested Angie. "Do you have any? If not, I know my grandma has a new box of Swiss Miss."

"We have some in our kitchen," said Kiki. "With marshmallows."

The porch was nearly dark now, shadows casting their images against the front lawn.

Kiki could make out her shadow and Angie's. She moved her arm as her shadow, a thin line, moved.

Angie, realizing what she was doing, lifted her hand, too, and waved.

Kiki giggled, waving her hand. "We are waving shadows," she said.

When they stood to enter Kiki's house, their lean shadows meshed together so that Kiki could not tell where she ended and Angie began. It was as though she and Angie were one big shadow, merging together, taking on a new shape. And although her hands were cold, her heart felt warm, like it often does when one is with a friend.

38

The apartment had never felt so lonely. Not even on that first day when he'd cosigned the lease at age sixteen, with Ormond as his guardian, did it seem this hollow and drenched with silence. The first night alone in this place had been a mixture of relief and uncertainty. He'd been under Ormond's roof for almost a year after leaving Carlisle and was glad to be out on his own where he could buy his own groceries and stock his own refrigerator. Yet the apartment held no familiar sounds. At least Ormond's had the purr of his two calico cats and the tick-tock of an antique grandfather clock he'd inherited from his father.

On this late afternoon, Gideon moved from room to room, hoping to hear something. *Comfort*, he thought. *I just need comfort.* Strange, he hadn't asked for comfort ever and now he wished that a voice—maybe even an audible one from God—would soothe his heart and give it the capability to relax. If only God would reassure him that he was not to blame. He waited. He entered the living room, sat on the couch, and strained his ears. Hearing nothing, eventually he gave in to his hunger and made himself a snack.

Spreading apple butter on two slices of toasted multigrain bread, he thought of how different life would have been if he would have stayed on the farm. He would not have disappointed his parents. Moriah would still be alive.

Perhaps.

But how could he have stayed under his father's rule? How could he have respected a man who whipped children and locked neighbor boys inside sheds, and later lying about it? He remembered how he'd told the whole story to Mari, Kiki, and Angie that afternoon in November, and how he had known then that he still harbored hatred. And he knew it now. It gripped his heart like barbed wire.

After the burial, that night as they left his parents' home, relief had filled him. He had entered their home once more, and it hadn't been as complex as he'd expected. There had been no harsh words with his father, no accusatory remarks. "I feel like he has no control over me anymore," Gideon said, referring to Father on the ride back to Twin Branches. Kiki, Mari, and the new boy, Lowell, had listened to him go on for miles about how he felt stronger and no longer a victim of his past.

He'd been the liar.

The sky darkened outside, and the first snowflakes began to fall. The image of his father standing far from his own son's grave haunted and embittered him even more. *What kind of father shows no remorse at the death of his child? What kind of beast stands off in the distance, refusing to participate in a funeral service?*

"I will not!" Gideon's voice bounced off the walls of his kitchen. "I will not be like him!" He swallowed his anger and resentment, but he was afraid that if he didn't let these emotions go, he just might wind up like his father.

Gideon watched the snow from his kitchen window as it fell across the lawn. The large flakes fluttered carelessly onto the patches of brown grass. *White as snow.* The phrase entered his mind, gently, like the snow. *White as snow. Jesus has washed our sins, so we can be white as snow.*

Pulling on his coat, he rushed outside. Without bothering to zip up, he made his way to the lawn. He noted the quiet chill in the air. A cardinal flitted past him and perched on a holly bush, its feathers matching those of the miniature red berries on the bush. "It's snowing!" he cried and expected the echo of his voice to scare the bird off, but the cardinal only cocked his head and watched Gideon open his mouth.

As the flakes landed in Gideon's mouth, he stuck out his tongue and let a flake melt on the tip of it.

Flakes spilled onto his head, his coat, the tops of his boots. He breathed in the crisp scent and as he took a few steps toward the road, he smelled the distinct aroma of a burning fire. He thought back to the fires his mother had built in the hearth at the farmhouse. He saw the bright flames, flames that made the living room warm even on the coldest day. Next, he saw Moriah playing with a wooden toy wagon, Moriah coming over to the table where Gideon sat nailing cedar blocks together. "He's making me a keepsake. Gideon is the best brother!" Yes, Moriah had said those words. And he'd hugged his older brother when Gideon presented him with the finished product. "I'll put my special toys in here," the little boy had said, his eyes filled with gratitude.

The snow was coming down harder now, building layers over the parking lot and the tops of the parked vehicles. He felt the solid crunch under his shoes as he walked toward the sidewalk that circled the complex. This time when he opened his mouth, a breeze blew and he got a face full of cold, wet snow in his lashes and nose. It was then that he heard laughter. Within seconds, he realized that it was his own.

Still laughing as the snow swirled around him like a stream of confetti, Gideon stumbled over a thick root of a nearby oak. His left foot twisted and he prepared to fall onto the ground. Instinctively, both of his hands shot out in front of his chest to brace his body. To his surprise, he landed against the trunk of the oak, his chin scraping the hard surface. Allowing his arms to stretch as far as they could around the bark, he hugged the trunk. It was as though God had put that tree there to catch him and to remind him that the Almighty's arms were wide and merciful enough to forgive even the most guilty of creatures.

Back in the house, he looked for the newspaper article Mari had told him to read. Ashlyn had written it and it was on the second page of the February first edition of the *Twin Star*. He expected something similar to a police report, listing times and dates and perhaps even a murder suspect, although he doubted she would have clearly accused Reginald Smithfield at this point. Not publicly, not until the trial which was set for sometime in March. But what he read was not at all what he expected. This was not a piece filled with cold facts, but a thoughtfully written column that brought back that lump inside his chest. The title was printed in bold letters, halfway down the page:

Who Was Moriah Miller?

Moriah Miller died on January seventeenth this year, the victim of homicide. He was only twenty-one. A newcomer to Twin Branches, most were not aware of who he was, not having had time to get to know him at the auto shop where he spent many days.

So just who was Moriah? He was thoughtful, funny, and generous. Moriah was the kind of person who brought donuts to the Russell Brothers Auto Shop one afternoon just because he felt it was an occasion to enjoy eating Krispy Kremes in the company of friends. Moriah was the kind of person who laughed at the brown bread I steam in a can, but although reluctant, tried a slice. And he liked it! "She makes the best bread!" he told customers at Another Cup one afternoon. "And it's steamed in a can. It's the perfect combination of healthy and sweet. You have to try it." Customers smiled at him, and a few laughed out loud. Moriah was the type of person who could make you laugh.

My fiancé and I spent a number of evenings together talking and laughing with him. Moriah loved a good conversation, always ready to comment and pose thought-provoking questions. I was glad that Moriah made the choice to move from his Amish home in Pennsylvania to join us here in Twin Branches, even if his upbringing on the farm in the small community of Carlisle caused issues and concerns he was unable to fully resolve. His decision to live in our town meant I gained a new friend.

Unfortunately, Moriah made some bad choices, too. He allowed methamphetamine to become part of his life. Pretty soon it was a daily companion. This highly addictive stimulant wreaks havoc with the mind and body. It clouds your ability to make good decisions. People die every day from meth.

The use of meth is not what killed Moriah, but it didn't help that he was under its addictive rule. Meth changed Moriah from a fun-loving, easygoing man into a ball of uncontrollable emotions and destructive actions.

Moriah was only in Twin Branches for a short while, but hopefully what he taught us through his life and death will be a reminder that—regardless of where we were born, our religious beliefs, or what we look like—we all are capable of reaching out a hand and heart to help those in our midst.

Some might think that a life like Moriah's was not as valuable as another's. They might feel that since he was an addict, he is better off dead. But I like to believe that every life has hope and that even Moriah, with all the wrong choices he made, was still entitled to have those he loved hope with him. I know I hold on to hope. Moriah was one of God's creations and with his death, God wept. And a mother's heart is broken forever.

Gideon carefully cut the article from the rest of the paper. He folded the newsprint into a business envelope and addressed it to his parents. *They need this realistic, yet heartfelt piece written by a reporter,* he thought. Even if she was English, Ashlyn's words could convey to them what he could not.

39

The new guy, as Kiki called him, was serious about applying at a grocery store. Gideon took him to the local Piggly Wiggly to get an application. A manager happened to walk by, his name tag covering the pocket on his starched white shirt. *Jeffery Madison* it read, but Gideon already knew the portly man. He owned a 2009 Mustang and had brought it to the shop for new tires two months ago. Gideon introduced Lowell to him. "He wants to run a cash register," Gideon said, "but I told him that he probably has to start out as a stock boy for the first few months."

Jeffery increased the width of one of his perpetual smiles. "That's right. You work hard and you'll move up to that cash register. Did you get an application?" He told the men to pick one up at customer service.

Lowell liked the sound of moving up to the cash register. He grinned, thanked the man, and followed Gideon to get an application.

Gideon observed how mesmerized he was by the electronic registers.

Even though his awe for the machines was a bit geeky, overall, Gideon was impressed. Lowell seemed to know how to handle himself, even among the English. "How about we work on that application at the tearoom?" he suggested. His longing for a hot cup of green tea was still there, and for that he was grateful.

Amos was the first to greet the two when they entered Another Cup. Immediately, he wrapped his arms around Gideon, offering sympathy. "So sorry," he mumbled. "I am so sorry."

Gideon felt tears sting the backs of his eyes and hoped that a few sniffs would cause them to back off. He guided Lowell to the counter where Della was telling a customer about the deer her husband had shot last week and how she was sick of eating venison.

"I just want chicken," she said. "Just a nice piece of fried chicken with a hot homemade biscuit, mashed taters, and gravy on the side. It's a good thing I work here where I can ask Alfred and Rex to cook me up what I like to eat."

From the kitchen, Alfred called out, "We live to make you happy, Sugar!"

With that, Della let out an infectious laugh. Even the customer listening to her deer story joined in the laughter.

As Gideon introduced Lowell to the group, Lowell held out his hand and shook Della's and then the customer's seated at the counter. "Call me Fresno," he told each of them.

"Fresno?" Amos ran the name over his tongue and then extended his hand. "Sure, Fresno." His smile was wide and warm. "Welcome to Twin Branches."

Fresno grinned and shook Amos's hand up and down, jiggling it like one would a water pump back on the farm.

Gideon made a mental note to himself: Tell Fresno that a solid handshake is all that's necessary. If he keeps up this pumping-style, folks will think he's an overly aggressive used-car salesman.

"What do you do, Fresno?" asked Della.

"Well, Gideon got me a nice apartment to live in. That's a big relief. Now I'm looking for employment."

Della winked at him. "We could use you here, Sugar." It seemed Della never met a man she didn't like. "Do you need a TV? I gave Amos my old one and then my husband went and bought a brand-new LED for Christmas, so I still have an extra."

"Sure." Fresno thought for a moment and then added, "I'd like a TV, just don't tell my parents."

"Ah," said Della. "There's nothing wrong with a TV, as long as you don't let it rule you. Moderation is the key to so much of life."

Mari made her way over to the counter, bringing Gideon a cup of green tea. Her eyes met his and he saw empathy, gentleness, and a glimmer of something else he could not place. She stuffed her hands into her apron pockets and glanced out the window. "I hope it doesn't snow again. I can't wait for spring."

Gideon took a sip from his cup as Fresno asked, "What are you drinking?"

When Gideon told him, he peered into the beverage. "Maybe I should try some. Is it any good? And is it really green?"

Mari thought he should give green tea a try and poured him a cup.

Fresno let his taste buds absorb the tea. "Hmm . . ." By the look in his eyes, it was clear he wasn't going to be a fan of green tea after all.

"Would you like pie today? Sandwich first?" Della was eager to wait on Gideon. Seemed all the venison she'd been consuming was giving her new vigor.

Feeling no hunger, Gideon said, "Fresno might want something. The tea is fine for me now."

"We don't want you wasting away," Della said. "If you're all weak and feathery, how can you work on my car?" She then said to the new customer, "What can I get you?"

"Pepsi!" Fresno gave a boyish grin. "In a glass with a straw, please."

"You're a real polite one," said Della and then smiled. "I wish some of our youngsters around here would learn those manners you have." Edging closer to Gideon, she looked intently into his eyes. "Sugar," she said, her usual husky voice laced with tenderness, "you know I'm sorry about Moriah. I just don't know what to say. I guess there will never be any good words to utter after a young man dies." She shook her head. "I hate all those trite phrases people shower you with. Like, 'well, it was meant to be' or 'you'll move on.' I just want to say how sorry I really am." Then she turned to fill a glass with ice and Pepsi for Fresno. "Here you are, Sugar," she said to the boy, and instead of spitting her gum into the trash can with a cough, she wiped her eyes with the hem of her apron.

Gideon wanted to thank her for taking the time to show her sorrow. One day he'd let her know that her condolences were well received. He knew he needed to help Fresno now. Moriah would want him to, so he took a pen from his pocket and had Fresno spread the application out on the countertop. "We'll get this taken care of," he said and began to read off the boxes for the young man to fill in.

Pretty soon, Fresno was on his own. He didn't have the typical hesitations that most of the escapees had upon seeing an application for the first time.

Mari watched him for a moment, smiling as his brow furrowed and tongue stuck slightly out as he concentrated. "I'll put in a good word for you," she said. "The manager at Piggly Wiggly comes in here every Tuesday at one for lunch."

Fresno thanked her, his eyes still intent on the application. "What's my address?" he asked.

Gideon told him, and Fresno filled in the appropriate lines.

Mari refilled Gideon's cup with hot tea, and he liked the way she was attentive to him today. He thought back to what a support she'd been for him ever since Moriah's death. The first time he'd entered this tearoom under her management, he'd been captivated by her poise and beauty. But over the last month, she had become so much more to him than someone to enjoy looking at. Ever since the trip to and from Pennsylvania, he felt stronger and more capable to do and say what he wanted to.

As she added more half and half to the pitcher on the counter, he decided to go for it. He'd been practicing in front of the mirror all morning. Perhaps now was as good a time as any. "Mari." He produced a tight smile and tried to make it more relaxed.

"Yes?"

What if she said no again? Gideon wished his doubts could be dismissed. "I see you took down the Christmas decorations."

"Well, it is February."

"Is it really?" He feigned surprise. "Mari?" *I better hurry and ask or else she'll think I'm a lunatic.* "I'd like to go to church with you and Kiki on Sunday." He was grateful that his voice didn't crack, even though his insides were feeling like twisted knots of bark.

"Church on Sunday?"

"Yes."

"That's it?"

Gideon lowered his cup. What was she getting at now?

"We spend days together driving up north, and all you can come up with is that you'll go to church with me?"

"I thought you wanted me to go to church."

She smiled. "I do, of course I do. I thought that was a given now that you know how I feel about my Savior. . . . But I was also hoping . . ."

He searched her eyes. They were like warm rays of sunshine. *She'd been hoping?* Was that what the extra glimmer was within those irises? "What were you hoping?"

She offered a slight smile. "Remember when you asked me out?"

How could I forget? He nodded, feeling even more nervous than he had that day—that day when he'd planned out his words and moves, only to have her say no, thank you. He'd never forget that blow to his ego.

"Well, I want to know something. Was that my only chance at a date with you, or do I get another?"

He smiled, reached over, took her hand.

Amos whistled.

Fresno stopped writing and said, "I drove all the way from Carlisle with these two. I could feel something brewing between them when they shared a milkshake at Burger King."

Gideon knew he'd better do this right. After all, he had an avid audience. One of Mari's silver rings that held an emerald jewel twisted, so he straightened it, noting as usual how dirty his own fingernails were. He could never deny what he did for a living, his hands told all. Just as he was about to say something about her many rings on her fingers, Fresno asked for another pen; the one Gideon let him borrow was out of ink.

Della handed the boy a pen from her apron pocket and said, "Sugar, today is your lucky day. And it looks like it's a pretty good day for our couple here, too." She winked at Gideon and Mari as Fresno took the pen and thanked her.

Gideon felt his heart beat like a woodpecker's beak against the bark of a pine tree. "I'd like to ask you again," he said, but the minute the words left his mouth, he remembered how Mari had once used Kiki as an excuse as to why she could not date him. "But who's going to take care of Kiki?"

"I'll send her over to Angie's grandma's. Kiki told me that Luva is a good cook, and she needs something besides my usual grub."

"You will?" He liked the way that she had given this so much thought.

"Yes." Demurely, she looked at him. "So are you going to ask?"

Clearing his throat, he felt his heart like the wings of a hawk soaring deep into the sky. "Mari, would you like to go out with me?" He hoped he'd asked the right way.

By the look of her face, he figured he had mastered this. She was smiling like she often did—dimples shining like two jewels from her cheeks. But today, this day, he saw more than just a friendly smile revealed in her brown eyes. He saw a future beckoning him to embrace it, to take the risks, to show his heart, to forgive and be forgiven, and to live.

40

Kiki paced around her desk until Mr. Lincoln ordered her to sit down. *What was the matter with him? He's getting too teacher-like this morning. Wasn't he ever a kid? Doesn't he remember what it's like to be nervous before making a speech?*

Although Mari had told her that she did a good job when she practiced at home last night, Kiki was fearful she'd forget one of the lines. With a green ink pen, she'd written them out on a pack of index cards. She'd printed as neatly as she could, and the tediousness of it made her hand cramp. Her sister asked why she'd used green ink, and Kiki replied that she could see better when things were written in her favorite color.

"Take it slowly," Mari warned her after Kiki read from the cards. "Breathe. But don't hold your breath. Stand up straight when you talk." When Kiki started over again, Mari instructed, "Look out at the audience. Out, not at your hands."

Out into the audience. This morning, Kiki swallowed and then looked up and out into the classroom. The other students were talking and laughing. They didn't seem nervous at all, and that wasn't fair. Why should she be the only one feeling like her heart was going to beat right out of her skin? Soon the adults, the guests they'd invited, would be here at school, right here at her middle school. And then, one by one, each student would be called up front to present their guest to the class. Kiki ran her fingers over the edges of her note cards. When Angie asked if she was nervous, her fingers clutched her second note card so tightly that it folded in half. "Yeah," she blurted so loudly that Mr. Lincoln told her to keep it down. Tapping her shoes against the metal foot of her desk, she straightened the card.

Mr. Lincoln walked behind her, his leather shoes squeaking until he stopped abruptly, a hand on her shoulder. "Kiki, would you like to go first? Would it be easier for you to get it over right away, or do you want to wait?"

Kiki thought for a moment. She supposed that her teacher was trying to be kind, but she'd rather not have the choice. "Just put me in the middle," she said. "I don't want to know beforehand when I'm up. Just put me in the middle."

Minutes later, Mr. Lincoln announced that it was time to go into the auditorium for the program. In a single file, the group of twenty-two eighth graders in Mr. Lincoln's health and well-being class walked down the hallway, past rows of lockers, past the media center, and in through the auditorium's double doors.

Inside the auditorium, dozens of adults were gathered, all seated in those stiff wooden chairs school auditoriums were famous for. Kiki spotted the back of Gideon's head. She knew it belonged to him because of the ball cap. Relief filled her; he was here. He had showed up. Mari was seated next to him. She seemed awfully close and as Kiki observed further, she saw that the two of them were holding hands! Kiki was tempted to whoop and holler like Ormond might, but she knew that there was a time and place for everything, and this was neither the time nor the place to cry out like an animal.

As the students filled in the first rows of the room, Mr. Lincoln made his way to the microphone on the stage. He welcomed the guests.

"Role models are vital for all of us," he said. "I recall the ones I had growing up. We might have a tendency to look up to celebrities or athletes, but a role model is a person we can come in contact with in our everyday lives. Today each of you is here at the request of one of my students. You have been invited because you are someone's role model."

Kiki thought back to when Mr. Lincoln first told the class about this event. She asked lots of questions to make sure she understood just what a role model is. She realized it had nothing to do with a good-looking man or woman on the cover of *Allure* or *Vogue* magazine. Apparently, a role model was a regular person that might have gray hair or a big nose and be fat or thin. This person was someone you knew and considered your hero. Kiki needed no further explanation after that. When Mr. Lincoln said the word *hero*, Kiki understood. She wrote down the name of her role model on her assignment sheet and smiled.

Kiki realized she'd been daydreaming. Quickly, she sat straight and directed her attention to her teacher. He was calling her name! Pressing her fingers into her index cards, she rose from her chair. This was it. This was her moment. If only Yoneko was allowed to be with her. Yoneko had such a calming effect on her, even though Dr. Conner reminded her that she was going on fourteen and needed to leave her puppet-cat at home more often.

From somewhere near her, she heard Angie say with enthusiasm, "Go, Kiki."

With feet that felt like boxes of Pennzoil, Kiki climbed the short set of steps onto the stage. She walked to the center of the platform just as her other classmates had done. The mic was her target. Once in front of it, she looked out at the audience. There were so many strangers. Their faces were all intently focused on her, just as Mari said they would be. She stepped closer to the microphone because Mr. Lincoln was gesturing to her to do so. Moistening her lips, she began. "Mr. Gideon Miller," she said and motioned for him to stand.

He smiled, stood, nodded at the others.

Now it was her turn. Other kids had shared who their heroes were and why. She must present Gideon to this group of people so that they would see just how important he was to her. "Gideon is my role model because . . ." Kiki felt all eyes on her. Her head spun a little like it did when she jumped to her feet too quickly. *Steady*, she told herself. *Steady*. She took in a deep breath. "He's my role model . . ." Her voice cracked over the PA system. This was not as she'd planned. With a look of *help me*, she found Mari's eyes. They were filled with affirmation, so unlike the two boys seated in the front row that were holding back laughter. She must pretend that she was rehearsing as she'd done over the last weeks. "He's my hero because he's my boss at Russell Brothers Auto Shop. He let me work there." She was not following her cue cards. Knowing that Mari was looking uncomfortable because she was way off track, Kiki tried again. Her eyes met Gideon's.

She saw his mouth move to form the words, "You can do it, Kiki."

With his encouragement, she felt fueled to continue. Speaking slowly, but not too slowly, she found a comfortable pace. Mari had told her to give her lines with confidence, using the same confidence she did when she put on her pirate hat, wielding her sword, and pretending to be seeking treasure. With those words giving her assurance, Kiki continued. "I met Gideon because I ruined his parking lot. I didn't realize that he'd just paved it, and I rode my bicycle around it. Someone told on me." In her original speech, she'd said that someone was Angie Smithfield, but Mari advised her to leave Angie's name out. "Gideon came into Principal Peppers' office, and that's where we met for the first time. I was embarrassed and nervous." Kiki paused, and then added without looking at anyone, "Just like I am now."

She heard some laughter from the audience, and it felt good to her ears. With her eyes on her index card, she carefully read her next line. "But the reason Gideon is my role model is because . . . Gideon forgives."

When the class and guests clapped, Kiki beamed. She looked around to see that even Mr. Lincoln was applauding. She could give a speech. She wasn't stupid.

"Gideon is talented, too. He makes keepsakes boxes." With that,

Kiki flew down the steps to her chair and from under it, withdrew the box. Flustered that she'd forgotten to take it up onto the stage with her the first time, she hopped back to her spot behind the mic. Lifting the box, she said, "Gideon made this for his brother." The box shone in the spotlight. As students craned their necks to see her visual aid, she removed the block of wood from it. "And one day, Gideon is going to make a pirate ship out of this piece of wood."

Although the class laughed, Kiki continued. "Right?"

Now it was Gideon's turn to say something, responding as each of the previous adults had. He stood, turning like the other adults had, facing partially toward the crowd and partially toward the stage. "I think it is interesting that Kiki has chosen me as her role model. Of course, I am honored." His smile grew then. "But the truth is, she's my role model, too. Sure, she can be bossy and silly, but her humor and persistence keep me on track. She is a hard worker—but more than that, she's a friend who keeps me in check. There are no neglecting responsibilities when Kiki is around. And I like that. With Kiki, I know I can't go wrong."

Kiki wanted to hug him, but she knew she had to keep cool. So she blurted, "Does that mean you'll make the pirate ship out of the wood?" *Say yes, say yes, please, for Pete's sake!*

"Sure," said Gideon. "I can do that."

When the audience clapped again, Kiki thought her smile would stick with her forever. From memory, she heard Principal Peppers' voice with the question he'd asked her months ago. *Are you happy here?* As she looked out over the audience, at the very back, she saw the principal standing along the wall. She wondered how long he'd been there, his arms crossed against his aqua-colored Hawaiian shirt. She thought about telling him that she was happy, but her teacher was telling her to sit down. Other kids needed to take turns to talk about their role models. Clutching the keepsake that rattled with the wood and her collection of arrowheads, Kiki stepped away from the mic. As a fellow classmate took her spot and introduced his role model, Kiki sat down.

Dr. Conner had said that good things could happen, she just needed to be patient. She looked around the auditorium and thought of how nice it would be if the choir from her church could be here to sing a few verses of "Amazing Grace." That would be a sweet sound. But for now, she'd just have to let the words play inside her head.

Angie leaned over to smile at her. Kiki smiled back. Today was a good, good day.

G ideon hopped out of his truck with a light heart after hearing Kiki's speech in front of a full auditorium. She's incredible, he thought. When he'd dropped Mari off at the tearoom, he confessed that it had actually been a blessing that Kiki had ridden through his wet cement all those months ago. That was the beginning . . . the beginning that led up to this moment.

Catching sight of three budding purple crocuses across the street in front of the hardware store, he stopped to admire their beauty against the starkness of the surrounding barren ground. As a kid, Moriah had always said that the first one to spot a budding flower was the winner. Although Gideon never knew what prize the winner received in Moriah's game, he now felt like he'd won.

"God," he whispered and inhaled the chilly February morning, "she has brought me back to You." The realization made him feel changed, different. This was even more monumental than the first time he drove a car or kissed an English girl. Compelled by some unseen force, he crossed the road to get a better view of the flowers.

The early spring buds sat low to the ground, bits of cedar mulch surrounding them. He observed their petals, the way the sun caught them in its pale light and the way the shadow spread over them when the sun sank behind a cloud. His intent gaze stopped as he studied the blossom in the middle. This flower was bent on one side—no, more than bent, two of its tender petals were limp, sagging, a darker shade of purple, obviously bruised from something.

"That's me," he said, feeling an association with the small flower.

"That's me. God, do You see my heart in that flower?" He raised his face to the sky and felt as though God was letting him know that it was okay to be wounded, to be bruised—that yes, one could still grow and thrive. In every blossoming flower, God left His mark, a sign that there was promise and hope in each new spring. In the snow, he had experienced the forgiveness of God. In this moment, he felt he could be the forgiving one that Kiki claimed he was. If God had given him the grace to forgive an autistic girl for ruining his cement, He could also supply the grace to forgive in even larger situations. He wondered what his heart would look like without the burden of bitterness for his father. Would it be able to flourish and be as attractive as even this bruised crocus?

Customers were approaching the hardware store, and he knew he needed to leave the flowerbead to get over to the auto shop.

"Finally, you're back!" Ormond greeted him as he walked through the front door. "The phone's been ringin' off the wall. I can't get no work done."

Gideon hurried toward the clanging phone and picked up the receiver. "Hello, Russell Brothers Auto Repair."

He heard silence followed by short breaths.

The hesitancy on the other end would always be familiar to Gideon. He imagined some young boy or girl crouched over a cell phone at a remote gas station, a lumpy duffel bag at his or her feet. "Yes?" He drew the receiver closer to his ear.

"Is this the Getaway Savior?" The voice was strained.

The word *savior* made him pause. All these years of being called this, and he'd been fine with it. But today—today he could not let it go. He might be Kiki's role model, but that was all. *There is only one real Savior without flaw, only one worthy of worship, only one who heals bruised hearts and fills them with peace and forgiveness.*

"Um, uh, hello?"

Slowly, with feeling, Gideon said, "I'm no savior."

"You can't help me then?" Fear gripped the youth's voice.

"Depends—if you want your car fixed, I can do that. Or if you want to start a new life among the English, I can help."

"I—I'm Noah. I heard about you. I'm from Lancaster."

Gideon knew Lancaster County. The people there produced some of the best apple butter of any Amish community. "Hello, Noah," he said in his friendly tone. "This is Gideon Miller. What can I do for you?"

The End

RECIPES

Ashlyn's Bread in a Can

½ cup whole wheat flour
½ cup cornmeal
½ cup rye flour
1 teaspoon baking soda
1 cup buttermilk
⅓ cup molasses
½ teaspoon salt
½ teaspoon nutmeg
½ teaspoon cinnamon
1 cup raisins

Stir flours and cornmeal together in a large bowl. Add baking soda, salt, nutmeg, and cinnamon. Stir. Pour in buttermilk. Add molasses and mix well. Stir in raisins. Pour mixture into one greased 1-lb. coffee can and attach lid securely. Fill large cooking pot with boiling water so that it covers the can halfway when placed in pot. Put lid on pan. Steam bread for two hours. Remove can from water. Carefully run a knife around the inside of the can to loosen the bread from the sides and then invert the bread onto a cooling rack. Serve hot in rounds with butter.

Gideon's Christmas Salad

1 ripe avocado, chopped
4 Roma tomatoes, diced
4 tablespoons onions, diced
1 minced garlic clove
6 oz. acini di pepe, cooked according to directions on box, drained
1 cup sour cream
2 drops Tabasco sauce
Salt and pepper to taste
1 teaspoon sugar

Gently mix cooked acini di pepe with salt and pepper. Add sugar and Tabasco. Fold in sour cream. Add avocado, tomatoes, onion, and garlic. Serve cold.

ACKNOWLEDGMENTS

As I've stated before, no novel is ever written fully alone. Others supply tidbits, facts, and wisdom along the way that beckon to enter my pages. Perhaps the most fun contribution from others was when I held a Name-that-Character contest on my Facebook Author Page. I asked my readers to come up with names for two of my characters—a waitress at a tearoom and the daughter of the local sheriff. Thanks to Sallie Deaton, who gave the name *Della* to my waitress and to Charlotte Stevenson, who provided *Ashlyn* for the daughter.

I was able to glean from the following books to help in my research of the Amish lifestyle—*The Amish Way* and *Amish Grace*, both by Donald B. Kraybill, Steven M. Nolt, and David L. Weaver-Zercher; and *Plain Secrets* by Joe Mackall. My research included various websites as well as documentaries about Amish youth who have left their roots to relocate in English neighborhoods. My four years at Eastern Mennonite University gave me much insight into the close-knit families, peaceful faith, and loving communities of the Anabaptists.

An abundance of praise to my agent, Chip MacGregor of MacGregor Literary Agency.

Thank you to the team at River North for giving me the platform to write this novel.

Much appreciation goes to my editor, Rachel Overton, for her keen eye to detail.

I belong to a very special group of writers called the Serious Scribes, and I appreciate the women I meet with every month—Katharine, Jen, Kim, Diane, and Catherine.

To my children—Rachel, Benjamin, and Elizabeth—I'm amused by the ways you always seem surprised/baffled/embarrassed when someone out in public recognizes me and wants to actually hear more about my novels.

To Carl, much gratitude for your support and encouragement, especially when the path is bleak and I am tempted to take up the habit of biting my nails or consuming too much chocolate.

And, to all my readers—without you, life wouldn't be as much fun. Thank you!

river north

FICTION FROM MOODY PUBLISHERS

River North Fiction is here to provide quality fiction that will refresh and encourage you in your daily walk with God. We want to help readers know, love, and serve JESUS through the power of story.

Connect with us at www.rivernorthfiction.com

- ✔ Blog
- ✔ Newsletter
- ✔ Free Giveaways

- ✔ Behind the scenes look at writing fiction and publishing
- ✔ Book Club

MOODY
PUBLISHERS

www.MoodyPublishers.com